Never Confuse Justice with Truth

Never Confuse Justice with Truth

A Novel

by

Edward Bessey

Library of Congress Control Number: 2011903138

ISBN:	Hardcover	978-1-4568-7685-2
	Softcover	978-1-4568-7684-5
	Ebook	978-1-4568-7686-9

This book is a work of fiction, and all its characters are imaginary. All references to actual places and institutions in Canada and other countries are for dramatic and creative effect only, invoked solely to draw attention to and/or give realism to possibly Canada's greatest social catastrophe, and are not in any way indicative of actual events, even though such occurrences may have occurred at the mentioned locations.

This book was printed in the United States of America.

To order additional copies of this book, contact:
Xlibris Corporation
1-888-795-4274
www.Xlibris.com
Orders@Xlibris.com
93870

Contents

Prologue

The Inuit and the Innu had lived in Labrador possibly from as far back as 10,000 BC. The Innu inhabited primarily the inland barren areas and hunted mainly caribou and various smaller animals and fished the rivers. The Inuit roamed along the coast and hunted mammals such as whales, polar bears and seals and collected wild berries, in addition to saltwater fishing. Both peoples led seasonal nomadic lives and depended on hunting for their food and clothing. Contact between these two peoples was limited to a few brief periods in summer when the Innu came to the coast to fish.

The Vikings, and possibly Irish monks, were the first white men to encounter the Inuit, the Innu and other first nation's peoples of North America. After the rediscovery of North America by Cabot, dozens of European nations joined the race for fish, furs, and whale oil. Among these were the Basque whalers who erected rendering stations along the Labrador coast.

From the beginning, the clash of such diverse cultures and philosophies was inevitable, and it was the Innu and Inuit who would receive the cultural shock. The Vikings in AD 1,000 sought land for settlement; the Inuit believed nobody should own land. The Vikings fought with the *Skrælings* at L'Anse aux Meadows over a cow that had wandered off. The Innu killed it, believing nobody could own animals, and if it roamed free, it was fair game. In 1501, Gasper Corte Real, unable to find gold, captured fifty *friendly savages* and took them back to Portugal to be sold as slaves. Thus, began the cultural tug-of-war, and it was the white man with superior killing devices that ultimately won.

But it was in the name of God and religion that brought the greatest impact.

These first brief contacts on the Labrador coast produced little influence until God's emissaries of the Moravian Church came to Labrador in the 1760s to established a mission at Makkovik to *civilize the indigenous heathens* of the coast, first reported as exceptionally friendly by Basque fishermen, who noted these *wild savages*, who had no written language and who had not yet discovered the wheel, had an innate curiosity for foreign innovations and showed undue respect for those who knew how to implement these new methods, making conditions ripe for an influx of Europe's overzealous religious soul savers to embark on *missions* to enlighten them of the ways of the white man's loving and merciful God. And, naturally, missionaries were sponsored by business ventures. Thus, began the forced evangelization of the Inuit and the decline of an ancient people and its culture.

First, the age-old Inuit practice of equality for men and women living communally in extended family units, or bands, intermarrying and sharing the chores and caring for one another was considered unhealthy and immoral by Christians, and they were urged—more correctly, coerced—into giving up their nomadic lifestyle and to settle down in single-family housing units in organized communities, near Moravian churches, of course, for better control and surveillance. A proven divide-and-conquer mentality, there simply being too much strength in communal living.

Second, the eating of raw meats was frowned upon and considered *savage*. Thus, the passive Inuit gave up their healthy traditional diets and, as directed, ate the salty, canned, sugary processed foods, conveniently supplied for them from the church trading posts in exchange for fish and furs.

Supplied with white man's firearms, thus began the mass slaughter of the several coastal species of animals for the clothing and hats of Europe's elite. And those unable to pay their bills were indentured as servants and, sometimes even worse, shipped overseas to be exhibited in zoos and freak shows. Such was the case of the devout Christian family of Abraham Ulrikab, who in Europe without their traditional family support died of abuse, despair, or diseases within a year. Their transgression was a £15 debt at the Moravian trading post.

The consequences were immediate. Robbed of their traditional source of food and clothing, they starved, froze to death, or died of despair. The *cultured* food in conjunction with a sedentary lifestyle brought diabetes, high blood pressure, and heart disease; and close association with God's missionaries brought whooping cough, measles, tuberculosis, scarlet fever, polio, smallpox, and every known form of silent invisible killer of the civilized world. And of course, alcohol—the blood of Jesus—was first introduced by the priests in communion; and syphilis was probably introduced by the same priests to the obedient youth just after communion, who were culturally indoctrinated into respecting their elders.

The Moravians, with their main priority—business—taken care of, could now move on to God and spirituality. The Inuit was required to give up their earthly, heathen gods with their dark-age belief that everything on earth had a spirit and demanded respect, the idea that no person could own land, and that one should just take only as much from nature as needed for survival. Veneration of Sedna, their sea goddess, who lived beneath the waters and who provided most of their marine animals, their main source of food, was openly ridiculed, an effective tactic of control in the religious world for humbling those dissidents who could not read or write. It became sacrilege just to mention the names of any Inuit gods or goddesses, whom their ancestors had worshiped for some ten thousand years. Schools were compulsory, and all children had to attend to be *civilized* and learn proper English etiquette. As a result, children were separated from their families for some ten months a year and subjected to severe discipline, a trait foreign to free-spirited nomads. Even their language was considered offensive; speaking Inuktitut was forbidden in public. To add insult to injury, the very name of their race was being deleted; they were now Eskimos. Communities now had English names. Children were forced to take Christian names. It was ethnic cleansing systematically carried out in the name of God.

Awed by with the white man's superior knowledge and power, and brutally subjected to their strict legal codes, the Inuit were soon made to feel like an inferior race. Those who objected became criminals in their own land with penalties enforced by foreigners with superior weapons. In return, they were guaranteed that the Christian God, who lived invisibly up in the heavens, would love and care for them if they converted and followed. And follow they did, like lambs to the slaughter.

Literally.

And God mercilessly collected his harvest by the thousands, young and old alike, victims of the Inuit's loving and forgiving nature. Of the estimated four thousand Inuit roaming the coast when the Moravians arrived, without immunity, 70 percent of the population had been eradicated by 1918. And of the remaining one thousand two hundred souls, 30 percent would die of the Spanish flu in just two months in the fall of 1918.

But it didn't end there.

In the spring of 1949, Newfoundland became part of Canada, and immediately, in the early 1950s, the Innu were herded together and mandated to live in designated communities such as Utshimassit on Davis Inlet or the Inuit to such northern points as Grise Fjord, a thousand miles farther north, to ensure Canada's Arctic sovereignty. A purported improvement to the reserves that existed at that time across Canada. Other religions, such as the Roman Catholic Church, soon invaded these communities vying for their share of lost souls. And worse, the new federal government placed further constraints on the Innu and Inuit's hunting and fishing rights; they now needed a license. And that came with a strict quota.

These additional oppressive changes to a traditionally outdoor, healthy, active, proud, and independent Innu and Inuit peoples deprived them even further of the very activity on which defined their culture: hunting and fishing. While it was not the ostensible native reserves as in the rest of Canada, the effect was no less severe. They lived in slum housing conditions and were denigrated as being dirty, stupid, and lazy, depending permanently on government assistance. Despair caused the suicide rate to skyrocket to twelve times the national average. But history has shown that it was forced inactivity that led to their excessive drinking, drug use, violence, child neglect, and their resulting low self-esteem.

As you read this tragic yet heart-warming, uplifting, multiracial, multicultural love story, it is imperative to understand that Inuit and Innu are distinctive races of people with unique cultures and to remember world opinion on these peoples was formed by the white man, who labelled the Inuit *Eskimos* and the Innu *Indians*, unaware or out of ignorance and arrogance of the diverse traditions and customs of these first peoples.

First Nations is the official term of ethnicity of Canada's aboriginal peoples who are neither Inuit nor Métis—interracial. They are believed to have crossed the Beringian land bridge between Asia and America during the last Ice Age, some fifteen to thirty thousand years ago.

There are currently over six hundred thirty recognized first nation's governments, or bands, spread across Canada, with a total population of eight hundred thousand people, whose individual group members identify with one another through a common heritage, consisting of a language, culture, sometimes religion, oral traditions, and beliefs. Being Caucasoid, many experts believe they came from Mongolia.

On the other hand, the Inuit of Canada, with a population of some fifty thousand people, is thought to be descendants of the Thule people who entered America over the ice, or by kayak, some six to twelve thousand years ago and are spread over a vast expanse from Alaska to Greenland, along the coastline, all sharing the same ancestry, that of the peoples of the Asia's northern coastline, some expert say Japanese. They are not considered first nations.

While white man can readily accept that Europe—half Canada's size—can consist of thirty or more separate nations, they seem unable, or unwilling, to grasp that the aboriginal peoples, who have been here for twenty thousand years or more, can consist of any more than just two nations: *Indians and Eskimos*.

Part I

Truth

Chapter One

The Code of the North

If you're old enough to bleed, you're old enough to breed.

June 30, 2000

The wind whistled through the seams in the broken walls, and the midnight sun illuminated the cracks in the tattered roof as Joella lay in her bed, cold and scared, hugging her teddy bear to keep warm and crying as her parent's friends yelled and fought one another in a drugged, drunken craze. She knew some of her father's friends would soon come to her bed, and she would have to fight them off. She was fifteen and had begun her menstrual cycle and was considered a woman and was now expected to have sexual intercourse—that was the code of the North: *If you're old enough to bleed, you're old enough to breed.*

Natuashish, Labrador, was as isolated from modern society as any place on earth and equally as lawless. The frozen wasteland offered few amenities to the young and restless, so they turned to drugs and alcohol for entertainment. Moonshine, glue sniffing, and marijuana use were the daily ingredients of life, even in elementary school, and anyone who did not participate was soon ostracized and treated with utter contempt and considered *stuck up* and often the target of their ruthless and senseless pranks; and most soon complied.

All that is, except Joella Adams, who was considered a hard nut to crack and was grudgingly gaining respect for her tenacity. She was at the top of her class in school and was competing with the Qablunaats, as the non-Inuit were branded. Many times, she had been detained by police for physically injuring local boys who had assaulted her. After each incident, she had cuts, bruises, or black eyes as proof and witnesses to substantiate that she was attacked, all with legitimate arguments to justify she was just defending her honor, but these were always casually overlooked. Relative to the level of lawlessness and chaos of the north, it was considered minor. She had acquired the reputation of a problem child by both the police and Social Services. Most young people now left her alone, having accepted the fact she was determined to control her own destiny.

A few years earlier, when her family moved from Utshimassit on Davis Inlet to Natuashish in Sango Bay, a town built for them by the federal government, life was good. With the world news media watching, she had food and clothes, and for the first time, there was peace in her life. But as the reporters filtered away and the community faded from the limelight, it reverted back to its anarchic past. Substance abuse quickly resurfaced and again took over her family, and her new home gradually became ransacked. Until now, it was just as dilapidated as their old hut back on Davis Inlet. And once again, females received less respect by men than their snowmobiles or the husky dogs they used for pulling their sleds and which roamed freely, often attacking people.

For years, Joella had kept daily diaries of the anarchy, describing all the violent incidents that occurred in the heartless community and the brutality caused by drugs and alcohol to her family, her wretched condition, even detailing the numerous sexual attacks on her by people of all ages and walks of life, and hid them at the house of her older friend, Lois, who was as unscrupulous as the worst of them but who protected her.

Joella wrote in her diaries in English, knowing, if discovered, most Inuit or Innu adults would not be able to read them. In them, she also envisioned a perfect life with her ideal imaginary boyfriend to whom she told all her troubles and called him My Naglingnig, her word for *snowflake,* since he loved snow and the Arctic way of life.

My Naglingnig was Todd Clarke, a white seventeen-year-old boy she helped with his socials homework, whom everyone called Simple or the Nerd. But she was smart enough to know he wasn't retarded, just shy and homely and a whiz in both computers and math. He was a hard worker and near the top of the class, thanks partly to her. This added to her predicament, anyone associating with a person outside the Innu race was labeled Apple, red on the outside, white on the inside, in short, a traitor to their heritage.

But Joella was not Innu; she was Inuit, a world of difference. Traditional enemies. Her race was a minority in the community. Historically, the Inuit avoided the Innu and lived along the coast. But in 1967, the government of Canada and the Catholic Church coerced the Innu to give up their nomadic way of life and settle at Utshimassit, which was on an island in Davis Inlet, where her ancestors had lived.

She refused to eat raw food, take part in ancestral Innu animism rituals like *Makushan, the Spirit of the Caribou* celebrations that worshiped animals, or any activity that degraded women, further exacerbating her snobbish image.

Unknown to her tormenters, fighting back was wearing her down. Anger and frustration was replacing common sense. Hunger was a daily struggle; most of the family welfare money went to alcohol. Her meager subsistence was the food Simple gave regularly for helping him with his studies. Her clothes were tattered, and she often wore her only parka and blue jeans to bed. That too was Simple's cast offs. Even her sanitary napkins were just stuffing from her now-skinny teddy bear. But she struggled on, praying each day to the white man's god, hoping for a miracle, determined to someday escape her private hell.

She was happy school was now out and could spend some time away from her family with Todd in their secret cave back in Davis Inlet. The brief Arctic summers were always the best time for her. She followed Todd wherever he went, and he fed her. She very much wanted to make him her boyfriend, but he was far out of her league.

She jumped up screaming in terror as the door came crashing down, and depraved Quinn entered, holding his full erect penis in his hand. Her survival spirit once more automatically surfaced, as she took a fighting stance and desperately scanned the room for some defensive object, but to her dismay, the room was completely bare.

"I just gave your father a flask of moonshine and two caribou skins for this fuck, and I'm going to get it," he snarled with drunken aggressiveness. "Now fuckin' open up, bitch."

"Leave her alone!" her mother, Aariak, yelled from the kitchen.

"Shut the fuck up," Tuk warned his wife. "Or he'll fuck you too."

Joella screamed for her parents to help, but her father shouted back, "Don't be a fuckin' baby!"

Quinn stood there panting like a bloodthirsty rutting ogre with a demanding look on his face waiting for her to comply. She could see his evil bloodshot eyes, his mottled wart-filled face, and rotten teeth, smell his greasy filthy clothes and body odor. It almost made her vomit.

She screamed again for help and backed slowly into a corner as he staggered toward her. He grabbed the front of her jeans ripping it open. She responded by clawing his face with both hands and with all the fierceness of a caged tiger, as he slammed her mercilessly to the floor and pinned her, his knee on her chest, nearly suffocating her. He forced his filthy, sore-infested hand inside her panties trying to insert a finger inside her vagina. She could feel the pain as she closed her legs tight and spate in his face.

"You're on the rags, bitch," he roared, slapping her full force with his free hand on the side of the head.

He pulled his bloodied hand away and wiped it on her clothes.

"You're going to suck me then."

She could hardly breathe as he grabbed her hair and forced his rancid penis into her mouth. She gagged, took a deep breath, and bit down with all the strength and hate she could muster. He let out an ear-piercing shriek and a string of curses as he pulled away, then hit her full force in the head again, knocking her nearly senseless.

"You're going to die for that, bitch," he snarled.

Her mother ran into her bedroom, grasped Quinn by his long greasy hair with both her hands, and courageously tried to pull him off. her father followed behind her cursing, grabbed her by the neck, viciously slapped her, and threw her out. She went sprawling on the kitchen floor, face-first, slamming against the woodstove.

"He paid for her," Tuk reminded his wife furiously.

Quinn slapped Joella again mercilessly against the side of the head and roared, "I'm going to fuck you even if you're on the rags, or I'll kill you, like I did Joe."

He again forced his hand between her legs causing her to wench in pain. She then noticed his hunting knife in a sheath on the back of his belt. Knowing she was unable to reach it, she relaxed and began to cry.

"Okay, let me take my pad off then."

He gave a vile, triumphant smile and released his grip. His wallowing in her humiliation incensed her even more. As he turned, she leaped up, grabbed his knife, and stabbed him with full force in the side of the neck. Blood spurted from his jugular vein, splattering her face. He stood up and hit her with the full weight of his body and with both fists. She staggered into the corner, barely conscious. He grabbed her throat with one hand and squeezed. She used all her strength and continued to stab blindly at his face, gasping desperately for air, while he punched her with his free hand for what seemed like an eternity. As she began to lose consciousness and slide slowly down the wall, she realized that he too was weakening from his loss of blood. It was running into his eyes, and he was now swinging wildly and hitting the wall. With renewed optimism and vigor, she managed to break his choke hold and slip behind him. Coughing and barely able to breathe, she continued to stab viciously at his back in a frenzied state, near insanity. Soaked in blood, the knife was difficult to hold, as she shivered uncontrollably with rage but carried on unconsciously like a preprogrammed robot. Her mother and father yelled for her to stop; she did not hear. Quinn slumped to the floor. She knelt on him and unrelentingly continued to stab him. Her mother tried desperately to pull her away, to no avail. Finally, Joella become exhausted, and her father was able to grab her hair and yanked her free, throwing her violently out into the kitchen.

Her parents stood speechless for a time catching their breath and staring in disbelief at each other and at the lifeless body in a huge pool of blood on the floor, the hunting knife still imbedded in its back. Both now sober from the urgency of their immediate problem.

"Call the cops," Tuk ordered his wife, terrified, "Or we'll be blamed."

"No! Get rid of him, you fuckin' coward! Bury him under the floorboards; he deserved it."

Oblivious of what had happened, Joella, in a state of shock, sat motionless on the floor, covered completely in blood, convulsing, severely traumatized from the vicious beating, barely able to see from her injuries.

Aariak scurried to the kitchen, hurriedly packed a knapsack of food, then gathered some of her own warm clothes. She put one of her Great Spirit dream-catcher packages inside and warned, "Joella, you can only open this at the lowest point in your life. Now go! And survive! The Great Spirit will protect you."

Joella, barely aware of her mother's directive, didn't move. Aariak lifted her up, put on her coat, placed the knapsack on her back, kissed her bloodied face, and sobbing added, "Go to your secret place near the criminal's burial ground where we put the flowers each year. A friendly spirit there will guard and protect you. I'll solve this, but you will never see me again.

Tuk, hysterical as well, yelled, "What the fuck are you doing? Quinn is dead. She killed—"

"She's going to hide in case someone misses the bastard!" Aariak screamed back, grabbing the bread knife and shaking it at him. "You caused this, you bastard! You sold your own daughter to a madman! You knew he was mental! If you interfere, I'll give you the same fuckin' medicine."

He had never seen his wife so hostile and determined, her voice resonated with desperation. As Joella staggered out the door, he made no attempt to stop her.

"She didn't have to kill him—" he finally managed meekly.

"Yes, she did! Someone should have killed the fuckin' mental years ago. Now shut the fuck up and do as I say, or I'll fuckin' tell what happened to Joe."

For two days, Joella did not show up at Todd's home as usual to scrounge for food or chat with him, and he missed her company and cheery smile. Rumors were circulating around the small hamlet that something tragic had happened at her house, and his fear of losing her gave him the nerve to go there on the pretense of asking her to hike with him to Eagle's Glide to take pictures. Photography was just one of his many and diverse hobbies, but Joella was his only true friend. He wondered if she were at Tammy's house.

Tammy Tulugaq, also Inuit, who lived next door to Joella, was the only other girl he liked, but she was only twelve. The few Inuit families had been placed together during the move for support. She came to his house once each month at night to ride with his father to the office to collect their family's welfare cheque. She would sometimes stay and chat with him about his coin or stamp collection. Like Joella, he found her smart, inquisitive, and very pretty.

At first, Todd found Joella's parents abnormally quiet and courteous. Even odder, they were both sober. He cautiously sat on the edge of a broken three-legged stool near the filthy, dish-laden kitchen table and stared all around hoping to see or hear her. Nobody spoke. She must be at Tammy's or Lois's house, he thought.

He was appalled; her new home was a dirty run-down shack. It gave him a creepy feeling. Something was obviously wrong. He looked questioningly at Mrs. Adams for an explanation.

"What are you doing here? You parents will be pissed. Joella's gone away to live with her uncle in Goose Bay," her father rudely advised.

But his wife, quickly realizing Simple was the only person who could help, would have none of it.

"Joella needs your help Todd—"

"Shut the fuck up!"

"Tuk killed Quinn, Todd. Joella got scared and ran away. She said only you can find her. She needs you. She'll tell you what happened—" she continued doggedly, talking louder to show her defiance.

"In the Polar Bear Cave," interrupted Tuk, hoping Todd would walk in on a mother bear and her cubs.

"Goddamn liar! Todd knows polar bears don't live in caves," her mother shot back, grabbing the kitchen knife. "Shut your fuckin' face, or I'll dump you too."

Todd was startled at their crude and vicious exchange. It was his first time at her house. He was puzzled how Joella could be so sweet and caring yet have such vulgar parents.

"She's scared. She needs you now, Todd," her mother pleaded, almost mournfully. She then whispered something in his ear, as her husband angrily pulled her away and slapped her hard. She fell backward unto the floor screaming. Todd jumped up, knocking over the chair, and ran from the house in a state of panic.

Arriving home in record time, his gentle mother, Melissa, noticing the horrified look on his face, warned him not to go to the Adam's house again because gossip was rampant that someone had stabbed Quinn and dumped his body in Wolverine Gulch behind his shack, and the police was returning from Nain immediately to investigate.

"Good, that scum was a menace to everybody," Todd muttered, knowing Joella couldn't possibly be involved in such a wicked deed. But the concerned expression on his mother's face indicated otherwise. To him, that was unthinkable; Joella was the most loving and kindest person he knew. For years, he had wanted her as his girlfriend but was always too shy to ask.

Having met Joella's parents, he knew the task he had to undertake and was acutely aware of the trouble in which he could become embroiled. He guessed she was by now hiding in their secret cave, back in Davis Inlet. They had spent most of their childhood days there together; his best memories were there with her. Fifteen kilometers was not a long walk for him, but he had to get across the channel to the island without a boat. With roaming polar bears, wolves, and numerous other animals, it was frightening, but he realized it must have been even more traumatic for her. She was less than one hundred pounds, a prime target for predatory animals. And if she were injured and bleeding, the wolves would quickly pick up her trail and track her to the cave. His concern for her was making him brave.

"I have to find Joella," he informed his mother, almost melancholically. "She's in trouble."

"I know you like her, dear, but getting involved is dangerous," she advised kindly. "Besides, Wilbert would be furious."

That was an area of trouble he had not anticipated; his father was always very authoritarian and demanding.

"And he's a pimp!"

"Hush, dear! Your dad has always had an affinity to help native girls. They need direction and discipline."

"She's more than my teacher, Mom; she's my only friend. I'm just Simple to everyone else," he answered with tears in his eyes.

She went and hugged him tightly. "I'll pack some food and warm clothes for her, dear. Take the small rifle—the .30-30 Winchester—an extra jacket, and lots of bear spray."

He kissed his mother on the cheek and hugged her. "I love you, Mom."

"Don't worry," she offered caringly, patting his back, "I won't tell your father. Go prepare before he comes."

After four hours trekking across the soft boggy muskeg, Todd became tired and sweaty and stopped to rest on a high pinnacle to rest and view his surroundings. His knapsack was heavy at forty pounds, but he had insisted on taking all the things Joella needed to survive until he could talk her into returning. As he picked and ate the partly ripe bakeapples and partridgeberries, he pondered whether he'd return if he had parents like hers. He felt sorry for her. Having been his only friend for all his life, he would do anything to help her. She had always treated him better than she did her few female friends, including her faithful soul mate, Lois Ikkusek—a promiscuous man-eater; but he was her only male friend. Others saw her as too independent and self-centered, but to him, she was a saint.

He knew it was reckless to travel alone in the open in full view of prowling animals. Paddling a kayak along the coast would have been safer, but too time-consuming. He had already seen two polar bears, but they did not scare him; they were white, easy to spot, and always trailed a prey to determine its weakness before a kill. He knew he was big for his age at five-eleven, 160 pounds, and bears shied away from large humans. It was the packs of roaming wolves that worried him most, and he carried his bear spray tightly in his left hand and his loaded rifle in his right in case of a surprise attack.

Worried, he knelt down and said a brief prayer that no harm had already come to Joella, then quickly picked up his knapsack, and trudged determinedly on. It was early summer; it wouldn't get very dark, and he figured he'd make it in a few more hours.

Arriving at the seashore three hours later, he was relieved to find several kayaks scattered along the beach. He dragged the nearest one into the water, threw his heavy bag into it, and paddled with a renewed sense of urgency, crossing the narrow channel in record time.

An hour later, as he rounded the side of the hill and began to climb up the steep incline to peer between the rocks to find their narrow secret cave entrance that was hidden in the tall grasses, he spotted her about a hundred feet away bathing in the cold water of Bear Creek below. His mouth fell open as he stared for a time at her developed nude body. He had never seen a naked female before and was instantly aroused. Then he felt somewhat ashamed, realizing that he was treating her like her other abusers. He abruptly turned around and began to quietly retrace his step, then to noisily return to spare her embarrassment. But she saw him first, covered her breasts with her arms, and gave a loud scream. Soon recognizing him, she ran toward him crying. He removed his knapsack and waited with open arms, spellbound, unable to stop staring at her unclad body.

Reaching him, she wrapped her arms around his neck and kissed him passionately on the lips. He responded as best he could. It was the first time he had ever kissed a girl. He noticed she had ghastly bruises all over her body, her face was deep red and swollen, and she had two puffy black eyes. All the skin around her neck was black with several deep cuts. She looked as if she had fought off a pack of wolves. He guessed her father had beaten her again.

"Oh, Joella, you have to get to a hospital—"

"No, Todd, love me," she whispered, instantly sobbing. He was troubled by her bedraggled state and strange behavior.

"I've always loved you," he replied bashfully, thrilled about his good fortune yet deeply concerned about her injuries.

"No, make love to me, Todd."

He was even more puzzled at her instant affection for him.

"I've never loved a girl," he almost whispered, blushing and bowing his head. "I don't know how—"

"I haven't either. I'll help you, Todd. I love you. They're coming for me."

He was both pleased and embarrassed at the same time. Everything he had ever dreamed about was materializing at lightning speed. He very much wanted to make love to her, but his concern for her welfare was stronger.

"Joella, you're hurt. What happened? Let's go, now."

"I'll tell you later. Let's do it before they come. I want you to be my first love. Mental almost was."

He had no idea what she was talking about and wondered why she would even let such a filthy person as Quinn near her. She began to undress him as she continued to kiss him.

An hour later, they lay exhausted on the blanket he had brought for her, basking in the afterglow of the greatest experience of their lives. He caressed her hair and hugged her small soft body close to him and felt that God was rewarding him for his righteous living. He was proud at having accomplished a feat where every other boy in the community had failed. He had found and made love to his dream.

"Does your dad know you're here, Todd?" she finally asked, concerned.

"No!" he answered surprised. "My mom helped me. She tells me everything. She's my friend. She likes you."

"But your dad hates me," she replied sadly.

"I know," he answered dejectedly. "And he's the devil."

She turned and kissed him passionately, then stated lovingly, "You're very kind and understanding, Todd."

"And stupid," he added.

She became angry.

"That's crazy, Todd! People here are bullies and mean. They say that because you don't do what they want. It makes them feel good putting you down. Stop it!"

He was surprised and somewhat amused at her instant outburst but pleased at her confidence in him. They became quiet for a long time as he held her tightly, cherishing her presence. He marveled how strong and fearless she was for someone so tiny.

Finally, she spoke again, forlornly, "Promise me, Todd, you'll go to university, become a lawyer. Help my people; they're lost."

Caught off guard at her impossible request, he did not know how to answer without hurting her feelings. He knew he would never be that smart, but his love for her was too strong to refuse her.

"I try my best, Joella. But I want you to become a movie star, like your mother tells everybody. I saw your dream-catcher packa—"

"I'm going to jail for life, Todd," she blurted out candidly, suddenly becoming hysterical. "I killed Quinn."

Todd was stunned.

For the next hour, he listened spellbound, sometimes shocked, sometimes angry, but always understanding, as she sobbed and poured out all the intimate details of her silent nightmare over the years. How nearly every male in town tried to rape her, including two of her schoolteachers and Pastor Cornelius, how she had to sleep with her door barred for fear of her father beating her in one of his drunken rages, how she was hungry and cold all the time, how the welfare money was spent on alcohol by her father, and by her mother on stupid dream-catcher packages to appease the Great Spirit. The list was endless. He was astounded that a person's life could be so miserable, yet she was able to smile all the time. She described in great detail how much he meant to her over the years and why she wanted him as her first lover.

Exhausted, she relaxed and pleaded for him to read her diaries after she got arrested. It was important to her that he knew the private hell she had endured and to try to understand her actions. She ended by kissing him and admitting, "My Naglingnig in my diary is you, Todd. You're my Snowflake."

Never had he been felt so lost and alone. He had just found his dream girl, and now she was going to jail? He could not even entertain that idea of losing his only friend. His mind began to work overtime.

"It was self-defense!"

"I'm Inuit, Todd."

Todd knew the law would not be on her side. Even worse, Quinn was Innu. "I'll take the blame; everyone thinks I'm simple anyhow."

She was smart enough to know the police would soon figure it out, and he'd be charged with obstructing justice.

"You can't help me now, Todd," she cried, putting her head on his chest and hugging him. "But you can get a degree and help my people. My life is lost. Just remember me please."

Tears came to his eyes as he held her tight and promised, "I'll get you help. God will help me!"

He then had a bright idea. "Come back with me; I'll hide you in our storehouse loft. It's not bad in the summer. I sleep there sometimes, and I can feed you and get help for your injuries—"

"You'll be charged with helping me."

"I don't care, Joella," he offered bravely. "I only have you and Mom."

"Lois and Tammy worship you," she muttered, hesitant to tell him.

"Lois?" he gasped, unbelievingly.

Lois was also member of one of the few Inuit families in the community.

But she'd probably eat me if I disobeyed, he mused.

Snuggled tightly into Todd's strong arms as he slept, she pondered her near-death encounter. She could not remember how she had crossed the channel or how she found the cave; these past two days were almost a blur, barely able to recognize her surroundings. She lay in blood-soaked clothes in the mud on the cave floor, hovering in and out of consciousness. Her eyes were puffy and barely open, causing blurred vision; her head pulsed, and she hallucinated, seeing red sunsets on the cave walls. Hunger and thirst racked her shivering body. When she awoke after a long sleep the second day, with filthy, blood-dried hands, she forced herself to eat some pemmican, even though her throat was swollen closed and it pained terrible just to swallow. But she never gave up hope and struggled on, believing God would rescue her and praying several times that day for a miracle.

Then this morning, she awoke sane enough to recognize her bedraggled condition and take a bath. The cold creek water soothed her bruised and aching body and returned her senses. Looking up into the warm sunshine, she saw her miracle hovering high above her. At first startled—it looked like an angel with outstretched arms—she soon recognized it was Todd with his large hunting knapsack waving to her.

Life's tragedy was bittersweet, she thought, only through adversity did she have the courage to ask him to make love to her, yet she had carved their initials in half the trees on the tundra or scraped them on all the large rocks on the seashore.

"Thank you, God," she whispered, kissing Todd, awakening him.

"Are you okay?" he asked, covering her snugly with his side of the blanket.

"Perfect," she answered.

She lay back and cuddled him, pondering her mother's statement, "A friendly spirit will guard and protect you there," and wondered if it were true. She had always questioned her mother why she placed flowers on a criminal's gravesite each year and why she always had to attend. But her mother's answer was always the same, "It's not yet time."

Todd quickly became Joella's savior. Never had she felt so grateful and loved. He fed her and patiently attended to all her injuries without a word, making her feel comfortable and loved.

But Todd's involvement troubled her. He had the most loving and respected family in the whole community. She tried frantically to emphasize how serious it was to associate with a criminal like her and how it could adversely affect his family. But loving her dearly, he casually dismissed it as good Christian values.

Greatly rejuvenated, the fourth day, they paddled their borrowed kayaks along the seashore to several of their favorite picnicking spots during the warmth of the day and reminisced, spending time photographing nature. They made a bonfire on the beach and cooked some shellfish, sang some old traditional songs in Inuktitut, made love in the tall grasses, then took a few pictures of each other in the nude.

Still panicking, she wanted to start moving south, but he was against it, noting the tundra offered little concealment; police dogs and helicopters would easily find her. And there was even greater danger from wild animals.

After another day of gentle prodding, he eventually persuaded her to return and hide in the storeroom until her injuries healed, and he and his mother could find reliable help. But she was still terrified he would become an accomplice.

Arriving home at four in the morning, the sight of the police helicopter on the pad and the sound of tracking dogs barking at the station pound sent a chill down her spine. Todd felt relieved he had persuaded her to return. And in the nick of time, the search was about to begin.

Slipping silently into the large storeroom, he painstakingly made her a comfortable bed of foam in the attic, then lovingly tucked her in, telling her not to worry; he and his mom would sort it out. She pulled him close, kissed him, and soon they were making love again.

An hour later, he got her a bucket of water for her bathroom and promised again things would work out. After he closed and locked the door below, she began to sob uncontrollably, her body convulsing violently, fearing that it was the beginning of a nightmare for both of them.

As Todd noiselessly crept into his house, he was surprised to see several heavily armed people surrounding his father as they prepared a search party for him.

"Where in hell were you? Have you been helping that 'skimo murderer's daughter?" his incensed father yelled.

He had never seen his father so furious and explicit, but, more so, taken aback and confused by the remark.

"The cops have arrested Aariak for murdering Quinn," his mother explained nervously.

Todd stood there speechless as his father lectured nonstop, but he wasn't listening; he was experiencing conflicting feelings. He did not know whether he was happy or sad for Joella's mother taking the blame. On the one hand, she was a filthy and crude drunk; on the other hand, she was trying to save Joella. Pastor Cornelius would lecture lying was a mortal sin, but his sense of justice would argue Joella was just defending herself. But now, he had just lost all respect for Pastor Cornelius. He struggled to decide if he should tell Joella.

"Where is she?" his father demanded authoritatively.

"I won't tell you!" he said defiantly, coming back to reality. "She didn't do anything wrong."

Shocked and angry at his son's defiant remark, he reached out to shake him, but his mother jumped between them.

Ironically, noticing Todd disobeyed his father for the first time and was standing up for himself, Melissa surprisingly felt a sense of satisfaction and pride. She was relieved her passive son was finally growing up.

Wilbert yelled at his wife, "I'm the welfare officer here! Our son cannot cohort with murders."

Todd was deeply hurt that his happy family was beginning to fragment like the Adams.

"Don't touch Mom, Dad," he warned coolly, moving toward his father. "Or you'll have to fight me too."

"You're simple if you get mixed up with 'skimos and Indians—" his father began.

Instantly, his mother slapped him hard across the face. Todd was stunned at his mother's ferocity and hurt that his father would make such a statement.

"Don't you *ever* say that again, Wilbert. He's the top of his class," she reminded him furiously.

Todd picked up his knapsack and said sadly, "I don't want to destroy your life, Mom. Dad had never treated me like a son; he only speaks to me when he wants something."

He kissed his mother and whispered in her ear, "Don't worry. I'm staying in the storeroom." Then, staring at his father, added, "Joella was right. She said you hate the Innu and Inuit."

"Where do you think you're going?" his father roared, pointing toward to his bedroom, now fuming because of the unexpected slap.

"I've tried all my life to please you, Dad, yet I've never heard a kind word from you. Now I'm pleasing you," he responded still calm.

His father took a step toward him.

"Don't try to stop me! I'm not a fat pig who sits behind a desk and pimp little girls all day, then come home, and drink a dozen beer. I don't want to hurt you." Then added derisively, "For Mom's sake."

Melissa was startled, speechless at his scathing remark, but noticed her husband's face reddened as he obediently backed off.

As Todd closed the door, he noted calmly, "I'm not simple, but you're a racist bastard." Then warned sternly, "Don't hurt Mom!"

Joella cringed with fear as and held her breath when she heard the storeroom door open.

"It's me," Todd whispered, climbing up the ladder to her bed. "I'm an outcast now as well."

She stared at him in disbelief. He had the ideal family, the family she always worshiped.

"What do you mean?" she asked dejectedly.

He calmly explained the turmoil developing in his family over the issue.

"No, Todd! You have a nice family. You can't help me if you—"

"I'm not stupid, Joella. I'm just scaring them into helping you."

Tears of joy came to her eyes as she realized that adversity was finally making him realize that he wasn't simple. She pulled him onto her and kissed him passionately, and within minutes, they were making love.

For the next two weeks, Todd stayed by Joella's side in the storeroom tending to her injuries and trying to cheer her up as they figured out a plan of action, going into the house only when his father had left for work. He struggled with the idea of asking his mother for help, knowing she'd agree, but it would split up his family. He knew how much his mother naively respected and trusted his father.

His mother kept him abreast of all the happenings in the murder investigation. The police had come to their house nearly every day searching for him, only to be told that he was on one of his typical summer photography and hiking trips. But with each visit, they were becoming more suspicious and aggressive. Each evening, he could hear his father shouting at his mother for refusing to tell him where he was hiding. He knew his mother was under severe stress and tried to think of a way to help her.

Each night, Todd slept with Joella cuddled in his arms. Both were content with the temporary arrangement. To her, it was much better than her home life; to him, he had his only love safe. Both were aware it would end when school began.

Melissa soon noticed Todd was accessing the first-aid kit a lot and preferring to eat his meals in the storeroom, taking much larger portions than usual. That was out of character for him; he liked to chat with her during meals.

Then one day, the police arrived at his house and informed Melissa that her husband had notified them that their son was living in their storeroom, and he would be arrested if he did not come to the station to meet the child psychologist to explain his actions in assisting a delinquent. Acting surprised, Melissa asked the police to wait in the house as she checked.

Melissa knocked on the door and related the police's request to Todd without entering. Joella, not wanting him to take the rap, decided to turn herself in, but Todd quickly persuaded her to remain silent until he determined how much they knew.

Inside the house, Todd readily agreed to accompany the police to the station for questioning, but surprisingly, his mother disagreed, insisting a lawyer be present. Nevertheless, she allowed him to go meet a child psychologist regarding a specific unrelated school matter, advising the police she needed some time to contact her husband for advice and would come along later.

When they left, Melissa went to the storeroom and called gently, "Joella, I know you're here. They've going to arrest Todd. I just want to talk to you."

"Oh, God, no!" she began to cry, quickly climbing down the ladder. "He did nothing, Mrs. Clarke. I'll turn myself in and tell what happened."

Mrs. Clark, though first shaken by her bedraggled appearance, hugged her, told her to relax, and advised against it until she could find legal representation for her. Sobbing pitifully, Joella sat on Todd's snowmobile and poured out her pathetic life story as Melissa held and consoled her.

After finishing, she stared nervously at Mrs. Clarke expecting her to be angry and evict her. But much to Joella's surprise, Mrs. Clarke advised caringly, "Come inside and have a bath, dear. Your injuries need attention. I'll give you some of my new clothes." Then smiling added, "It'll fit better than Todd's."

Joella managed a smile. She wished she had such a mother.

Todd returned to the storeroom to find her gone and, believing the police had apprehended her, in a panic, rushed inside to tell his mother, only to find Joella smiling and eating a meal with her at the table. Tears came to his eyes again. He went and hugged his mother and repeated, "I love you, Mom." Then added, "You knew all along, didn't you?"

"Yes, dear. I love you too," she responded in her relaxed, affectionate tone. "She's badly hurt but has to stay hidden until we find a way help her. Your father must not know; he'll turn her in."

Joella got up and hugged them both. Todd had never felt more affection for his mother.

Melissa, knowing Joella's levelheaded mentality for years from practically living at the Clarke household and Quinn's despicable reputation from continuous brushes with the law and his openly discussed mental instability, readily believed her story but knew she required a lawyer urgently to escape incarceration. And much to the chagrin of her husband, for the next three days, Melissa did nothing except frantically seek out friends for help or make phone calls to legal agencies, until she eventually secured services for both Joella and Todd. Only then did she go with Todd to meet the police and child psychologist to answer only those questions their lawyer specified, but none regarding Joella until their lawyer showed up in person.

Gossip was now rife in the small hamlet that the Clarkes were becoming involved, and the strain was openly showing on their marriage. Melissa knew her constant disagreement with Wilbert might create an irreconcilable rift, but she could not come to grips with losing her only son, who almost worshiped her. She was still irritated at the callousness of her husband for turning his own son over to the police and at a lost to understand his instant hatred for the Inuit, with whom he had been raised and had helped all his life. At one time, he even wanted to adopt native twin girls, but she persuaded him to wait to see if she could have any more children. He was even more furious when he learned that Todd had used his $2,300 savings for his new snowmobile on a lawyer to help Joella, who was just another rebellious, runaway Inuit and who was still at large.

Melissa was acutely aware that gossip always spread like wildfire in such abnormal circumstances, but one rumor kept reoccurring, and it bothered her. It involved her husband's association with young girls. She wondered if Todd had spread it in retaliation; he had often alluded to his father's unfaithfulness. She was positive her husband wasn't involved with teenagers. But now, in an unusual move, Cecil had sent Lois in person to warn her that Todd was right, that Wilbert knew where Joella was hiding, and he was about to pimp her to two of his friends, recommending she keep it confidential and trap them.

Melissa knew that Lois, though rough and abrasive, was always a reliable source. And even though her brother, Cecil, was a hardened criminal, she knew from her counseling sessions with their family, they were very close-knit, and he had always protected his sister, who liked Todd. Out of desperation, she reluctantly agreed to Todd's plan, still believing he was just being overprotective of Joella.

Next morning while eating breakfast with his father, Todd informed his mother he was going to the cabin on the seashore back in Davis Inlet for a few days to take photographs of migrating

Beluga whales. His mother hugged him and reminded him she couldn't pack for him since she had to work at the women's shelter for the day. They both then rushed off. As planned, after they saw Wilbert leave for work, they both returned to Todd's bedroom, which overlooked the storeroom, and waited.

With them gone, Joella prepared to turn herself in to police to prevent further animosity within Todd's family. She was hurt by his family fighting, knowing it was her fault. As she began to dress, Wilbert burst into the storeroom.

"Here's the greasy meat eater," he informed his two accomplices who eagerly entered behind him laughing. "She's all yours, boys. Get your money's worth. I'll watch."

He slammed the door closed, opened his beer, and sat down on Todd's old snowmobile to enjoy the show.

"I'll take her first," said his friend, Carl Parker, laughing as he bolted for the ladder.

"We can both take her," contradicted Jimmy Snowdon. "She's a 'skimo; she likes doubles," he added as he raced enthusiastically close behind.

Joella screamed for Mrs. Clarke as she grabbed the bucket of slop water and threw it. The nearly full bucket of stinky sewage hit them directly in the face knocking them both backward unto the hard wooden floor. Wilbert slapped his knee and laughed hardily at the lively spectacle; he felt he was getting more than his money's worth.

Sputtering and cursing in a fit of rage, Carl jumped up, grabbed the dog whip from the wall rack, and cracked it, narrowly missing Joella's face. He continued to swing it her as she screamed for Mrs. Clarke and tried to defend herself by angrily hurling anything she could find down onto them. Jimmy quickly got another ladder and placed it adjacent to the first, and they both began to race up together. Wilbert was exuberant, applauding and enjoying the unexpected show. He knew from Pastor Cornelius that Joella could be a spitfire, but this was an over-the-top performance.

As Carl and Jimmy reached the top rung of their ladders, they stopped abruptly upon hearing the storeroom door slam open and two guns click simultaneously behind them. Turning cautiously around, they stared down into a double-barreled shotgun, with both barrels cocked.

"Believe me now? I told you Dad pimped Inuit and Innu girls! Everyone knows," Todd reminded his mother emphatically, heading angrily for his father first, but anxious to fight all three of them.

"No, Todd. Get the police. Hurry!" Melissa ordered, grudgingly having to accept his bizarre story. In an instant, he was racing to the station.

Relieved it wasn't the cops, Carl and Jimmy relaxed and came down, laughing and mocking her, as Wilbert walked casually toward his wife, instructing her to put the gun down. Although scared, she gritted her teeth and pulled the trigger, blowing a huge hole through the wall near him. The recoil slammed her against the wall, nearly knocking her to the floor and terrifying his two friends. Joella watched speechless from above, now too terrified to tell her why she was calling. Melissa gained her composure, quickly reloaded the barrel, and calmly ordered, "Stand together please."

They reluctantly complied. Pointing the barrels directly at all three of them and staring at her husband, who was both puzzled and fuming at her uncharacteristic behavior, she sneered disgustingly, "Not only a pimp, a pedophile! Taking advantage of poor children. You're sick! And you wanted to adopt twin girls! What kind of a coward would turn his own son in to police and not help him?"

"You're just as simple as Todd if—" he began somewhat warily, testing her resolve.

"One more word and I'll blow your nuts off, freak!" she responded, this time tersely, raising the gun to her face, putting pressure on the trigger, and pointing it directly at his crutch. He stopped suddenly, swallowed hard, and cautiously raised his hands, shaking them to show his compliance as he backed slowly against the wall.

Hearing the shotgun blast, a crowd quickly gathered outside, obstructing the doorway. Some were shouting obscenities and crudely recounting her husband's abuse of young girls, whereas others were simply cursing him and egging her to shoot the *womanizing bastard*. Hearing their vulgar statements of his past abuse on children firsthand only made her more ferocious, until she really did want to kill him.

The police arrived in typical grandstanding fashion: speeding with sirens blaring and lights flashing. With guns drawn and crouching behind their vehicle doors in movie-land style, they yelled orders for Melissa to drop her weapon and lie face down. She obeyed. Joella scrambled down from the storeroom loft. They rushed in and roughly handcuffed both her and Joella, who now was standing motionless and still traumatized.

Todd got out of the police car, intervened, and tried to explain they had arrested the wrong persons, as Wilbert and his friends kept contradicting him, claiming they were only trying to capture Joella. Anger escalated rapidly as everyone shouted over one another with arguments and counterarguments, struggling to get their points across. The crowd, eager for details, was pushing through the storeroom door and yelling even louder to lynch Wilbert, Carl, and Jimmy.

The mêlée went on for a time before Todd, frustrated at his father's lies, punched him full force in the mouth, sending him flying heavily backward over a pile of stacked firewood, then gave him two or three more solid punches to the face. Blood squirted from his nose. Carl, quickly coming to Wilbert's assistance, received a vicious karate kick to the head with Todd's steel-toed hiking boots, toppling him over the oil drum that was used as the storeroom stove. Hot embers went flying across the floor, and smoke began to fill the room. Melissa and Joella both screamed for Todd to stop. Seeing the police were hesitant to get involved, Jimmy waded in to help his friends, only to have his arm caught and twisted, to receive the same hard boot to the crutch and a chop to the back of the neck, before being brutally slammed face-first onto the wooden floor.

The crowd outside cheered and clapped, egging Todd on. The police, aware they were rapidly losing control, began to panic, slammed the door closed, and barred it for their protection.

The police were stunned at Todd's instant change of character from a sensible, quiet teenager to an aggressive karate expert. They found it surreal but were nonetheless impressed at the way he was easily manhandling three adults but, more so, alarmed at his refusal to surrender, fearing they might have to shoot him.

Amid the smoke and noise, the police waited cautiously for their chance. With Wilbert and Jimmy now beaten into submission and lying motionless on the floor, they tackled Todd from behind as he turned to finish Carl off. With Carl's assistance, they managed to scuffle him to the floor, drag him to the snowmobile, and handcuff him to the handlebars. Joella and Melissa were now crying and screaming for them not to hurt Todd.

A person standing on a wooden box outside watching through a window gave the impatient crowd a blow-by-blow description of the unfair one-sided battle taking place inside. Infuriated, they kicked the door open, entered the storeroom, and surrounded the police, menacing them and demanding Todd's release. The floorboards were now beginning to burn, and the air was dense with smoke. Mass confusion ensued as the two office officers tried to control the crowd and still protect Wilbert and his friends.

The police backed into the smoke-free corner of the storeroom and, with guns drawn, ordered the crowd outside. Nobody obeyed. It only infuriated them more. Beginning to panic, one officer fired a shot into the ceiling. Still, nobody complied. Instead, the crowd challenged the police to shoot them. The anarchy continued unabated as the floorboards burned with Melissa, Joella, and Todd, all handcuffed to objects in the storeroom. The police fired another shot into the ceiling and threatened to use their weapons on the crowd, but to no avail. It continued unabated until the obnoxious fumes and the threat of gas in the snowmobile tank exploding persuaded the mob to move outside. However, it still took another tense ten minutes before the police, with several bystanders' help, could douse the flames and adequately secure the area to escort Joella and Melissa to one of the police cars.

It took even longer for both officers, with bystanders refusing to help, to wrestle Todd inside the other police car, who with hands and feet cuffed, was still viciously struggling to get at his father and his two friends.

Within an hour, all, except Todd, was corralled into one small room like pack animals at the police station as the two junior police officers tried to make sense of what had happened. Todd was segregated and securely chained to the bars of an adjacent cell, with cuffs still on both hands and feet.

Whereas Melissa, Todd, and Joella refused to talk until they had legal representation, Wilbert, the respected welfare officer with his impressive reputation for helping natives, gave a convincing argument that they were just helping capture a runaway. The police readily accepted his reasoning, apologized for their error in judgment, praised them for their courage and civic duty, and released them, calling an ambulance to take them to the clinic for emergency medical treatment.

As the chaos abated, Todd and Melissa listened silently as the police compiled their report. They afforded Joella all the respect of a mangy husky dog, recommending she be sent to St. John's to be adopted by a non-Inuit family to be civilized and get a proper Christian upbringing. She was denigrated to the level of a radical as her past infractions were dredged up for injuries to several boys in the town. She was maliciously convicted as they verbally discussed openly the proper wording of their official report based on the testimony of Wilbert and his two friends. Not once was she asked to comment on her actions or to sign the report.

Joella sat quietly, dismayed at the gullibility of the police, whom she knew were blatantly racist and with whom she had utter contempt. She became even more mystified at their naivety when she learned that, as a minor, she was only being apprehended to be put up for adoption since her mother had already been arrested and charged, having publicly confessed to the murder, and was presently awaiting trial in St. John's.

Mrs. Clarke summoned the two police to her cell and courteously tried to bring them down to reality by informing them that her lawyer also represented Joella and she was also under orders to remain silent, pointing out that anything a minor might say was inadmissible without legal representation, and that their report, as written, was inaccurate and discriminatory, not being based on proven facts. But that embarrassed them, irritating them even further. They stubbornly returned to their desk and modified their report to record her lack of cooperation as well.

Later that night after the police finished their report and had their coffee and donuts, Mrs. Clarke was read her rights and informed she was to be detained for a host of crimes ranging from contributing to the delinquency of a minor to the unlawful discharge of a firearm. Todd was unshackled and told to go home and reappear tomorrow for questioning on his assisting a runaway; none of the people he attacked and injured wished to lay charges against him. But he refused to leave his mother or Joella, vowing that, if released, he would kill his father and his father's two friends. That gave the inexperienced officers the excuse they needed to detain him as well.

Near midnight, the local priest, Pastor Cornelius, showed up to give his firsthand assessment of the situation. Being the second most respected person in the community, he felt his input could be of assistance to Joella but unknowingly further degraded her by explaining to the police that her pathetic upbringing was the cause of her criminal delinquency.

Todd, sickened by the hypocrisy of the priest, shocked his mother by interjecting sarcastically, “You’re a damn liar. You tried to rape her too, a year ago, and she clawed your dork.”

The police looked up in surprise at his unexpected allegation.

“How dare you make such a false accusation against God’s representative of the church trying to help?” the priest asked, flushing.

“If I’m lying, there’s no scratch mark on your dork. Show the police your penis!”

Melissa had never seen her obedient son so crude and verbal, guessing his resentment was a case of frustration boiling over due to the community’s complacency toward his father’s activities all these years.

The two officers looked at each other questioningly, somewhat amused. While Todd was referred to as Simple, they, like most, knew that moniker was fueled by the envy of the community bullies, because he was always very quiet, courteous, and a model student with many active hobbies. He had an unblemished record of being brutally honest and dependable, and it raised their suspicions. They stopped talking and nodded for him to elaborate, but once again, his mother intervened and gently advised him to wait until their lawyer arrived.

Joella by now had resigned herself to her fate. At fifteen, she guessed she was facing life in jail without parole, realizing once again the truth would fall on deft ears; it always had. Her only consolation was that Todd loved her and his mother believed her. She was fully aware they had little influence to change things, but for once in her life, she did not feel alone.

She cried silently, knowing that when her lawyer came, she would tell the whole story exactly as it happened; it was the honest thing to do. With her mother, it was a love-hate relationship. Her mother was a stupid drunk, but however much she despised her lifestyle, she had always tried her best to protect her. Whereas she had always hated her father, it still hurt to think he valued her so little that he would sell her to the filthy community criminal, whom everyone openly called *Mental* and whom everyone considered lower than the animals.

The officer stood up and yelled, “Lights out!”

Joella walked to the bars and motioned to Todd.

Before she could speak, Todd whispered, “Don’t say anything, Joella. Nobody knows that you killed Quinn, and they won’t be able to prove your mom did it.”

“No, Todd. I know. That’s not justice for our people. That’s just being like them.”

Heartbroken at the thought of losing her, he asked, “What do you want me to do, Joella?”

“Go with other girls, Todd. Enjoy life but wait for me. Lois is the best here. She’s crude, but she has a good heart. I swear I’ll never love anyone but you,” she whispered, kissing him through the bars.

“I promise. I’ll always love you, Joella. Don’t worry; be patient. Mom will solve it.

Noticing his mother sobbing uncontrollably, Todd went to the opposite end of his cell to say good night. He reached through the bars, hugged her, and encouraged, “Things will be okay, Mom.”

“How long have you known about your father?” she managed, convulsing.

He could see she was in sheer agony. “Ever since I can remember.”

“Why didn’t you tell me?”

“I tried. Many times. You wouldn’t believe me. I knew you loved Dad, and I loved you too much to hurt you.” He paused. “And I didn’t want you to think I was simple.”

“Our lives are going to change, Todd. Understand you’re now a man. Take control but don’t hurt your father. He’s a good man. Let God take care of him. Promise?”

Todd hesitated.

She knew his silence meant he disagreed, not wanting to disappoint her. Yet she was pleased that the real Todd was finally emerging. “Please? Please promise me, Todd,” she sobbed.

He had no intention of letting him escape justice and answered ambiguously just to pacify her. “I’ll never let you down, Mom.”

Chapter Two

Cast to the Wolves

God helps those who help themselves.

The helicopter ride to Goose Bay was noisy and rough. Melissa and Joella sat together with eyes closed, each reliving their own personal hell.

Melissa tried to rationalize that threatening to kill them was evil, that her firing the gun was an overreaction, that maybe they would not have raped her. She was desperately searching for a reason to modify reality, but her conscience dictated otherwise. How could she have been so gullible all these years? Was she was a victim of her own stupidity? Her cozy world had come crashing down so fast and unexpectedly that it left her disorientated. Not being allowed to say good-bye to her only loving son made her feel like a criminal, that she had abandoned him.

Joella had her own personal crisis, not that she had killed Quinn, in that she felt she had no choice and wasted no time trying to justify her actions; but her mother, whom she despised, had willingly taken the blame for her. That meant her mother truly loved her. Her father she now despised with a burning passion for letting her mother take the rap. He was truly an animal, just as criminally insane as Quinn.

But more disturbing was that she was his daughter. Her mind processed dozens of logical and indisputable reasons why she was distinct from her father. But the troubling reality remained; she had just killed a person.

Obviously, I must have taken after my mother, who's stupid but not crazy, she finally rationalized. *I cannot possible be insane and love Todd so passionately. All I want is to be left alone in life, with him.*

As they landed, seeing Joella's suffering, Melissa took her in her arms and hugged her as she cried. Although severely anguished herself, she found the courage to vent her true feelings.

"If I had a daughter, I would want her to be just like you."

"Where does the love of God go in times like this, Mrs. Clarke? I prayed every night so he would always protect me," she sobbed. "Even our pastor lied."

Like Joella, her faith was also being tested to the limit. The shock that her husband had been abusing Inuit children for years and even wanted to adopt twin Inuit girls left her utterly crushed and violated. She could not remotely fathom how he could hate her enough to frame her after twenty years of marriage bliss. She now knew the source of his bliss. She felt like a stooge. She recalled Todd trying to forewarn her on many occasions, but her love and respect for Wilbert was so strong it clouded her senses, until at times she too thought Todd was a little simple.

"I don't know, sweetheart; maybe he's testing our faith."

"What's going to happen to me? Todd and Lois were the only friends I ever had," Joella whimpered, barely able to speak.

"We'll survive, Joella. We both have each other, and we both love Todd. He has my heart. He will always love you. Promise me you will keep studying; get a good education."

"Yes, but I'm scared for him too, Mrs. Clarke; he's too kind."

"Adversity changes people. He's quiet, not stupid; he'll rise to the challenge, as I will. You will too. Keep praying and fighting."

"Time to go," the policewoman announced, as the pilot opened the helicopter door. Touched by their plight, she added, "I'll keep you two together until your flight to St. John's. You might be here for a few weeks for preliminary arraignment." Then with encouragement, "It'll not make you feel any better, but I believe both of you."

"Thank you," Melissa offered gratefully, but Joella, who was not so trusting, just sneered and remained quiet.

Melissa and Joella were thankful to be allowed to stay together in Goose Bay in a double cell. They talked all night, revealing each other's intimate secrets. Although a generation apart, they were now united in adversity. Joella expressed regret for involving Todd into her troubles and begged Melissa to read her diary to understand her plight.

"I'm Inuit," she apologized, as if it were a mortal sin. "But still, I'm a person. I'm still human and shouldn't be raped."

"You did nothing wrong, and I'm proud of you. Whatever happens, keep remembering the happy times with Todd," consoled Melissa, hugging her. "You're a good person, and he has always loved you."

"Mrs. Clarke, Todd deserves better. Maybe there's no place in heaven for the Inuit; we're just too bad."

"Hush! All people are equal. You study hard. He will too. I know him."

"But, Mrs. Clarke, I broke up your marr—"

"You did no such thing. You opened my eyes. Wilbert is a sick man."

"I'm not strong like you, Mrs. Clarke."

"I once read, 'In the darkest hour, the soul is replenished and given strength to continue.' Remember, we can't give up. We must shape our own destinies. Promise?"

"I've always obeyed you, Mrs. Clarke."

"Cheer up, Joella. Let's make the best of the next two weeks together. Things will get better."

Being a minor and having confessed at the brief preliminary arraignment next day, Joella was judged a special and complex case that could best be handled with proper legal representation.

Whereas Melissa, at a separate hearing, was deemed high risk to escape and reoffend, if released back into the community. Thus late evening found them both crying and hugging each other at the airport as they were separated and boarded onto different flights to St. John's.

But life did not get better for Joella, and two incidents in the next two weeks came close to being catastrophic. Arriving at St. John's late, Joella was temporarily assigned a private cell in an adult jail designed for hardened criminals, where her newly appointed child-welfare lawyer, Mrs. Crosby, found her next morning, tired and drab, after cowering all night in the far corner of her cell, as two lesbians argued and fought in an adjacent cell over who was going to get her.

Within hours after the court opened, Mrs. Crosby had obtained an order to have her moved to an all-girls group home for juvenile offenders where she was paired with a teenager named Tara, who was incarcerated for inadvertently poisoning her cheating boyfriend.

Tara was eighteen, five foot ten, one hundred and eighty pounds, a kind-hearted giant, who was prone to exploding into a violent temper tantrum if jokes were made about her manly appearance.

Assuming the role as Joella's mentor, she took time to condition her for prison life, even before allowing Joella to get any sleep. She patiently explained the social hierarchy in the detention culture, warning her she would have to be assertive and fight back because the inmates would test her resolve sooner or later when the opportunity presented itself; otherwise, she would soon become their servant or, even worse, a sex toy for them.

Her test came sooner.

After sleeping for twelve hours, Joella got up, took a shower, donned her reformatory-issued, uniform, and shyly went for breakfast in the common area. She searched but was unable to find Tara, whom she desperately needed to coach her the first week. She picked up her meal from the cafeteria and timidly went to sit in the only vacant chair.

She placed her meal on the table and began to sit, when a blonde girl sitting to her left pulled her chair away, causing her to fall heavily onto the floor, striking her head on the chair edge, and sending it across the room. Blood ran down her neck from the wound. Everybody roared with laughter.

"Move! You're at the top table, 'skimo," shouted the brunette to her right.

Hurting badly and instantly angry, Joella's survival instinct again emerged. She jumped up and yelled, "No, you move!" She grabbed the blonde by her long hair and mercilessly jerked her head backward sending her sprawling onto the floor and her chair flying. The adjacent brunette jumped up to help, but Joella grabbed her hot tea from the tray and threw it into her face.

Everyone scrambled away from the table as some pitched in to help Joella, causing a commotion that attracted the staff.

The blonde grabbed a knife, just as Tara rushed out from the kitchen, where breakfast preparation was her officially designated daily chore, carrying a large butcher knife. Seeing Joella bleeding, she barked, "Do you need help?" The brunette, like Joella, stared in horror, as Tara pushed the butcher knife into her belt, held her arms out straight, cracked all her fingers at once, and demanded angrily, "Who's the troublemaker?'

Two wardens appeared and saw the blonde holding a knife and tea stains over the brunette's white uniform and attacked, "You two causing trouble again?"

"I think they were teaching me to protect myself," offered Joella meekly, not sure if an olive branch would work. "But I want them to say sorry for pulling my chair away. It hurt, and I'm cut," showing them the blood on her shoulder.

"Is that all, Sheila?" the warden asked the blonde, guessing Joella was too scared to tell the truth.

"No!" Sheila responded. "I don't want 'skimos at my table."

"Let's go!" ordered the second warden.

Sheila resisted and was dragged away screaming, lying about what happened.

"What about you, Joy? What do you have to say for yourself?" demanded the chief warden, staring at the brunette.

"I'm sorry," Joy apologized to Joella. Then, turning to the warden, "You know I'm scared of Sheila. Everyone is! I want another cell mate."

"And who are you?" the warden asked Joella in an even angrier tone.

"Joella Adams, ma'am. I'm sorry. She hurt me."

"Come with me," she ordered sternly, as other inmates began to loudly object, explaining it wasn't Joella's fault.

After having her head wound attended at the infirmary, the chief warden took her to the disciplinary office and explained the centre's procedures for handling bullies and warned her she wouldn't get a second chance.

"Pulling Sheila's hair is one thing," she admonished angrily, "but had the tea been boiling, Joy would have been blinded. She's not the bad one!" Then she noted in a kinder voice, "Be careful. Follow procedures, and you'll be okay. And remember, when someone is nice to you here, they want something. You being the youngest, I gave you our best cell mate."

"Thank you, ma'am," Joella responded timidly

Melissa found her jail cell noisy and the inmates repulsive, so she kept to herself and read the Bible. Within days, the prison chaplin recognized her as a good person and persuaded the guards to permit her daily use of the staff amenity room.

Each night, she sobbed pitifully as she prayed. She could not understand how she could be detained but not charged, believing that a person could be held for only two days. She didn't trust or believe her court-appointed lawyer, Mrs. Fowler, who seemed to be only a mouthpiece for the prosecution. Her lawyer staunchly justified the crown's perspective by stressing the serious nature of her crimes, and as a result, the court had the right to hold her indefinitely if they considered her mentally unstable and a threat to herself or to others.

Even worse, she was not allowed to talk to Todd, knowing by now there was probably an outright war between him and his father. All news was being filtered through her lawyer, who was tracking Todd through Social Services, which supposedly was capable of supervising him.

To add to Melissa's sorrows, her sister's sixteen-year-old daughter had just been killed in a car accident and she could not go to England to attend her funeral, the court permitting only a ten-minute phone call on compassionate grounds. And she was too ashamed of her actions to explain her situation to her sister.

She felt like a mouse in a cage, completely at the mercy of society.

Todd sat on his makeshift bed in the secret hideout in Davis Inlet, staring blankly at Lois sitting in Joella's favorite driftwood chair, dazed by the turn of events. He had wanted to come alone to escape reality and relive his few brief moments of love with her, but Lois was adamant that Joella wanted her to take care of him until he was more mature. He pondered how in just two weeks he had gone from the protected community simpleton to a rejected problem kid, and he had done nothing, except try to help. It distressed him how he could have digressed from a sniveling coward, avoiding even minor confrontations, to an aggressive instigator, attacking and injuring three adults in one fight. He knew it was pent-up frustration caused by his father's long mistreatment of his mother. He was now ashamed of his evil compulsions.

Those weeks had been disastrous for him as the web of lies and deception spun by both his father and other people in authority spiraled out of control until his family disintegrated and he was left to fend for himself.

The morning after Joella and his mother had been arrested, they had been whisked away by helicopter without him having said good-bye or informed of their destination. Then a week later, he had been brutally advised by Social Services that both his mother and Joella were to be charged with attempted murder and manslaughter respectively. To add insult to injury, the police had ordered him to live with his father, at which point he again threatened, if enforced, he'd murder him, thus giving the police the excuse they needed to kept him in custody for both his father's protection and for his own stubborn refusal to allow Social Services to place him in a foster home away from Natuashish.

Then the police, served with a habeas corpus by his lawyer and without an offense with which to charge him, were forced to release him back into the community, fully aware he was capable of revenge. With nowhere to go and no friends, he had accepted Lois's suggestion to come and live with them but first decided to spend a few days in the cave. This gave Lois an opportunity to try to persuade him to change his passive nature.

Lois's family, the Ikkuseks, although civilized relative to Joella's parents, were still barbarians by his standard, and their house was mediocre at best. Lois was not of his mentality. Although always neat and clean, she was crude and as rough and tumble as any man in the community. At seventeen, she was as strong as him and needlessly aggressive. Besides being conniving and a compulsive liar, she was just as abusive to men as men were to the females and just as apt to punch out a man as she would a woman. She was in perfect tune with a lawless community that lacked any shred of morality. She always wore tight blue jeans and a loose-fitting lumberjack's shirt, showing her cleavage. She drank, smoked, spate, and cursed at the drop of a hat. Just being seen with her embarrassed him. He seldom spoke to her. He did not know how to converse with females, other than Joella, Tammy, and his mother.

"The court is deciding my fate; they're trying to send me away to a foster home," he finally mused aloud after a long silence.

"You're seventeen, for fuck sake, going to college next year, Todd. Tell them where to fuckin' go. Start making your own decisions."

Her ungodly words sent chills down his spine. He did not know how to respond.

"Joella told me to help you. If you're going to survive in this fuckin' shit hole alone, you're going to have to toughen up and fight, like you did. You already fuckin' know how. They're all proud of you."

"Fighting is not the kind of life I want, Lois," he explained calmly, yet somewhat irritated.

"You think I want this kind of life? If you want something bad enough, you have to fight for it. Joella will wait for you. She's not like me. She's not only pure; she's honest and dependable."

He remained quiet, wondering how long she, or his mother, would be away. He missed them badly, and it was beginning to hurt just to talk about them.

"You're smart and strong. Fuckin' use it or you *are* fuckin' simple," she added to jolt him.

He found himself flush at the word *simple*. Her vulgar language was offensive to him. His mother would advise him to avoid people like that, but he now had little choice.

"God will help—"

"He didn't fuckin' help Joella or your mother. And they're saints. God helps those who help themselves. And that means there's no fuckin' god in this stinking hole!"

"How?" he managed cautiously, disgusted by her wicked statement.

She went and sat by him and smiled. "You can start by fuckin' me."

"You love Shark Fin," he reminded her, almost repulsively.

"Love?" She laughed sarcastically. "Which world are you in? Grow up! Shark Fin is just my fuck. I'm yours if you want me."

She kissed him on the lips. He quickly pulled away, repulsed at the foul taste of nicotine.

"Okay," she said, going back to her side of the cave to her bed and lying down. "I've always wanted you, but I won't rape you. I'm here if you want me." She then raised her head and added kindly, "In Inuktitut, we have a saying for the dreams of people like you: 'Searching for the moon in the water.' Look around you. This *is* the real world. Good night, Todd."

He did not answer. If this were the real world, he wanted no part of it, preferring to live in a cave like a hermit. He lay back and thought of how Joella was coping and was soon fast asleep.

He woke at four in the morning and saw her sleeping peacefully and wondered why she was so kind to him; nobody else ever was, except his mother, Tammy, and Joella. He stared at her slim perfect body. *She is really pretty*, he thought, *but her foul behavior overshadows it*. He wondered if she really did have good heart and her competitive mentality molded her that way. He recalled how her eyes often sparkled with mischief and fun when she teased him. He knew his mother had shielded him from the outside world.

Well, if this is truly is the real world, he mused, *I may as well start living*. He stood up, took a deep breath, went over, and kissed her softly on the lips. She awoke, smiled, and pulled him onto her.

"Nerds are not good lovers," he ventured timidly.

She kissed him and ordered, "Stop fuckin' yourself and fuck me."

Returning two days later, Todd soon learned that his father had volunteered to go to St. John's to testify against his mother.

Incensed, he went home to challenge him but found the house empty, his father's private office unlocked, with his laptop computer still on. He browsed it and was astounded to find his father had been accessing teen pornographic Web sites; his hard drive contained dozens of underage nude photos and movies. He was almost traumatized, realizing his father was not only a pimp but also a pedophile, like his mother had accused him. He stared in disbelief at the preteen nude girl in the picture, sickened at what his father was doing to her and at the masked cameraman filming it. Then after viewing a few more pictures, he realized the pretty girl was from his school.

He quickly stood up, took several deep breathes to calm himself, almost too appalled to continue. Upon closer viewing the girl's tear-stained, tortured face, he was positively stunned, finding it almost too mind-boggling and disgusting to believe. The pretty girl was Tammy Tulugaq. And only twelve.

He again sat down and stared at the photo with his mouth open for a long time. It was almost too repulsive to comprehend. He really liked Tammy, and she liked him. He wanted to go to his father's office and beat him senseless but realized he would have to keep her identity a secret for her sake.

An unlocked desk drawer revealed stacks of CDs. He scanned a few and saw they were all sex movies. Only on a few old floppy disks did he find welfare files. Two other drawers were packed full of old VCR videotapes. It became obvious why nobody was permitted into his father's office, which was supposedly off-limits because it contained confidential government files.

In a quiet state of disbelief, he took the laptop, all the CDs, and any money he could find, then hurried back to the Ikkuseks to read Joella's diaries, anxious to see if his own father had tried to molest her as well.

After an hour of scanning, he realized the CDs were all filled with sex movies, and it would take weeks to view. He went back to his home and collected all the old VCR tapes as well.

With his father now the opposition, he had no money for even the basic necessities. So while his father worked, he spent the time gathering all his belongings from their storeroom to have a fire sale for money to visit his mother and Joella. He hocked everything from his beloved kayak and old snowmobile down to his collections of coins and stamps.

After toiling and haggling for a week, and getting less than a quarter of the value of his precious belongings, which had taken him a lifetime to accumulate, he realized the people were much poorer than he had imagined.

He needed at least $12,000, and the depressing total of his life's belongings only came to $4,300. He felt defeated. And worst, even that amount was mostly due to the generous help and of the Ikkuseks, mostly the not-so-subtle persuasion and double dealing of Cecil.

Lois, who by now was falling for him, came up with the idea of blackmailing his father. At first, he was appalled at her vile suggestion but then became confused at his own evil impulses to exact revenge. After recalling Tammy's ordeal, it didn't take long before his resentment and indignation toward his father became so intense, little convincing was required, realizing his laptop files was a smoking gun.

The next day, he made a copy of all the files and returned the computer, minus the hard drive with a note pleading for $10,000 to help his mother.

Unexpectedly, his father contacted police. When confronted, Todd confessed and readily answered all the police questions and concerns honestly, stressing that he took the files only as evidence his father was a pedophile and that some of the files contained pictures and names of local underage girls with whom his father had had sex. The police, while not disbelieving him, knew the files were illegally obtained and, not wanting another scandal, already being overworked, ordered him to return the hard drive and CDs, as well as any videotapes he might have taken

For the next two days, Todd spent all his spare time making two backup copies of the hundred or so videotapes, CDs, and floppy disks, storing one copy in the Ikkuseks' shed and the other in his secret spot in their own storeroom under the floorboards.

He then complied with vengeance, adding a full-color printout of the disgusting picture of Tammy being molested as proof and wrote a note on the back saying he had two copies of every last file, and if he had not received the money in two days, pictures of him with other local teenagers would be posted on the on the Internet, giving him the exact Web site location. He included the names of three other girls for shook effect.

Wilbert stared in terror at the incriminating pictures, shocked his own son had the courage to bribe him. He had already unceremoniously learned that Todd was a silent tiger from the beating he received in the storeroom. Aware Todd was a computer geek, as all his own computer knowledge had come from him, he knew Todd was capable of doing much more.

Having grossly underestimated both Todd's physical and mental tenacity, he began to panic, now at a loss on how to resolve it. Realizing such a disclosure could bring his career crashing down, he phoned his friends, Carl and Jimmy, who were also still recovering from the beating, for advice, only to find they had even graver concerns. Namely, Todd was living with the Ikkuseks, whom both the Inuit and the Innu community respected for their track record of toughness in protecting their aboriginal heritage. And since Todd was now dating Lois, to disturb him was to upset that whole community who liked him and possibly bring the wrath of Cecil down on them, stressing Cecil had already killed one person. They were even having second thought about testifying and wanted no further involvement.

Wilbert hung up, got a beer, and sat dejectedly in his leather armchair and stared in disbelief at the smiling picture of Todd over the burning fireplace. His *simple* son had single-handedly defeated him in just a few weeks. Still stunned by his son's viciousness, he had but one option to mitigate his losses and still save his honor and integrity in the community. It was now a lose-lose situation.

Lois watched with excitement as Todd quickly ripped open the envelope from his father and stare agape at his name on a $10,000 certified cheque, amazed it had taken only two days. Ecstatic, he hugged Lois and kissed her at the post office, as several people watched and applauded.

Rushing to the bank, he deposited the money, retaining $100 to throw a party at the Ikkusek household to show his gratitude to Lois and her family for accepting him as a member. With her insistence, he invited all the Innu and Inuit people that she recommended, which included the mayor and all the council elders.

That night, he drank his first taste of alcohol as a toast to the Ikkuseks and the Inuit and Innu. Then after bravely toasting Lois, he awkwardly danced with a girl for the first time: Lois. He knew she was not his type, but she was sure dedicated to helping him and figured she would be an ideal travel companion, for protection as well as company.

Before the night was over, he was drunk, had shed his shyness, and, for almost an hour, in perfect Inuktitut that astounded the elders, bared his soul, relating how both he and his mom were always fascinated by the aboriginals and their rugged survival culture. While that was the catalyst that had gotten him involved in photography, he noted that it was Joella who had persuaded him to study to become a lawyer and help their people deal with white man's arrogance, which he now found equally as offensive.

Though Todd was young, the elders realized that he was a hardworking, conscientious person with a commitment to the North. He would finish high school within a year and go to college. That was the kind of person who could help in their struggle in the future. Seizing the moment, the elders unanimously agreed to make him an honorary Inuit and, in a brief ancestral ceremony in the name of the Inuit sea god, Sedna, christened him with Joella's favorite name, Naglingnig.

As the group applauded, he ate the ceremonial raw walrus meat in Joella's honor, and although drunk, tears came to his eyes, recalling how much he missed her. He then decided to give Social Services $5,000 to make her life easier in detention, since his lawyer had twice hinted rich people get preferential treatment, including better study facilities.

He was beginning to experience and understand life's shadier side and liked it. Nonetheless, his conscience bothered him, appreciating how embarrassingly easy it was to stumble into a life of crime. In reality, he was now a criminal, his infractions being no different from the others he despised, just that he was smart enough not to get caught. In order to survive and help Joella, he realized that this would likely not be his last.

Fearing Todd was going to keep blackmailing him and that proof of the malicious rumors now in circulation could mushroom and be investigated, Wilbert Clarke notified police that he had exercised his option for a promotion to Social Welfare Administrator, located in Goose Bay, a gratuitous post that had been made for his assistance in finding Quinn's killer. He burned all the CDs, videotapes, floppy disks, and had his hard drive reformatted to destroy any traces of his abuse on children. Then, as a goodwill gesture to silence Todd, he requested that Social Services permit him to live in the house with a caretaker, explaining his son deserved a decent place to live, and he would adequately support him until he reached legal age, which he knew was less than two years.

Social Services, knowing Mr. Clarke's honorable reputation and Todd's reliability, readily agreed on a trial basis, even though Todd adamantly refused a caretaker.

Throughout the remainder of the summer, Todd and Lois became inseparable. Her foul manners began to moderate, whereas his rapidly deteriorated. They were referred to as the *Odd Couple.* She took a keen interest in photography and enrolled in karate classes to be near him. She could already defeat him at kayak racing and proved to be more accurate rifle marksman. He now accepted her as an equal and had become conditioned to her offensive manners. She unknowingly became his shadow, and he appreciated it.

The government-appointed caretaker appeared periodically unannounced at his home to monitor him and was pleasantly surprised to find Lois, who was helping him, could cook and was keeping his home spotless. They considered him responsible enough to continue alone, unaware that Lois practically lived with him as his wife. Lois enjoyed her new popularity and respect, and with Todd's ability to speak Inuktitut fluently, he soon became the star of the Ikkusek family, who in turn elevated his image among the Inuit and Innu.

Though friendless for nearly a month, Joella was safe from any rapist, had warm clothes, plenty of food, and a clean decent place to live, even if it were a family-group home, their politically correct term for her prison. The summer weather in St. John's was warmer than back home, and she spent a lot of time outside with the others in organized activities.

She was surprised, but happy, to be given a large private bedroom, neatly organized as a virtual classroom. There was a computer and a large screen complete with two-way communications with her remote teacher. Since there were no restrictions on grade levels or study times, she engrossed herself into her grade ten studies all summer, aiming to complete high school in just two years, at times studying until well after midnight.

She did not know why she was separated from the others and given preferential treatment but guessed it was because they considered her dangerous. It bothered her that her trial was taking such a long time. Nonetheless, she had Tara as a trusted friend during their outside chores, disciplinary lectures, and compulsory exercises.

The conditions were much better than she had anticipated, but she was beginning to panic about another problem. In September, she had missed her second menstrual period and was having morning sickness and believed she might be pregnant, realizing that would be the worst-case scenario for her. However, she still held out hope it might be a false alarm, but subconsciously, she was intelligent enough to grasp she was most likely in self-denial. She now felt guilty about asking Todd to make love to her. She shuddered to think she would have to go through a pregnancy alone at her age, then have Todd's child taken away. She knew she should tell her lawyer, but she did not trust her.

She desperately wanted to talk to Melissa but was prevented from communicating with anybody, other than her lawyer, and many nights she would wake up crying for Todd, only to have the night watchwoman rush in to investigate. But each morning, she would kneel and pray, go with the others to eat breakfast, then valiantly go to back her desk to study.

Shark Fin, sitting in the restaurant section of the large community general store with his friends drinking, saw Todd and Lois enter. After two months, it still riled him that the local simpleton had stolen his girlfriend. He was two years older than Todd, but not as big or as physically strong and was hesitant to challenge him. It was also rumored that Todd was beginning to fight back, even against the police. Even worse, Lois was taking karate, and she was already vicious enough to attack a polar bear with her bare hands.

But with his drunken friends by his side for support, Shark Fin guzzled his fifth beer, turned to them, and boasted, "Watch me have some fun."

There was a commotion as his friends began to talk and laugh as he prepared for the confrontation. He shouted aloud for all to hear, "How was Lois after I got finished with her, Todd?"

Everybody in the store became quiet, turned, and looked. The clerk, knowing Shark Fin's spiteful reputation, sensed trouble and quickly phoned the police.

Lois was instantly furious, but before she could defend him, Todd yelled back, "Excellent! It didn't take *long* to get past the *used* part."

The store roared with laughter at the unexpected response from Todd, and there was an instant chorus of jokes and scorn, this time aimed at Shark Fin.

Lois smiled at Todd's new assertiveness, thrilled her plan was working.

Shark Fin, embarrassed, angrily stood up and staggered toward him. Glue Gun, Shark Fin's sidekick, stopped him. After seeing Todd beat his own father and his two friends to a pulp in the storeroom, he knew Shark Fin was no match for Todd, eagerly took his place, and sneered, "You fuck Joella, and you're a hero. What makes you such a fuckin' stud all of a sudden?"

Todd, incensed at the insult on Joella, clinched his fists, walked angrily toward them both, put his face inches from Glue Gun's, and stated scornfully, "Ask your wife!"

Again, a thunderous din erupted, as they now clapped, rapped on tables, and ridiculed Glue Gun. Todd soon realized they were like a pack of wolves, willing to follow the strongest leader. Encouraged by the crowd, and seeing Glue Gun too humiliated to answer, he egged him further, "Or one of your twin sisters!"

Glue Gun, caught off guard by his tenacious stance, was speechless, at a lost on how to react, hesitant to fight Todd. Just then the police stormed into the store and strode directly to Todd.

"Is there a problem?"

"No. I was educating the drunks."

"Who's drunk?" asked the officer. The store went quiet again, as they waited for him to snitch—a cardinal sin among Inuit and Innu.

"That's your job. You figure it out. I'm simple. Remember?" He turned and walked to the clerk and calmly placed his order.

Lois, in an unusual display of affection, hugged him and whispered, "I'm proud of you." Then, seizing an opportunity to exact revenge, turning to the senior officer, shouted angrily, "Since I went with Todd, I found out Shark Fin is a criminal. You should arrest him."

Once again, you could hear a pin drop.

"On what grounds?" he asked seriously.

"His dork is too small!"

This time the whole store roared with laughter, including the two police officers.

As they left the store, Lois knew Todd was deeply embarrassed at her yet pleased by her actions. She gloated, "That's how it's done, Todd. They'll think twice before challenging you again."

Todd gave a rare smile.

She added, "We're a good fuckin' team. Joella would be proud of us."

Todd wondered if it were true.

Unknown to Todd, his disrespect for the police had earned him the credentials needed for survival in such a desolate place. Lois was secretly approached by the local *wolf pack* for her to persuade Todd to hang out with their popular group. But he spurned their acceptance. These were the same cowardly lowlifes who had previously attacked Joella and provided falsified court affidavits, contributing to her present incarceration. He swore to God the day she had been arrested, he would get restitution from every last person that hurt her.

Aware he had to be patient and wait for an opportunity to exact that revenge, he accelerated his martial arts program and was learning military techniques from Lois's renegade brother, Cecil, however repulsive he found him.

Cecil was indeed a nasty hooligan who had been dishonorably discharged from the army for stabbing a person in a drunken brawl, and everyone gave him a wide berth for fear of guilt by association. He had several other charges impending for break and enter and robbery.

His father's two friends, Carl and Jimmy, who were leaving for St. John's to testify against his mother, were already avoiding Todd, having already tasted a sample of his ferociousness. And the area was abuzz with gossip that Todd was stalking them. They were now always seen together for protection.

His aim now was not just to study enough to obtain the academic college level for a law entrance, but to become a martial arts expert as well. By not smoking and being an avid outdoorsman, he was already ahead of most of the community dopeheads and drunks, at any age. He knew his threat would come from the middle-aged hardened criminals who saw him as a threat to their predatory schemes for molesting young females. He was aware they would love to catch him alone on the open barrens or on the ocean. But Lois, with her best friend now in jail, was more than eager to help and had plans of her own for retaliation against several of the other local bullies. She had her own dark secrets.

At the end of September, Joella was moved from her group home in St. John's to the hospital for psychological analysis, and she felt alone and lost in the huge building. For nearly a week, doctors subjected her to a battery of tests as to assess her physical and mental condition. The injuries from her confrontation with Quinn were serious and most still visible, but not life threatening. She heard how she had suffered from malnutrition over the years, something she knew all too well, and was put on a long list of vitamin supplements.

She again laboriously recapped her miserable life as they listened attentively, asking only a few questions. She explained that she was grateful that the detention centre staff was kind and courteous to her but stressed that she missed Todd and Mrs. Clarke and wanted to talk to them about a personal problem she was having.

The three psychiatrists were puzzled at her maturity and intelligence for a fifteen-year-old. Both her mechanical aptitude test and IQ test scores were higher than the average of most college entrance students. Not once did she contradict herself in their mental profiling assessment cross-examinations. They considered her kind, disciplined, and courteous, a model teenager. How or why a person with such a calm personality would kill someone was a mystery to them, and had she not confessed, they would have argued in court she was incapable of such a deed. They found her congenial and loved chatting with her.

The psychiatric report to Social Services unanimously emphasized that she was not a threat to herself or to the public if released into a foster home. Their only stipulation was she be kept away from her father for her own protection.

In the final analysis, the only conclusion they could draw, or concoct, was she had honestly defended herself against a monster but overreacted as the result of a lifetime of abuses.

By the first of October, Lois's grades in school began to improve with Todd's help. The community left them alone, word having circulated that Cecil would send anyone bothering them to the bottom of Davis Inlet to visit Sedna's Inukshuk. Todd was smart enough to know an ally and helped Cecil with his welfare documents or unemployment insurance forms and faithfully bought him a bottle of rum every week.

When alone and distressed, he read Joella's diary. He could now identify with her grief.

> My Naglingnig,
>
> Tonight I am crying in my bed, a prisoner to my five senses. I see only evil. I hear only evil. I feel only fear. I smell only the mildew of my cold wet bedroom, and I long for the taste of food. God has deserted me in my time of need.

Lois returned from class and saw Todd crying. She had never seen a boy cry and felt oddly sorry for him. She hugged him and asked him what was wrong. He said nothing. It felt strange for her to feel another person's grief.

"Tell me, Todd. I'll get Cees to blow his fuckin' head off."

"I got a phone call. It's a private hearing. We can't go to see Mom or attend Joella's trial."

"What? Your mom's not a minor."

"They do what they fuckin' want!"

Surprised, she smiled at him. It was the first time he had ever uttered a four-letter word.

"I'm getting even with Carl and Jimmy," he vowed venomously.

Seeing he was becoming desperate, she tried to moderate his temper. "Let's do it together."

He hugged her for a change and said forcefully, "Okay, but first let's fuck."

I may have overdone it, she mused happily.

When the trial began, Melissa's outlook was optimistic, her lawyer having assured her that she would be back home within a few days. Now, on October 15, three weeks later, as she sat silently in the court listening to her beloved husband testifying on behalf of the crown, blatantly lying regarding the events of the shooting, she was depressed and doubtful if she'd be home in a month.

She stared at her husband and sobbed silently as he calmly explained that he always believed his wife was mentally ill and Todd had unfortunately inherited those same genes. Yet, even though he was lying, she still loved him, forgave him, and would probably take him back after she was acquitted. She desperately struggled with her feelings. How could she still love someone so evil? Or was she really simple like people often accused Todd? But, if she were retarded, why wasn't she remanded for psychological assessment? All the cards were stacked against her; she felt lost.

Wilbert's two friends, Carl and Jimmy, subsequently substantiated his testimony, followed by several affidavits laboriously presented on behalf of several witnesses of Natuashish and summarily accepted by the judge, even though most were mere fabrications by juvenile delinquents with petty criminal records seeking a lenient sentence for outstanding infractions, the same youths she had helped over the years. She seemed to be sinking deeper and deeper into the quagmire of lies being spun by the prosecution.

She heard the ex-mayor explain how she was a role model to the youth of the community, how she taught them to be resolute in dealing with bullies, how he believed that because Joella almost worshiped her and Todd, and that was the motivation Joella needed to murder Quinn.

Pastor Cornelius stated she was a staunch Christian and found no fault with her and didn't believe she tried to kill anybody. But, as not to tarnish his honorable credentials, he made a blanket statement, noting that several other members of his parish were *also* handicapped in some way.

The prosecution went on endlessly. Melissa was appalled, having no idea people were permitted to lie in court with impunity. She was horrified at all the derogatory statements made against her. There seemed to be no end to her inferior status and evil ways; yet until now, most of the community youth looked to her for guidance and support.

Todd was prevented from testifying by his father's lawyers who had painted him as being mildly retarded and as a result was known in the community as Simple. Todd's handwritten submission was permitted but heavily edited by his Social Services legal counsel to prevent him from being forced into a foster home.

What concerned Melissa most of all was that all her prime witnesses were rejected. Joella's affidavit was submitted by her lawyer and immediately dismissed by the crown, in view of the fact that she was a problem child and had freely confessed to murder.

Melissa could not humanly comprehend how such a sweet child like Joella could be so demonized. Justice did not enter the picture; it was merely a game of egos between competing lawyers to win Brownie points, and her lawyer was definitely a Brownie.

Finally, she got her turn on the stand and related the events chronologically, precisely as they occurred, without regard for her own welfare or making mistakes. When cross-examined, most prosecution questions centered on why she threatened her husband and fired a shot at him. She heard the words from Joella's official report twisted and taken out of context, such as Joella admitting she did not hear any of her attackers say that they intended to rape her, that they had not put a hand on her.

Melissa admitted threatening her husband but adamantly denied trying to shoot him. However, she was positive Joella's attackers intended to rape her and naively admitted she would have shot all three if they continued to rape Joella, and her lawyer did not stop her.

Her time on the stand took only half a day, whereas her prosecution took three weeks. By midafternoon, the hearing was complete, the jury charged and sequestered.

As she left, she was told the decision would take several days, but next morning, she was recalled to the courtroom, a decision having been quickly reached. This raised her hopes, but she was still nervous, knowing the all-man jury would find her guilty of the unlawful discharge of a firearm, and she would get a fine and possibly house arrest, but no criminal record. Contributing to the delinquency of a minor was a charge she knew would be dropped; she had used Bible principles. On attempted manslaughter, she would be found innocent; it was an asinine charge. She figured that was fair justice.

That's had to be the reason the jury decision was so swift, she mused, as she stood up to hear the decision. She would soon be home like she planned to look after Todd and help Joella. She was relieved and upbeat, smiling for a change.

"Has the jury reached a decision?" queried the judge.

The jury foreperson announced, "We have reached unanimous verdicts on all three charges, Your Honor."

There was a longer-than-usual pause as she opened her notes. Melissa held her breath.

"On the charge of unlawful discharge of a firearm: guilty."

The courtroom remained silent.

"On the charge of contributing to the delinquency of a minor: guilty."

The courtroom stirred to show its disapproval.

On the charge of attempted manslaughter: guilty. The jury recommends she remain incarcerated until sentencing and during any subsequent appeal."

The courtroom stood up, became noisy, some shouting *fraud.*

The judge hit his gavel on the bench. When the noise abated, he queried the jury foreperson unbelievingly, "Guilty on all three charges?"

Yes, Your Honor."

"Even the attempted murder charge?"

"Yes, Your Honor."

The courtroom remained deathly silent waiting for his rebuttal. After a brief silence, he responded halfheartedly, "The people have spoken. Sentencing will take place at 2:00 p.m. Friday in this courtroom. Escort Ms. Clarke back to her cell, sheriff."

Melissa sat slowly down, stunned by the decision. All she could think about was what was going to become of Todd. She knew that even though he was a gentle soul, upon hearing the *guilty* news, he would undoubtedly seek revenge against his father and his father's friends. She had absolutely no idea where to look for justice.

All her life, she had helped lost Innu and Inuit youth; now she was the one lost.

Without parents or community support and having confessed at her closed hearing, Joella's government-appointed lawyer acted more like a prosecutor than her defense, counseling her to accept the court's decision and not appeal any sentence they might give her, noting it would likely be minimal since it was her first conviction.

There was actually no trial, more of an ad-hoc committee of medical and legal professionals brainstorming some spur-of-the-moment procedure on how to civilize and constrain a savage animal before rushing off to their more important golf games. They did not seem to care whether she was guilty or innocent; the emphasis was placed on her past infractions, her present personal economic circumstances, and how best to rehabilitate her.

There was not one Inuit in the group or any person that understood the mentality of the North. Joella found it easy to interpret from their repetitive derogatory terminology with words like *those people, Indians, and Eskimos*. She was deemed a lower form of life, and she was being cast to the wolves.

She listened silently, afraid to even whimper, as they casually discussed her future, knowing she was completely at the mercy of people whom she distrusted as much as the incompetent police, who had recommended charging her. She saw them all as oppressors without compassion as they tried to pressure her into agreeing to the plea bargain made by her lawyer.

She was shocked to learn the plea bargain was five years' detention for self-defense, even if it were at a special youth centre in British Columbia so she could first attend a good school and then go to college while still being incarcerated in a minimum security facility.

However hard they tried, she refused, knowing—if she were pregnant—that if she moved so far away, Todd and Mrs. Clarke would never see her, and they were all she had in the world.

But in the end, the panel finally concluded that was the best possible option for her. The judge mysteriously reappeared and unceremoniously sanctioned it.

She sat motionless, almost numb. There was no defense, no trial; no one spoke on her behalf, as if there were no legal process. It resembled one of her disastrous school plays, designed by the students, where each had unlimited input; then the principal approved their ridiculous contribution without question. Every government employee from the corrections officer to the judge, in addition to all the hired experts, had unlimited power over her fate.

She felt like the little wolf puppy that she once found under a rock after its mother had rejected it, alone and frightened, wanting someone, anyone, to care for it. She now knew how it felt.

Chapter Three

Vigilante Justice

The end justifies the means.

—Karl Marx

By late October, Todd had been notified that his mother had been convicted of attempted murder and sentenced to six years to be served in a federal penitentiary in British Columbia. Soon after, he learned Joella Adams had been sentenced to five years in a correctional institute for young offenders at an undisclosed location. He was now panicking. With no family and a corrupt justice system, he knew vigilantism was his only option and was spending a lot of time scheming with Cecil to speed up his revenge.

He reread Joella's diary and, with the information, meticulously made a list in his computer database program detailing the demographics of all her offenders: age, race, sex, motive, address, hobbies, sports, and education, even to their favorite foods, some thirty males and four females, to more accurately determine their weaknesses. In another file, from Joella's diaries, he made a detailed description of all her abuses: the dates, severity, and location, etc. In a third file, he listed a series of appropriate responses to similar incidents. He then linked the files together and produced his integrated functional *hate* list.

He wanted to exact revenge in order of severity, but he had already initiated harsh responses against some on his hate list, which as yet had to bear fruit; but his father's penalty, which was his number one priority, bothered him the most. He was the epitome of evil and deserved the harshest punishment, yet he had promised his mother he would not harm him, and he was his only source of legal support, and bribe money, if needed. Tuk was a close second followed by his father's two friends, the masked cameraman, and the originators of the false affidavits. He was fully aware they were the hardest to access. Hitting the small fry first could possibly land him in jail, and the big fish would get away. He agonized long hours over the best strategy and, in the end, decided to strike whenever and wherever the opportunity presented itself.

Anxiety was already growing in the community. Gossip was rampant that the Nerd had hacked into everybody's computers, including that of his father and the police, and had copied confidential files on all the residents. That raised the fear that many other illegal acts could be uncovered since Lois's brother was in on a lot of them, and if all the facts were to become known to him, Cecil could possibly be enticed to testify against them in exchange for a more lenient sentence.

Though false, the rumors provided Todd with a brilliant idea. For the next week, he patiently taught Lois computer skills and urged her to work as a part-time secretary at the police station as part of the Community Youth Program to obtain their access code to the police computer database. The knowledge could not only give him a bargaining tool with the criminals but would reveal the trial venues and dates of Joella and his mother.

He was now on a mission. Not just for restitution, he wanted revenge so badly he often dreamed about it.

The police soon began to receive reports of vandalism; crime rose sharply. Carl's speedboat had been cut from its mooring in an early autumn snowstorm, had drifted out to sea, and was lost.

A 12-gauge shotgun cartridge had been concealed in a piece of his firewood; it exploded causing damage to his woodstove, and burning his new hardwood floor. Soon after, all his prized racing huskies had mysteriously perished of distemper, some say poisoned.

A week later, someone had put sugar in the gas tank of Jimmy's new snowmobile, causing his motor to seize. And now, Jimmy was in hospital with a broken ankle, having stepped into a bear trap that had been placed near his door. Tuk and his wife, who has just returned from jail, had been frightened into fleeing to Sheshatshiu to live with relatives, after hearing a rumor that the shaman had predicted he would die soon in a seal-hunting accident.

Todd and Lois were the usual suspects, but all was too afraid of Cecil to accuse them.

The police was also deeply concerned and was carefully monitoring Todd for Social Services but noticed nothing abnormal. Quite the opposite, each Sunday, he attended church services, as usual, and willingly assisted the pastor. Lois was accompanying him and was becoming civilized. They were hesitant to accuse him of anything sinister without just cause, especially since he was now alone.

At the church, Lois distracted the pastor while Todd copied the church computer files and planted a simple virus on the hard drive to erase all the files in two days. He planned to spread a rumor that Pastor Cornelius was being audited for fraud and had erased his donation records intentionally. For good measure, he put Ex-Lax in the minister's private wine supply.

Lois was more than willing to help but was concerned he'd get caught, and she was becoming nervous. He was now openly aggressive, and she was worried he would be forced to kill someone in self-defense. Not wanting to lose him, she coaxed him to slow down and let her help him, believing she had now created a monster.

On Remembrance Day, Todd got his long-awaited break. Social Services had received documentation from his new legal representation, whoever that was—they seemed to change monthly—disclosing that his mother's lawyer had informed them that her sentence was to be appealed, and for reasons unknown, his father, who was petitioning the courts for a divorce, was not going to appear as witness for the crown in her appeal. Even more bizarre, neither were his friends, Jimmy or Carl. And without their input, it was almost certain her charges would be stayed.

Equally encouraging, Joella's legal counsel had e-mailed them that her sentence was also being reviewed. Todd shook his head in amazement; the political and legal system was a jungle of bureaucracy, and Joella wanted him to be a lawyer.

Buoyed by the good news, Todd immediately volunteered to pay for a legal escort to accompany him visit Joella, but it was strictly forbidden. He offered to write her a letter to be approved by the court, but that too was prohibited. The Social Services lawyer was to be Joella's sole contact with the outside world. Todd soon realized that Joella's lawyer was a gofer for the court and was doing little to help her.

While not being permitted to give him the location of the detention centre or the courtroom, she did advise him of the hearing date.

With Lois working in the police office and subtly flirting with the young police officer, obtaining the password was a sure thing. And knowing the hearing date, Todd didn't take long to determine Joella's trial venue.

On reading her file, he wasn't surprised to learn from the court records that Joella had soon exonerated her mother—Joella was a kind person—or how she willingly revealed the details of her own life or her actions in the attempted rape; she had always been candidly honest. What really shocked him were the caustic responses of the prosecution to her truthful submissions and how her incompetent counsel did little to defend her. Even more astounding, the official records showed Tuk, who precipitated the disaster, was asked by the prosecution to testify against his own daughter in exchange for not being charged for selling her, a point overlooked by Joella's lawyer in the sham trial, and incredibly, he readily agreed. Luckily, he was prevented from being subpoenaed and testifying because the court psychiatrist considered him mentally incompetent. However, Joella's mother, who tried her best to defend her the only way she knew how, by taking the blame, had spent two months in jail for contempt of court and perjury. Todd felt there was absolutely no justice in the world.

Cecil, in one of his cantankerous moods, wanted to use his underground contacts to spring her, but Todd knew that was equally incompetent and unrealistic. Lois wanted to send thousands of e-mails to try to solicit public opinion to embarrass the courts. Todd had no idea what to do. Reaching an impasse, he decided on a surprise visit during her appeal and hoped for a miracle.

Even that simple task presented an insurmountable problem. How could he and Lois travel to Vancouver and sneak inside a well-guarded secret trial without being apprehended, since neither had ever been away from home and knew little of the outside world?

That problem was soon solved when Cecil, who had travelled half the world with the army and hitchhiked the other half as a hobo, knew all the shortcuts, including the undesirable ones. Todd invited him, as much for their security—his looks alone could instill morbid fear—as for guidance, to attend not only Joella's review—whatever that meant—but also to try to visit his mother. Cecil would pretend to be Joella's uncle.

However, it cost him $1,200 for a plane ticket for Cecil, plus $500 to buy both Cecil and Lois respectable clothes.

Joella had no idea what fate awaited her as the plane touched down in Vancouver. She was apprehensive about this special facility for indigenous people that they kept bragging about. She knew the people in British Columbia were not Inuit, but from various, diverse first nation's cultures and wondered how she would fit in, knowing most white people believed all aboriginals were of the same background. Most Canadians did not know the difference between Innu and Inuit, much less Tlingit, Haida, or Salish.

She had established a comfortable routine in St. John's and had adapted to her new reality and didn't want to start over. She was not adept at making friends, and Tara had been both a loyal friend and flawless security.

The next few hours revealed many surprises. It was December. There was no snow on the ground, and flowers were still in bloom along the highway. The correction facility was located in a wooded valley at a place called Mission. It was designed as a minimum-security refuge, a home-away-from-home type of environment for academically high-achieving nonviolent students, of which she figured she didn't belong. It was almost laughable; she wondered if they had her mixed up with some rich white person.

She found it was more of an open, expansive, guest ranch, surrounded by a temperate rain forest, complete with every amenity: a golf course, baseball pitch, tennis court, and a basketball court. The fenced enclosure contained no barbed wire, and its four gates were always open and unguarded; inmates wandered freely.

Her personal space was a miniapartment with all the amenities: a bedroom, bathroom, living room with fireplace, full kitchen, and a cozy study den complete with computer facilities, all impeccably clean. There was a list of mandatory chores posted on her door and a set of guidelines to follow. She perused the rules and found she had a choice of two public high schools or a private school. She was even permitted to use all public facilities once each week: skating, movies, theatre, and bowling. The only criteria being a two-day advance notice, for which she could apply on her computer.

Even more pleasant, her young guard and designated counselor, Susan Kamanirk, was actually an Inuit from Tuktoyaktuk, who was once incarcerated in the same facility and could speak Inuktitut. She began to relax for a change.

"Wow!" she exclaimed, managing an astonished smile to Susan. "This is like a resort."

"Only for the rich though. You got their elite private suite; your parents must be wealthy and famous," Susan said impressed and somewhat sarcastically.

Joella smiled cynically at the embarrassing remark. *I'm separated because I'm a dangerous murderer, stupid*, she thought.

They were all welcomed surprises, except the last and most revealing of all. She was required to complete a full medical and physical examination, and after five months, it would be impossible to conceal her pregnancy

"You're my very first assignment," continued Susan, smiling. "After I leave, turn the dead bolt on your door and push that red button next to the lock; it sets your security alarm. You're monitored in the office, but they're asleep half the time." She stopped and pointed out the cameras overhead.

"The cafeteria's down the hall. You can bring your meal back here. The meeting room is next to it. It's where the moderates hang out. We'll talk tomorrow. Good night."

Thrilled to have her own private place, she sat down and scanned her surroundings. How nice it would have been to have a happy family in a clean home like this, she mused. This was how Todd lived. Coming back to the real world, she hastily began to unpack and saw her mother's Great Spirit *dream-catcher* package. Tears came to her eyes. She stopped, sat down again, and stared sadly at it for a long time contemplating why her mother would lie to save her. It hurt to think her telling the truth had caused her mother to have a criminal record; life was so unpredictable and cruel.

She wanted to see what was inside such a stupid package but recalled her mother saying it had to be the lowest point in her life, and she figured that would be when they took her baby away. She reverently placed the package into the drawer and closed it, then went and kneeled at the bed to pray for her.

With her communicative skill and ultrareligious faith, Melissa soon became the sweetheart of the jail wardens. She was honest, dependable, and could be entrusted to do any chore without supervision, including using knives in the kitchen, a jail's highest level of trust. And with her sincere praying and pitiful crying daily, she received the sympathy of even the most hardened inmates, who considered her imprisonment a classic case of injustice, the victimization of females by a male-dominated establishment, and the male wardens were taking verbal abuse because of it. As a reprieve and to keep her away from the other inmates, she was given free access to all the staff facilities.

She longed for the clear, crisp Labrador nights with the Northern Lights dancing overhead and the rambunctious youth coming crying to her with all the problems they could not tell their parents. She knew the Innu and Inuit youth were in a void between two worlds and needed professional guidance. In their church open-chat sessions, she often explained to them where the dangers of such a lack of identity could lead them. Now they had nobody to run to. They were totally lost. As was she.

She prayed for Todd, Joella, and Wilbert several times a day, in spite of still openly struggling with the realization her husband did not love her all these years, whereas she adored him.

The prison chaplin was working with the parole board to reverse the visiting restriction and the communication blackout with her son. Even the wardens found that injunction extraordinary and oppressive and, with her lawyer's help, had persuaded the courts to bring forward her appeal date by three months, to be heard in February.

During the prison festivities on Christmas Day, the retiring prison chaplin made her a lay reader in recognition of her having successfully organized a religious pageant, in which nearly half of the inmates participated. It was a massive undertaking and a first for the maximum-security prison.

Christmas was a stark departure from past years at the Clarke house. Todd felt nostalgic for the smell of his mother's delicious holiday cooking he loved so much. He even missed the obnoxious guests that attended his father's government-sponsored parties that he hated so much. Most of his time now was consumed in concocting a scheme to see Joella and his mother on his next trip and shortening his hate list

Lois kept him in touch with reality by having several parties in his house basement or in the storeroom. The only participants were Inuit adults with Cecil maintaining strict law and order, with all conversations in Inuktitut; but she knew Todd enjoyed them.

However, at these parties, he was not happy about Tammy showing up uninvited and using lame excuses just to see him; it was bothering his conscience. He was also troubled by her excessive consumption of moonshine and twice thought he smelled glue on her clothes. She'd often stare at him, and when he'd notice her, she'd look embarrassed and blush. He was perplexed that she would come to his home, a place that caused her so much abuse, but then realized she was lonely, and he knew how that felt; so he often danced with her.

However impressive her surroundings, in the next two weeks, Joella realized the *moderates* were less than fair and treated her very mean. Their group home was a revolving door for problem kids; most being street-smart but uneducated drug users from broken homes, who ran away at the first opportunity. The few who stayed formed their own protective group, and she made no attempt to assimilate. She was despised and ridiculed because of her Labrador accent, that she had her own personal *rich-bitch* pad, had accepted a private Catholic high school, and studied most of the time. For these reasons, they nicknamed her *The Virgin Mary.* Being pregnant, she found that hilarious.

But she was respected by the staff and well-protected by Susan. She liked cooking and prepared many of her own meals in her unit, even those for her high school class cooking credits.

On Christmas Day, she was delighted to see such a huge variety of food dishes of different nationalities in the cafeteria and decided to taste all the foods she had never eaten. She filled her plate with small portions: salmon sushi, Indian tandoori chicken, three kinds of Chinese dim sum, a Turkish shish kebab, and Italian spaghetti and meatballs.

After slowly testing and enjoying all the delicacies for an hour, she suddenly felt weak. She stood up to walk back to her unit but cringed with cramps in her stomach, then threw up onto the table, and collapsed onto the floor.

Joella was quickly whisked away by the onsite ambulance. At the hospital, the medics assured the doctors that she had severe food poisoning. The doctors agreed but were puzzled when she refused any medicine for it. They immediately reported back to the institute that she was being uncooperative and disobedient and requested legal permission to force treat her. Susan Kamanirk persuaded her supervisor to refuse their request, explaining she had a common Inuit problem that was not life threatening, and she agreed to give her free twenty-four-hour monitoring instead.

She then sarcastically reminded her supervisor that food poising was not instantaneous, and any doctor worth his salts should know better. They embarrassingly agreed.

Later that night, after recovering for a few hours, Joella recognized Susan sitting by her bed reading a book.

"How are you feeling? Are you okay to talk?" asked Susan kindly.

Joella nodded.

"Joella, here you're free as long as you're responsible. Otherwise, they'll transfer to a secure jail. And I promise you, from experience, you won't like it! Tell the truth, and we'll help you. Remember, your case is being reviewed."

"Thank you. I'll try."

Susan stared patiently, waiting for her to continue. Joella, embarrassed, bowed her head and remained silent.

"Do you have anything to tell me?" queried Susan piercingly.

Joella shook her head. Tears came to her eyes.

"You'll have to trust someone soon. I know you don't have food poisoning."

"How?" Joella whimpered, starting to cry.

"Tara was a good friend. She guessed you were pregnant and tipped us off."

"How would she know?"

"She was your sundries supplier."

Joella already knew that but was confused how that was relevant.

"Everybody is monitored, Joella. Here you must be protected from others and yourself. Detailed records must be kept; it's the law. You gained fifteen pounds, and she said you didn't use any sanitary napkins in four months."

Joella began to instantly cry.

"I know they'll make me give up Todd's baby. Please help me."

"I'll do everything I can. But the courts usually put our children up for adoption."

"Our?" she asked confusingly.

"We're Inuit, Joella! I've been there. I lost my baby the same way. We don't get rich white man's justice," she responded disdainfully. Then mused aloud, "I don't know how *you* got this celebrity suite."

Neither did Joella.

Although nervous, Joella was relieved that her problem was out in the open, and she had a friend who understood her predicament.

Early January, Todd awoke one Sunday morning, after a huge snowstorm, to see a crowd of people shoveling snow from his driveway. Realizing they were mostly the tough troublemaking community bullies who were awaiting trial, he became nervous, got his gun, and awakened Lois.

Snarling like a cornered husky dog, Lois stormed outside with axe in hand, demanding to know what sinister game they were playing this time. She was soon relieved to learn from her brother that yesterday, they all had received notices from the police that their criminal charges had been stayed. The main computer systems' server in Goose Bay had inexplicably crashed, losing all the files, and the Natuashish office kept no official records. They believed Todd did it to help them, and they wanted to thank him.

Todd smiled to himself. At least, fate was smiling on him for a change. But the only virus he had planted was on the church computer, and that was a dismal failure. He was not impressed; they were the same scum that caused Joella's long record. If this were their pitiful attempt at restitution, he wanted none of it, and brandishing a gun, ordered them to leave. They obeyed, but surprisingly, some of the more reasonable ones thanked him for his help. Cecil slapped Todd on the back and, still jubilant, praised him in Inuktitut.

"You're now a real fuckin' Inuit, Todd, one of us."

Soon after every misfortune that befell any of the hoodlums in the community, Todd received the credit or blame. The police were beginning to treat him as if he were an auxiliary member of the force and secretly accrediting him with making the community more civilized. But Todd wanted revenge on them even more. It was their indifference, or stupidity, that implicated his mother in the first place.

Todd's and Lois's life had changed drastically. She was now madly in love with him and insanely jealous. Glue Gun's younger twin sisters were hounding him at every opportunity for dates, and he, who now attended every school party, danced with every girl purposely to cause dissention. Lois kept very close to control his actions, and theirs.

Todd noticed that Tammy also hung around him, asked him to dance, and praised him at every chance. He desperately wanted to talk about the pictures and apologize for his father's abuse but liked her too much to embarrass her, and she was still too young for dating. Knowing her hurt, he could see her pretty, tearful, pain-filled face in that picture every time he saw her.

He casually refused all their advances, fearing entrapment, and patiently assured Lois she would be his only girl until Joella returned.

Half of the local youth now worshiped him, while the other half wanted his hide. Even worse, nobody was challenging him anymore. They would even stand aside when he asked their girlfriends for dances. He was becoming a handful for Lois to control. She now knew she had indeed created a monster, a disaster waiting to happen.

Cecil staggered into the courtroom with a bottle of liquor in his hand, yelling he was Joella's uncle and that she was innocent. Joella was surprised and relieved to see someone from home for a change yet angered by his brainless actions; that would not help her cause. She tried to speak, but the court commotion drowned her out.

As the sheriffs were evicting him, Todd sneaked into the courtroom and headed directly to Joella, who was standing before the bench. She was well-dressed, had gained weight, looked older, and very distressed. There was more chaos, this time from the judge, as there was nobody to protect him. The prosecutor stood in his path.

Joella emphatically explained to the judge that Todd was peaceful and, crying mournfully, begged her counsel to let her speak to him. The judge was about to agree when the prosecution objected and urged a private meeting. They huddled at the bench and argued for a few seconds before acquiescing to the prosecution.

Joella, guessing correctly they did not want her pregnancy to become public knowledge, became impatiently and shouted,

"I love you, Todd. I'm pregnant. I want your mom to adopt our daughter."

Todd pulled away, walked to her, and kissed her on the lips before the returning sheriff managed to separate them.

She added, "They're going to put her up for adoption."

"I love you too. Mom went to jail for six years," he responded dejectedly. As the sheriff's deputies surrounded him and shuffled him away, he looked back and promised, "Whatever happens, I'll find our daughter and marry you. Someday."

The judge slammed his gavel on the desk, ordered him evicted, and took a recess.

Todd added, staring at her legal counsel, "You're not a lawyer. You're just an idiot, the court gofer."

"I was just standing up for our rights, sir. I only want justice," Joella begged the judge, without moving, as the judge began to leave.

"I'm afraid, Ms. Adams, in our courts, you get the law, not necessary your rights," he informed her sympathetically.

"But I only defended myself, sir. I don't want revenge."

"Control your client, Ms. Crosby," he said calmly and left the room.

It was an embarrassed and dejected bunch of misfits back at the hotel as everybody drank somberly from Cecil's rum bottle and quietly discussed their disastrous results. Cecil was relieved he was not arrested for cursing and pushing the sheriff. He knew from experience the reason being he was considered just another incorrigible, penniless, drunken Indian, who would just take up jail space.

Todd, embarrassed by the amateur blunder, knew his emotion was overriding his common sense. But most troubling was the revelation that Joella was pregnant. He felt her agony and had to find some way to help her, other than just paying money to his government-funded lawyer to get her better jail conditions. Even worse, he did not know if she was actually getting any service for that money. Most likely, her lawyer was taking a sizable slice. He did not trust lawyers. Without his mother to care for his daughter, he knew she would be adopted by some unidentified family. His life was slipping further and further toward the edge of an abyss.

Lois felt guilty for the joy Todd's tragedy had brought to her life and a deep sorrow for her best friend's incarceration. She knew Todd would now be even more vengeful and uncontrollable.

There was only one minor bright spot. While standing watch in the lobby as Todd and Cecil forced their way into the courtroom, Lois met Justin Patey, a burly two-hundred-pound twenty-four-year-old from the University of British Columbia, who was a trainee at Joella's institution. During their conversation, she learned he already had a criminology degree and was slated to become a male psychologist there when he graduated in May with his master's degree in applied social psychology. Because of his size and strength, he was temporarily assigned to assist the female wardens in dealing with the more aggressive inmates but was scheduled to eventually take over the position of the present director, who was leaving within a year. He listened patiently as Lois blurted out Joella's pathetic story, then promised her to keep an eye on her, and to e-mail her biweekly with as much information as law permitted, which he warned wasn't a great deal. Nonetheless, it raised Todd's hopes a little.

To visit his mother, Todd decided to use the legal route, but after dozens of phone calls and two days of niceties and begging, the result was the same: permission denied. Even worse, they now knew he was in town, and he guessed his mother's movement was restricted since he had spent a full day outside the maximum-security prison in Abbotsford hoping to catch a glimpse of her, but she did not participate in any outdoor activities. He could not remotely imagine his gentle mother in orange criminal-prisoner's fatigues and ankle chains, being paraded with murderers, and was somewhat relieved that image was spared him.

Now desperate, he was anxious to return home, with an even greater desire for revenge.

Back home after a disastrous trip, to keep his mind off Joella's pregnancy, Todd continued to diligently plan to carry out his revenge with crisis fervor and studied even harder to raise his grades to all As to qualify for the college of his choice, now determined to become the lawyer she wanted him to be.

In February, Providence began to shine on him for a change. Jimmy and Carl, who were longtime wilderness tourist guides, knew the precise location of roaming polar bears from their tag monitor beacons and, during their *slow* period, were poaching these same bears for their hides and penises for the black market.

Cecil, knowing this, tailed them whenever possible, usually to bribe them for a third of the spoils. And on one of their illegal expeditions, while he was scouring with his binoculars along the open patches of water near the edge the ice fields, he happened upon them having just shot two polar bears. He was about to pounce when he recalled how Todd had managed to get all his latest charges dropped, leaving him without a criminal record. He could identify with Todd trouble; he felt a strange closeness to him. This was his rare opportunity to repay Todd for rescuing him.

For once in his life, he found it a tough decision to choose between good and evil: help Todd or collect a possible $20,000. At first, it seemed a no-brainer. Then again, his sister loved both him and Todd. But $20,000 could get him that Arctic Cat snowmobile he never had.

He couldn't decide.

Like those bureaucrats at Joella's kangaroo-court trial, the brass at his own army court marshal knew his killing was in self-defense, and his brief jail time had been forced upon him by the military as a result of political rules and regulations beyond their control; and even though they eventually expunged his criminal record, the trauma had caused his life to spiral out of control since then. He now had the opportunity to break free again.

"I'm getting fuckin' soft," he mumbled to himself, as he quietly retreated and went to Todd's school to fetch him.

Less than an hour later, strategically concealed behind a high ice pinnacle, an excited Todd, with his camera's telescopic lenses, surreptitiously photographed and videotaped Jimmy and Carl laughing and drinking beer as they casually skinned the two animals. He wondered how he had gotten so lucky. It was a clear bright day; the pictures would be crystal sharp.

He sensed sweet revenge.

For the next week, with Lois's help at the station, Todd daily accessed the police computer in Ottawa. On February 15, he hit the jackpot. He located the confidential records of the two local officers. It was disappointing to read both were highly respected, but one officer had twice previously been reprimanded for keeping confiscated liquor. Even though Todd knew that such minor infractions were likely the result of inexperience, he wanted revenge nonetheless.

He meticulously digitally superimposed the offending officer's picture into a still photograph of Jimmy and Carl, positioning him strategically, such that the officer appeared to be a sentinel for them. For sentimental value, he added two cubs waiting in the background, hoping the public would not know that a mother bear was always alone with her babies.

He had Cecil's friend, on his next trip to Goose Bay, mail a copy to police headquarters in Ottawa, along with a letter, claiming the local police were trading in illegal bear hides at $10,000 per skin and bear penises for an equal amount, on the Asian market as aphrodisiacs. He knew these trivial details because Cecil had done the same thing and, when drunk, had a habit of boasting about his obscene profits. Todd also sent a hard copy, along with a videotape, to several newspapers.

The pictures first made front page locally, then soon became a world news sensation and instant fodder for fanatical environmentalists. With the uproar generated, within a week, both local officers were unceremoniously recalled for consultation, with the international news media standing by, hounding them for answers.

The community's temporary police replacements, incensed at the force being cast in such an embarrassing light, raided the property of both Jimmy and Carl and found several hides and penises. They were summarily arrested, detained, and charged with killing endangered species, illegal possession of bear hides, and subsequently dismissed from the federally funded wilderness tourist bureau.

Todd finally had his first major victory and was euphoric. He threw a party for Cecil and his few friends at the Ikkusek household and, in grand style, scratched off the first four major names from his *hate* list. He gloated over how he and Cecil were the perfect team and bought him two bottles of liquor for his assistance.

Everyone, including the new police officers, recognized that locally only Todd was capable of such sophisticated photography. This made Lois nervous, knowing Todd and Cecil had gone way too far, now sure she was going to lose him. The community would certainly gang up on Cecil; a fair number of the indigenous population depended on the illegal sale of skins of various animals, mostly seals, to supplement their income. Retaliation was only a matter of time.

But ironically, the council realized that Cecil, who practically lived outdoors, with all his charges stayed, would be an ideal candidate for the guide position and offered it to him, with a fair increase in pay. He initially thought they were mocking him and refused. But Todd hounded him for days to accept, recognizing it was their way of assuring honor among the thieves. He volunteered to teach Cecil how to compile his records and do his Internet advertising for him free of charge for a year. Still, Cecil refused. Todd used all his contacts to pressure him but to no avail. Cecil felt he was not qualified. Todd offered to arrange a date with Prissy, the schoolteacher, for him, his dream fantasy. That got his attention; she was the only woman who was ever kind to him.

Cecil, still uncomfortable with becoming an honest citizen, finally agreed on a trial basis and was afforded free use of the bureau truck, snowmobile, boat, and other items required to carry out his official functions. With government medical and dental insurance, and at Todd's annoying insistence, he got his rotten teeth repaired, his face warts removed, his hair cut short, had a clean shave daily, wore a clean bureau uniform at all times, and even went to church. His parents were amazed at his miraculous transformation.

Soon the whole community was praising Cecil for turning his life around and respecting him for the first time. But for them to say anything mildly negative about Todd would bring a swift rebuttal from old mean Cecil.

To add to Lois's fear, the police were uneasy about Cecil, a supposedly reformed criminal who was deemed too tough for the military, carrying sidearms and a scope-equipped, high-powered rifle that fired tranquilizing darts and was begging her to monitor him and report back.

At the annual winter celebrations, Todd was induced as a full-fledged Inuit, and Lois watched wide-eyed with amusement and disgust, as he willingly throat sang and ate raw walrus meat to confirm it.

With his flawless Inuktitut, he was invited to attend the Northern Games in Greenland as an observer, and he readily accepted. Lois and Cecil were paid to accompany him. To the Ikkusek family, their change in fortunes was incredible, and it was all as a result of their helping Todd.

Joella was angry that a disciplinary hearing was convened to deal with her delinquency for not revealing a pregnancy since, even she, wasn't aware of it before she was arrested. Every girl she knew back in Natuashish had had sex before she did. She did everything the courts asked of her, and she was still considered a troublemaker.

Susan had forewarned her that the hearing would be condescending and unforgiving and had coached her on how to answers the questions professionally without getting angry. But she was already angry; she felt treated like a piece of garbage.

For ten minutes, Joella valiantly controlled her frustration as the warden monotonously lectured her on the parole procedures, the limits of her rights and freedoms as a convicted killer, and her responsibilities to comply. Eventually, she tired of his endless subtle verbal abuse and exploded.

"A two-hundred-pound *Mental* tried to rape me in my own bed. I defended myself. Why is everyone treating me this way?"

"Why did you inform Todd of your court date and place—" began her psychologists calmly, changing the subject, realizing she was being overreprimanded.

"I did no such thing."

"Who did then?" asked the supervisor.

"I'm in jail. How would I know? He's a computer genius; he figured it out—"

"Juvenile detention: not jail. We're here to determine what to do with your child," interrupted the director. "We'll move you if you contact Todd again."

"Not jail?" She sneered silently. As usual, nobody believed her. Move? This infuriated her even more; she went into her survival mentality.

"What I do with my baby is my business."

They all looked up at her extreme change in attitude. Until this morning, she rarely spoke rudely, and her agreements were mostly reluctant nods.

"I'm keeping her. God says don't kill. And nobody, except him, will stop me."

The physician explained that it was quite moral to have an abortion as she was the victim of rape, and since Quinn was unstable, her child could be handicapped.

"I told everybody a dozen times. Quinn didn't rape me; I killed *it* first."

"It?" asked the warden, smiling.

"I told you; he was an animal!" she repeated emphatically.

Her psychologist laughed and asked, "Who's the father?"

Joella saw him as the only reasonable person in the group. She calmed down and, for twenty minutes, related chronologically all the events following the incident, her relationship with Todd and his family, and the code of the North.

They were all impressed by her honest and elaborate descriptions, awed by her intelligence for a person so young, grasping she was certainly not the average teenager.

Finally, the physician spoke, "I agree with you, Ms. Adams. At six months, an abortion is out of the question. And from your forthright disclosures, Todd appears to be a dependable person."

Joella managed a smile; the first obstacle was achieved. But her hopes were soon dashed when the Social Services representative stated categorically that based on her heinous crime and that as a fifteen-year-old Eskimo in detention, the courts would force her to put the child up for adoption.

Joella began to cry and stood up, just as defiant. "I know the pregnancy was my mistake. But I'm not a murderer. I defended myself, and if anyone here tries the same thing, I'd do it again." She began to walk to the door.

"We're not finished, Ms. Adams," noted the warden.

Joella turned and sarcastically noted, "All my life, I was subjected to white man's justice. We have no say. I already know what your answer will be."

"By *we,* you mean Eskimos?" asked the director, now angry.

"We're Inuit, not Eskimo, ma'am."

"You are unable to care for a child here," stated the social worker sarcastically. "Adoption is the only option."

"You do that, and you *will* make me a criminal," she promised as she slammed the door and left.

"She's a problem," noted the social worker disgustedly.

"No. She's a victim," responded her psychologist quickly.

"Victim?" asked the director, somewhat confused. "She murdered a person."

"She's a precocious fifteen-year-old, who defended herself against a madman and admitted guilt to save her mother," the psychologist recapped forcefully. "She's a victim of her culture, a victim of our social system, a victim of our courts, and . . ." He paused, stood up, and looked directly at the director. "I fear a victim of this institution too."

"We enforce the law, Mr. Patey, not make it," she reminded him determinedly. "You're new; you'll learn." She then addressed the hearing, "We conclude Ms. Adam's be denied any further sentencing reviews for serious breaches of this institute's protocol."

After making love, Lois was unusually quiet, cuddled Todd's back tightly, and kissed him on the nape of the neck.

He knew from her abnormal behavior, something was troubling her. "What's wrong, Lois?"

"You're like your mom, Todd; you're quiet but strong." Then after a period of silence to conjure up the courage added, "I love you. I don't want to lose you." She could hardly believe she finally told him. She cuddled him tighter.

As he had slowly come to know her better, he realized Joella was correct; she did have a good heart. Cecil was like that too. They, like him now, were victims of a harsh, unforgiving environment.

"I'm sorry, I'm promised to Joella, Lois, but I know I love you too." He paused for a time. "Until she returns, please stay with me."

"I will, but I'm worried. You're too close to Cees. He's pretty mean and can turn on you if—"

"No, Lois, Cecil's lonely, like you. You're not mean, just doing what's needed to live. Without your help, I would have been lost. I don't want to lose you either."

She felt only love for him, and it bothered her that he would eventually leave her. "I never thought I could fall in love," she whispered shyly. "I love Joella too; she's my only real friend. I told her all my true feelings. She was younger, but more mature than me."

Both were quiet for a long time, and finding the nerve, she added softly, "Don't take this wrong, Todd, but you and Cees can't take on the whole world."

"The police bugging you?"

"They're not a problem. But Cees knows all the criminals, and they know him. He was their hero. Now he's their enemy; they're scared."

"Cecil's not stupid. He'll still turn a blind eye to killing seals, poaching caribou, and stuff like that."

"I know my brother, Todd. When he likes and trusts someone, he protects them, like he does me. He's not educated. You made him into a respected person. He'd kill someone if they hurt you now. Let your list lie for a while."

He could tell she loved her brother too.

"I told you, Cecil's not mean. He has the job that suits his lifestyle. He won't cause any more trouble. Now that he looks civilized, he asked me to try to arrange that date with Prissy for him."

"Really? Yeah, pretty Prissy likes him." After pausing, she mused, "Why, I'll never know."

"I do. I despised you at first too. Because I didn't know the real you."

She hugged him tighter. "He needs a lot of help, Todd. Do you know how he told his last girlfriend that he loved her?"

"He had a girlfriend? He told her that? Gee, that's nice, Lois—"

"He wrote it in piss in the snow in front of her father's house."

Todd laughed for a long time. She was pleased to see him happy for a change. He noted, "All guys write in the snow."

"Who was the young girl in the picture, Todd?" she asked concerned, abruptly changing the subject.

"I can't tell for her sake," he whispered thoughtfully. Then, in a sudden angry outburst, "And I promised my mother not to hurt the scum ball."

He could feel her tears on his back. Knowing the tiger was mellowing and scared and he might lose her help, he turned and kissed her.

"Just help me with one more big takedown: Pastor Cornelius. The Ex-Lax, the loss records, the audit, none of it worked. Seduce him for me; let me record it, to prove to the courts that Joella was correct. Then I promise to be more careful and deal with the small fry."

"What!" she exclaimed, repulsed at the vile suggestion.

He smiled.

"Cecil agreed to be on standby so he won't touch you, just undress you. I know it may not work."

"Oh, I'm positive it will," she answered adamantly. She wanted to tell him a secret about herself but reneged, feeling he already had too many problems.

"Did you hear rumors about the preacher then?" he asked surprised.

"Cees will murder him if he hurts me, you know that," she whispered, still unsure, kissing him. After a brief silence, she added, "Okay then. Now, let's make love again."

"I love you, Lois," he said seriously. "And I promise I won't write it in the snow."

She laughed and hit his arm as a new round of lovemaking began.

It took some time for the seduction of the pastor to happen, almost as if he were forewarned by divine intervention. But on a classic dark stormy March Labrador night, the opportunity presented itself in storybook fashion. A sudden north easterly gale had unexpectedly blown in and forced all the housewives to rush home after delivering their cooking for the pastor's regular Friday potluck fund-raising dinner, and he had to phone Lois for help in storing and packing the meals, since his wife was away. She agreed, but only as an opportunity to help Todd.

Within ten minutes after arriving at the church, she sneaked Todd and Cecil through the rear entrance. They went and hid on the balcony for a clearer view. Todd carefully selected a strategic viewpoint and set up his video camera, as Cecil lay on the floor and drank straight from the bottle of rum Todd had bought for him.

Lois worked for ten minutes packaging the food for distribution to the poor, before the pastor arrived. It was warm inside, and she had removed her lumberjack shirt, leaving only a skimpy tank top showing her cleavage.

The pastor came and thanked her, staring at her breasts as she worked. He helped for a while and finally said, "Take a break, my dear, and have a wine with me."

She looked at him inquisitively and answered shyly, "I'm only seventeen. What if someone walks in?"

He went and locked the doors and got two glasses of wine. Returning, he sat beside her on the front church pew and said sternly, "Don't play games; I've seen your past with men."

She cringed at the statement but smiled and took the wine.

After chatting for a while and drinking the wine, he put his arm around her and touched her breast. She smiled robotically, pretending to enjoy it. Encouraged, he kissed it and slowly removed her tank top. After feeling her breast, he unbuttoned her jeans and removed them. He took off his shirt and collar and laid her on the pew. As he touched her panties, Cecil, watching angrily, could tolerate it no longer, jumped up, and sent his half-empty rum bottle smashing to the floor below, yelling, "You miserable son of a bitch, I fuckin' murder you too."

Without looking up, the pastor, without his shirt, bolted outside in the storm and headed for the manse, as Cecil, who could barely stand, staggered toward the steps, eager to get his hands on him. Todd scrambled from his hiding nook, grabbed Cecil, and desperately tried to calm him, explaining the idea was to get restitution by bribing him. After several tense and uncontrollable moments and after promising to buy him two more bottles of rum, Cecil began to settle down.

Lois, almost crying, quickly dressed, went to Todd, and hugged him. He kissed her and apologized, "I'm so sorry. Cecil's right; I waited a bit too long. I love you, Lois."

“I did it,” she gloated, relieved.

“How did you know he’d bite?” asked Todd, his mind working overtime. Again, she wanted to tell him but stopped just short.

“Just help me control my brother and keep your promise.”

Chapter Four

The Appeal

Extreme justice is extreme injustice.
—Marcus Tillius Cicero

Todd tossed and turned in his bed, unable to sleep; Joella's pregnancy was bothering him. He stared at Lois sleeping contentedly beside him and felt a tinge of shame and guilt about his love for her, while Joella was thousands of miles away, terrified and alone, struggling through a pregnancy. He kept her pregnancy a secret from everybody, not wanting any pity. If she didn't have an abortion, she was now eight months pregnant. He felt he was cheating on her. It had not entered his mind a girl could get pregnant so quickly.

Like Joella, Todd was abandoned by all his relatives. His only true friends were an Inuit family, the Ikkuseks, a family he utterly despised just a year ago. However poor and uncouth, they were protecting him as if he were their own blood. He had nobody with influence to help him either. The courts would not permit him to talk to his mother or Joella. If his mother were free, she would know how to handle it. He considered talking to his father to prevent his daughter from being put up for adoption, but his disgust for him overruled his good sense. He was at rock bottom. He had to figure out a way to help Joella. They were both like the leaves of a tree, cast to the wind, completely at the mercy of the world.

Next morning, he reluctantly revealed his insomnia problem to Lois but still could not tell her Joella was pregnant and asked her to let him spend a few days alone to think and sort out his life. Lois thought it a terrible idea; sure he was setting up another sting operation with her brother but nevertheless agreed for two days. He also wanted to confront the pastor without involving her, knowing she was scared yet willing to do anything for him. But first, he had to figure out what the appropriate penalty should be.

Since he was a kid, Todd was amazed with the grandeur of the frosty northern nights in Labrador. Silence filled the air. The dry snow felt like sand and squeaked under his feet as he walked. It was as if he were standing on the top of the world watching creation unfold. Atop Caribou Lookout, the complete dome of the sky was an endless canopy of bright flickering stars in a cold black abyss.

At times, he would stand there for hours and watch the forever-changing kaleidoscope of light covering the sky from horizon to horizon, as the Northern Lights lit up the crisp night and danced as if some magical god were shaking a rippling curtain of color, all the way from the peak of the orb down to the pure white blanket of freshly fallen snow on the ground. The air would whistle and crackle with static electricity as it cavorted on the snow. His fine hair would stand on end like a birch broom; he could hear Joella giggle and call him Einstein.

Here he felt alone and one with nature. And never more so than tonight. He recalled her telling him that in Inuit folklore, these sounds were caused by *sky livers*, who hovered in the heavens, trying to communicate with humans, begging them to save their soul from impending doom, and that these *soul catchers* should always be answered in a reverent whispering voice. He could also hear her laugh amusingly as he told her that in white man's tales, if you whistle to them, they would dance on the snow and chase you.

Life was forcing rapid and profound changes in his young life, and he was responding the only way he knew how: self-preservation. He knew he was losing his Christian faith because here he felt close to a new god, an unknown god, and he had come all this way to pray to it. He did not know why this cold, dark, lonely peak gave him such a good feeling, but Joella had told him Nature was a god of love for the Inuit, and somehow he connected with it. It was an ancient symbiotic relationship. Nature provided love by supplying all the necessary ingredients of life, and the Inuit responded with love by taking only as much from it as required to survive or help others.

He whispered a prayer to the *sky livers* to take good care of Joella and his mother and to help heal the wounds of the young girls his father had abused, especially Tammy.

Emily Howard sat with her husband, Winston, on the patio of their country estate just outside Oxford, England, basking in the early spring English sunshine, sipping a spot of tea and nibbling on crumpets, as she scanned the *Newfoundland Herald* on her laptop.

> Headlines for March 10, 2001
>
> PROTESTERS SURROUND SEAL FISHERY SHIP IN ST. ANTHONY
> LABRADOR WOMAN WINS APPEAL

Labrador woman? She was startled to read:

> Melissa Clarke, who was found guilty here in October for the attempted murder of her husband and his two his friends, has been granted an immediate appeal. Six months ago, a renegade Inuit teen from Utshimassit murdered a local resident of Natuashish, and Mrs. Clarke hid the delinquent on their property. Upon being discovered by her husband, Wilbert, and his friends, she attempted to shoot them and was apprehended by the local police.

> Mr. Clark is also petitioning his wife for a speedy divorce. He has been promoted to regional manager of Social Services for the area and is to receive a civic award. Their son, Todd, also arrested for assisting a fugitive, was released into the custody of the Social Services and is living at home alone.
>
> In a separate hearing, the five-year murder sentence of the fifteen-year-old juvenile is being reviewed. Being a minor, her name and location is being withheld but is also believed to be somewhere in BC.
>
> Mrs. Clarke, who is presently incarcerated in Ferndale, BC, is to present her appeal on March 18, in BC Supreme Court in Abbotsford. It is not known why both were moved to the West Coast . . .

"That's next week!" she whispered, looking at the calendar.

"Did you say something, dear?"

"We have to go to Canada to see my sister," she stated abruptly.

"A splendid idea, but good grief, woman. It's March. Labrador is an icicle this time of year," he responded in disbelief, removing his pipe from his mouth and blowing a stream of smoke. Then added pensively, "'Tis strange though. She hasn't called since the accident nearly six months ago. Before, she called every fortnight." Noticing his wife crying, he continued, "What's wrong, love? We can go somewhere else. Portugal is a tad warmer."

"She's in prison in Ferndale, BC, Winston."

He smiled, sure she must be joking, and mocked, "Isn't that Club Fed, where the inmates eat caviar and play golf year round?"

He knew their daughter's death at only sixteen in a car crash was weighting heavy on her. Unable to have more children, she was now pestering him to adopt a baby girl. Then in a kinder tone, he added, "Blimey, woman, that bloody Coronation Street is getting to you. Let's go to our condo in LA. I've just invested heavily in MGM . . ."

He stopped, noting she was almost sobbing. "The market fluctuations have been causing my ulcer to act up, Emmy."

"For murder," she whispered softly in anguish, handing him the laptop.

Smiling skeptically, he removed his pipe, casually tapped the ashes in the tray, and placed it on the table. He put on his spectacles and read with astonishment, then said calmly, "That's queer, love. She didn't say anything to us."

"That's why she missed the funeral."

"Where's Todd?" he mused aloud, refilling and relighting his pipe, deep in thought. "Good Lord, Emmy, he and his father don't see eye to eye." There was an extended silence as they pondered the negative possibilities. "That Wilbert is a perfidious black hard," he noted, nervously, staring at his wife. "I'll phone Todd to see if he's okay." He stood up and yelled, "Miles!"

Miles immediately appeared with fresh pot of tea, placed it on his table, and bowed. Seeing Mrs. Howard crying, he asked, "Is everything okay, madam?"

She shook her head.

"Miles, arrange a flight for me and Emmy to Vancouver, Canada," ordered Winston.

"Would that be for after Easter, sir? Convention dictates you give the opening address Good Friday, April 13, at Lord Thurston's—"

"Tomorrow, old boy. Extenuating circumstances."

Arriving back home late from Caribou Lookout and comfortably snug in his warm bed late at night, Todd was unable to sleep; he now missed Lois too. Life wasn't getting any easier. He recalled his mother telling him when all else fails, pray. But Christian praying didn't help her or Joella. Defeated, he felt that praying to the Christian god as well would not hurt and decided to give it a try. He got up, went to the family room, and knelt before his mother's large picture of *The Last Supper* over the fireplace.

"Heavenly Father, like Daniel, I've been cast into the lion's den—" The phone interrupted his train of thought for a second. He continued, "And like Daniel, please protect me. But my mother and Joella needs you even more. They're falsely in jail—"

Again, the phone rang, causing him to lose focus. Irritated, he jumped up, grabbed the phone, and snapped, "Lois, it's two o'clock! The answering machine shows you've phoned me ten times tonight—"

"Is Todd there?" came a heavy English accent on the line.

"Who's this?" he answered warily, believing someone was stalking him.

"His uncle Winston, in England."

"I'm Todd," he quickly answered.

"We're going to Vancouver tomorrow to see your mum and heard you . . ."

Todd now knew what he wanted from Pastor Cornelius. He took a deep breath, looked at the religious picture on the mantle, folded his hands reverently, and said, "Thank you, God!"

"'Tis not God, me, boy; 'tis your uncle, Winston."

For the next two hours, Todd poured out his heart to his aunt and uncle of his real living hell and begged desperately for them to adopt his child until he graduated college and could provide support.

"It's a girl?" asked his aunt excitedly.

"Yes."

"This may be the miracle of my prayers, Todd. I'll do my best."

"The *sky livers* will protect you," he promised.

"Sky livers? You've been alone too long," warned his aunt, concerned. "We'll phone you in a couple of days from Vancouver."

Pastor Cornelius was surprised to see Todd at the altar praying on a school night and welcomed him, "The heavenly father will forgive you, my son."

Irritated at his calmness, Todd stood up and attacked, "For what? I did nothing wrong. But will he protect you from Cecil? Lois is seventeen; you're fifty. Statutory rape—"

"I see you're here on a mission. What is it you want?" he angrily demanded.

"You tell the truth about my mother and Joella. And four tickets, and hotels in Vancouver to visit Mom and—"

The pastor was incensed and stated incredulously, "Nobody would believe the Ikkuseks. They're filthy, destitute criminals; nobody wants them."

"I want them! And my video shows you wanted Lois."

"Video? What video?"

"I was there!" He stressed *there.*

"You're bribing God?" he asked infuriated, barely able to control himself from attacking.

"No. A devil playing God. But it didn't work, so I'll give the tapes to the newspapers." Todd began to walk away. "And your wife, of course, when—"

As he opened the door, the pastor interrupted, smiling cynically, "Wait. Will that be the end of it?"

"Yes." Todd answered decisively. "But we also eat."

The pastor glared and nodded hesitantly as Todd left.

"Business class," snapped Todd, retaliating for the Ikkuseks being cast in such a disparaging light.

Cecil and Lois were joking and telling their parents about the pastor's predicament, when Todd walked unexpectedly into the Ikkusek household.

"Where were you? Why didn't you answer any of my calls? Did I do something wrong, Todd? I did all you asked. I love being at your place—" attacked a disappointed Lois, walking toward him.

"We're going to Vancouver," he announced, almost triumphantly, dismissing her concern and handing her and Cecil airline tickets. Cecil and Lois looked at each other confused. They had never seen him so happy.

"How did you get tickets without money?" asked Lois curiously. "We have school until—"

"I'm a big shot now," interrupted Cecil, sticking out his chest, taking a big drag on his cigarette, and blowing smoke rings. "I have to lead the Caribou parade."

"Okay. Prissy will be disappointed though. She was pretty happy when I gave her the ticket you bought her."

Cecil smiled, got up, and slapped Todd on the back.

"Dad'll cover. Where the hell did you get money for . . ." He paused, and staring at the tickets exclaimed, "Business class?"

"You'd never believe me, but I got a phone call from the *sky livers*. And I have another surprise when we get there," he joked, laughing.

His curious, relaxed, and talkative behavior astonished them.

"The money, Todd?" urged Lois loudly, impatient and nervous, fearing he had hacked into someone's bank account.

"Pastor Cornelius liked my photography," he said amusingly, trying unsuccessfully to act surprised. Then grandstanding, added, "So much he bought us all tickets, even agreeing not to testify at my mother's appeal."

The whole family roared with laughter.

Cecil congratulated him, "Jesus, Todd, I'm a fuckin' amateur compared to you. I'll do the honors of crossing the bastard off. Twenty-nine more, isn't it?"

Relieved, Lois hugged and kissed him, readily agreed, then warned, "Now keep your promise!"

"Most of the rest are small fry," he boasted. He kissed her back and whispered, "I missed you, and I'm horny."

"We have to go to Todd's house," Lois suddenly announced, equally as horny, disappointing her family, as she hurried to get her coat.

"Thanks, Todd," said a now hyper-appreciative Cecil as they left. "I'll sure as hell repay you for this one."

"We're even. That's payment for losing your bear penises. Now use yours. And name your first kid after Mom," he shot back.

The cantankerous old judge complimented Dorothy Woodward, Melissa's new defense lawyer, after she finished her long detailed submissions on the prosecution's opportune fabrications and on the unreliability of the witnesses at the original trial but had snapped repeatedly at the unprofessional behavior and pointless interruptions from Horace Cane, the prosecution lawyer.

The judge then demanded angrily, "If this isn't true, Mr. Cane, please explain why all of your witnesses are refusing to testify."

"They say they are busy, Your Honor. It's also March 18, sports week in—"

"Busy? In March? Aren't most of these people unemployed? We have subpoenas, Mr. Cane. A person is incarcerated based on their testimony, and they're busy enjoying winter sports? This case has all the earmarkings of tampering and borders on contempt of court."

Melissa was impatient and fidgety after sitting several hours alone in the box, unable to concentrate, barely listening and seldom understanding the monotonous legalese; her mind had been on Todd since her lawyer had received a phone call last evening from his social worker notifying her he had gone missing. They also reported he had committed this infraction before, with the Ikkuseks. She tried to understand why he would leave Natuashish, a place he loved so dearly, or why he would even associate with the Ikkuseks, known criminals. Most likely to get away from his father, she guessed.

She finally came alive when she heard the judge say, "Based on the evidence presented, Ms. Woodward, there appears to have been a gross miscarriage of justice perpetrated here. This court has no problem ordering a new trial."

There was instant disapproval from the prosecution. The judge hit his gavel hard on the desk and said irritably, looking at the court clerk, "At the earliest date, April twelfth, if possible?"

"I'll make it possible, Your Honor," agreed the clerk eagerly.

The judge continued, dismissing the prosecutor's objections, "Are you prepared for release today, Mrs. Clarke?"

That question created an instant uproar, and for the next hour, the tenacious prosecution adamantly refused to agree to her release, arguing the defense lawyer's statements had not been verified, believing Melissa would shoot her husband, and that he could persuade the previous witnesses to appear. The judge reluctantly acquiesced and ordered she remain in custody but permitted communication with her family, but not Joella.

Hearing that, Melissa was eager to find Todd, but her lawyer was now wasting more precious time trying to justify a request for a forty-eight-hour escorted weekend pass for which she had not applied, had no money, no friends, and no place to go. However, she was impressed at the persistence and aggressiveness of her defense, believing if she had been professionally represented initially, she would have been found innocent.

She was even more surprised when the judge readily agreed to the pass, refusing to entertain any further objections from the prosecution, and adjourned the hearing.

Melissa, exhausted, made a deep sigh of relief as she robotically followed her lawyer, who never seemed to smile, out of the courtroom. Her lawyer ordered her into the waiting room, saying that her escort group was inside and that she would contact her again on Monday, and quickly left. Confused at the sudden brush-off, Melissa obeyed, as the sheriff opened the door and directed her inside.

Inside, she was surprised to see no guards waiting, instead her sister, Emily, holding a big bouquet of flowers standing in the middle of the room smiling, and her husband, Winston, calmly smoking his pipe in a nonsmoking area. Thoroughly embarrassed at being seen in prison fatigues, she began to sob immediately, almost choking as she attempted to explain.

"I didn't do anything wrong, Emma, I swear. Wilbert framed me. I just stopped them from raping Joella . . ."

Emily hugged her, also crying, and gave her the flowers, as she continued to vent between her sobs. "'Twas a nightmare—"

"I'll have to teach you to shoot," Winston interjected stoically, hugging her warmly. "You missed the bloody black hard."

"Winston!" chided his wife.

"I'm sorry about Sarah. I couldn't attend her funeral—"

"We understand, Melissa," interrupted Emmy, desperately trying to calm her, with little success.

"Why would Wilbert do that after twenty years? It hurts, but I still love him though. Am I stupid?"

"Yes," quipped Winston. "For not shooting the bloody bloke."

"Winston, that's not helping," repeated his wife, this time somewhat irritated, staring at the sheriff.

After the furor abated, they chatted for some time before Melissa eventually calmed down, and they could explain that they had two pleasant surprises for her, one at their hotel site and another at their hotel in a week or so.

But Melissa wanted no more surprises; she was concerned about Todd. She finally relaxed when Winston hugged her again and promised her that Todd was fine, having talked with him for several hours in each of the last few days. He then warned her, "But the next time, tell me, and I'll—"

"Don't say it, Winston!" warned his wife again, shaking her finger at him.

He whispered to Melissa, "Shoot the bloody bastard for you."

She finally smiled. She was very tired but decided to go to their suite out of courtesy.

Melissa was almost stunned when the sheriff noted that the Howards were her approved escort and that she was to report back to him in two days, then left.

As they entered the dark penthouse suite, Melissa was startled to see a large group of people, as Winston calmly proclaimed, "Surprise number one."

As he switched on the light, the crowd began to applaud, all yelling, "Congratulations."

However startled, she was quick to recognize Todd, ran and squeezed him, crying, "How's my little boy?'

"Tough," he responded, almost crying himself. "I'm no longer a boy, Mom. I grew up damn fast."

"Thank you, God," she whispered.

With everyone crowding around, talking simultaneously and discussing a myriad of past events in record time, the commotion soon expended itself, and Melissa, at last, got around to properly welcoming Lois and Prissy. Then, gingerly turning to Cecil, asked politely, "Are you my new parole officer?"

Todd and Lois exploded into laughter and continued to laugh so loud that it confused his mother. Even Winston and Emily were nearly hysterical. She was disappointed that her imprisonment was being treated so casual.

"It's my boyfriend, Cecil," explained Prissy, between her giggles.

"Cecil who?"

Everyone roared again. She blushed bright red and became annoyed.

"My brother." Lois laughed. "Todd gave him an extreme makeover."

Now embarrassed, knowing Cecil had spent time in prison, she sat down to calm herself, unhappy Todd was associating with a hardened criminal.

"I sorry, I didn't mean to insult you, Cecil. You look and act like a real gentleman."

"Thank you, Mrs. Clarke. That's the nicest thing anyone ever said to me." He went and hugged her.

"And he certainly is, Mom. It was him and Lois that made me a man," declared Todd emphatically. "I was a lost puppy. The Ikkuseks and the Inuit adopted me."

"Your father's not at home?" she asked astounded.

"I'll tell you about the cheap scum ball later; tonight let's celebrate."

While taken aback by his crude remark, Melissa still felt as if a storm cloud had just moved away from the sun. She stared at her son and smiled with satisfaction. Yes, he was now a man: her man.

Todd and Lois went to Joella's group home hoping to see her, only to be reminded she had been previously reprimanded for revealing her location and that would she be transferred to a secure prison if he persisted and did not leave immediately. As Todd pleaded, almost in tears, for just one minute, Justin Patey appeared. Lois, overjoyed at seeing him, hugged him and asked him to help.

Justin took them to a nearby restaurant and tried to make them understand the negative impact of their actions on Joella, stressing she had already been denied any further sentencing reviews based on Todd's appearance at her initial hearing. He guaranteed them that she was fine given her circumstances and that he, and Susan Kamanirk, an Inuit, was personally watching over her. That he was not at liberty to discuss her private condition but would keep in touch with Lois and report any change, noting his options were limited, and that even he had to work within the law, however unjust.

He tried to impress upon Todd that he misunderstood her incarceration, and although unjust, it wasn't a tragedy. The legal system, however flawed, had acquiesced, thanks to the recommendation of her initial examining psychiatrists who recognized her unique intelligence and potential and moved her all the way across the country to the best facility in the nation, so she could get a degree while at the same time live relatively normal life, expense free, and without the poverty of her hometown. All Joella had to do was control her fierce independence, just hang in, and get revenge later. The institute was not being malicious, just following orders, and any help would have to come from outside, suggesting Todd secure a lawyer to have her taken out of the inept Social Services' custody, and made a ward of the courts; that way, he could interface with her more freely.

Seeing Justin's rationale, Todd, now troubled by the revelation that his interference had caused her more grief, accepted the inevitable, and thereafter, the meal became a two-hour social affair on how best to help her.

Justin volunteered to drive them to the airport and promised Todd that he'd work hard for her and e-mail him pictures of her each month so he would be close to her. In appreciation, Lois asked him to visit Labrador to see their poor communities to better understand Joella's plight, inviting him to stay at her humble home. Surprisingly, he graciously accepted.

Todd stopped briefly at the hotel and said good-bye to his aunt and uncle who were staying for a month until the baby was born. As he returned to the car, he saw Justin chatting happily with Lois and Cecil and wondered if he had told them Joella was pregnant. He wanted to keep, not only her pregnancy but his father's pedophilia and the names of all the young girls he had sexually abused a secret until he figured out to best way to handle all the dissention and hurt it would cause.

Chapter Five

The Secrets

Rape: a crime where the victim is guilty until proven innocent.

Back home, Todd had to study harder to make up a week of loss classes but was still agonizing over Joella's unfair treatment while the callous criminals who put her there were enjoying life.

After a four-hour study stint, he spent more hours browsing his father's sex pictures attempting to unravel the mysterious identity of the cameraman. But the cameraman appeared only briefly in a few scenes to help control an unruly victim, and he always wore a mask, which meant he was intelligent and easily recognizable.

On a large chart, Todd tabulated all the background scenes from all the various locations and discovered all the incidents involving the local girls took place on a black leather sofa, which sat on a tiled hardwood floor and against a birch-paneled wall. He knew of no such place in the community. He rechecked, and in each of these settings, he found a large clock with a faint picture of a man with a walking stick on it, located just above the couch, and the time on the clock always indicated eight o'clock or later. None of the tapes showed scenes from his home.

He abruptly switched back to his class assignment when he heard someone enter the house.

"Sorry for barging in on you, Todd. Did I scare you?" Cecil asked, in an unusual serious mood. "I just came to tell you the police caught drunk Ski-Dooers tonight and—"

Todd smiled and remarked emphatically, "Good!"

"I figured you did it. Next time, pick your targets, Todd. Not everyone here is your enemy," he continued in an ever graver tone. "Tammy and Leslie were among them; they're good kids, just drink a little."

Todd stood up and nearly fainted. Before he could question him further, he was gone.

Lois entered a few minutes later and saw Todd sitting pensively in front of the fireplace with his hands on each side of his bowed head.

"What's wrong?" she asked tenderly, hugging him. "I finished late at the station. I'm sorry. I had to process the eight people the police caught driving snowmobiles tonight while impaired. I think most are on your list."

He looked up blankly at the wall but said nothing. His eyes were watery.

"What's wrong, Todd?" she asked again, now concerned.

"I tipped off the cops about their party," he responded, still despondent.

"Good. Now there's only six left on your list," she responded, happily removing her coat.

"Lois," he said, nearly crying, "I've gone too far."

She could see he was in pain and reminded him, "But they hurt Joella."

"Little Tammy was among them. Now she'll have a record. She's not my enemy."

"You want Tammy?" Lois asked, surprised and a bit jealous.

He said nothing.

"She's barely thirteen."

He got up, hugged her tightly and kissed her, then mused aloud, "No. I'd be lost without you."

"What then?" she asked, confused.

"I can't tell you. But if I could, you'd understand."
"Maybe I already know," she responded sadly.
Todd doubted that.

According to the resident doctors, Joella's pregnancy, though initially secretive, was a model for any female, especially a teenager. She ate nutritious meals, didn't smoke, drink, or use drugs, exercised daily, and was ahead in her study schedule. Her child psychiatrist concluded any mental stress over fear of adoption was a minor component, since she had accepted her fate without complaining. They praised her for her maturity.

But in the last few days, she had been having some hemorrhaging, and Susan, who kept very close watch on her, revealed her problem to the staff. They moved her to the hospital for monitoring, where a team of doctors informed her that it was subchorionic and could possibly lead to a miscarriage, advising her to have a C-section immediately to prevent unforeseen complications; and with it being a large baby and she a small person, it would be a difficult natural birth.

Social Services had for weeks been encouraging—actually subtly pressuring—her to sign release forms for the adoption, saying that it would take years for an adoption to happen, if at all, and in that time, she would be allowed to have daily access to her daughter. But she always stubbornly refused conceding any rights. She knew, all too well, what happened to Inuit children who were adopted by white people. Visiting rights wasn't what Joella wanted, and no amount of pressure could make her change her mind.

Joella trusted her doctor and psychologist and agreed to a C-section but despised Social Services, even refusing to talk to them. To her, Susan was still an unknown factor; she was helpful and friendly but too dedicated to her job, and that meant pleasing her superiors, who were interested only in their own selfish interests.

In reality, Susan was deeply troubled, already having read Joella's file, knowing Social Services had given official consent to the hospital to proceed with the operation and that Joella had no say in the matter; explaining her options was just a legal formality.

Susan's conscience bothered her even more when she found out Joella's child already had prospective white adoption parents, and Joella was being deceived. Like Joella, she was an Inuit who had lost her baby twelve years earlier under similar circumstances. She wanted to tell her but knew that she would be dismissed. The best she could do was to identify the adopted parents to tell her later.

Joella awoke from her operation to see Susan's smiling face. Sitting next to her were her social worker and the warden, both looking glum.

"Is it a girl?" asked Joella groggily. "Can I see her?"

The social worker came to her bed and caressed her hand softly.

"Yes, it was a girl," she answered sympathetically. "But we have some bad news about the baby."

"What are you talking about?" interrupted Susan, baffled. The doctor had told her everything had gone flawlessly and showed her the baby. She had held it in her arms and had read the tag on the baby's wrist: "Adams, Joella: April 4, 2001: 11:30 PM," on the baby's wrist.

The warden ordered Susan outside. She refused. The social worker continued, "We're sorry, Joella, but your child was stillborn. You can visit her gravesite at Shady Lawns Cemetery after you recover."

"What! That's a damn lie!" exclaimed Susan as the warden grabbed her and hustled her out of the hospital room. She could hear Joella choking loudly on her sobs as she left.

"What the hell are they doing?" she screamed at the warden in the corridor. "I held the baby in my arms. He was as healthy as a horse!"

"*He?* If you value your position, control your tongue."

"What the hell is wrong with you? You're just a two-bit warden!"

"Yes, two-bit warden under orders!" she retorted. "And a black single mother with two daughters to support. You fucking think I agree?"

Susan knew Joella would be devastated. Hovering between intense anger and overwhelming sympathy, Susan exclaimed, "The agony of losing to adoption is one thing, but the torture of death is unbearable. She's barely sixteen. I know how she feels."

"Yes, it's cruel, morbid, and illegal, Susan; but you're still not telling her."

"Eskimo justice," Susan snarled. "Being black, you should understand. I suppose we should be grateful that he wasn't smothered and buried in a butter box under the floorboards."

"Be that as it may, it's illegal to tell her."

Susan glared at her in defiance as she turned and walked away. "This is not the end of it."

The Howards' attorney approached the bench and presented a $1,000,000 surety to the judge as proof they were capable of supporting the child. The Social Services lawyer advised the court they had initially reached an agreement on the adoption after several days of legal negotiations but only yesterday had discovered that pursuant to the initial terms of the court order of Joella's internment, severe restrictions had been placed on visitation and contact and that the identity of the adopted parents were to be kept strictly confidential. Todd, his mother, or Joella would not be permitted in the presence of the child.

The Howards assailed the Social Services' shady, double-dealing antics and strenuously objected to such harsh conditions, angrily demanding an apology and a retraction. The Social Services' lawyer, just as tenacious, argued that Joella was an inexperienced juvenile Inuit and a murderer, that Mrs. Clarke was convicted of attempted murder; and Todd was closely associated with both of them. That was their minimum acceptable criteria, as children were first offered for adoption in their country of birth. But this case was deemed a marginal exception, since the Howards were relatives, British peers, and financially independent.

A brief intense argument ensued with the Social Services' lawyer finally laying down the law: take it or leave it.

The Howards, fuming, huddled for a time with their counsel, then agreed, after being advised that Canadian courts had no jurisdiction in Britain. But their Christian beliefs and sense of justice were causing them great stress with such a deceptive decision, fully aware Todd already knew.

Signing the adoption papers, clause by clause, they were stunned to learn the child was a boy. Winston was ecstatic, but Emily was mildly let down; her heart had been set on a girl in memory of Penny. However, she instantly agreed, eager to again have a child in her home. Yet both knew that the child would revert back to Todd when he finished his degree, as they had promised him. Nonetheless, they were happy to have a legal heir to their estate.

Melissa stood nervously before the judge in civilian clothes, curious why there was nobody in the courtroom, except her lawyer, the prosecution lawyer, and court staff.

Within seconds, the court was called to order; the judge appeared and spoke briefly, as if he wanted to get the contentious issue quickly disposed off. "Mrs. Clarke, the prosecution was unable to produce credible witnesses to challenge your appeal. I asked no subpoenas be issued. This court has no alternative but to stay all charges against you. As of noon today, April 12, 2001, you are hereby released. Good luck, Mrs. Clarke."

Then, in an instant, he was gone.

The short unexpected proclamation left her speechless. Amazed how fast a person's life could change on the words of just one man, she just bowed to the vacant bench and slowly left.

Melissa entered the hotel room to see Emily holding an infant and Winston, not smoking his rancid pipe for a change, talking to her.

"You've adopted a baby girl," said Melissa, overjoyed, hugging her sister. "This day really is a gift from God."

"Todd wants him named Joe Ellan Clarke, after Joella's father."

Melissa smiled at her confusing statement, took the baby in her arms, and chided her sister, "Joe is a boy's name, Emma. And your surname is now Howard, not Clarke. Joella doesn't have a child. Besides, Tuk Adams is Joella's father. What's happening to you?"

"Surprise number two, dear," said Winston, happily, hugging them. "It's a boy, and it's your grandson."

Melissa dismissed his foolishness and started to talk to the baby.

"Please sit and listen, Melissa," requested her sister solemnly. "Todd is the baby's father; Joella is the mother. And his surname will be Clarke."

She sat down quietly, still thinking they were joking.

As per Todd's insistence, for half an hour, Winston and Emily patiently took turns describing Todd's dilemma since she left home. Todd had requested they tell her everything, being too embarrassed to tell her personally of the criminal acts he had committed for survival, but mostly for her to understand how much his life had dramatically changed before she returned home, to prepare her for their new reality. How his father had deserted him and the numerous underage girls his father had raped. How he had found the sex tapes, how he bribed his father for travel money, how he also blackmailed Pastor Cornelius, how the Ikkuseks had adopted him, how he lived at home with Lois, how he carried out his vigilante justice, and finally how he wanted her to go to England with them to care for his child while he studied law at Oxford. He wanted his mother to know every minute detail.

Melissa was both appalled and impressed, amazed at the extreme changes in his life and his uncanny ability to survive.

"But he's now an ungodly criminal," she eventually gasped, inundated.

"Hell no, Melissa." responded Winston emphatically. "He's a bloody hero. He's now a Howard." Then smiling, added, "Time you bloody grew up too."

Emma handed her husband and her sister each a crystal of Winston's expensive hundred-year-old cognac. "This is a special occasion. Let's have a snort to celebrate."

They clicked glassed and drank. It was Melissa's first taste of alcohol. For once, she felt she needed it.

Todd arrived home to see Lois decorating the house with Christmas decorations, and it was only Good Friday. He stared at her, his mouth opened in silent surprise, demanding an answer.

"We're having a party, Todd. We only have three more nights together."

"What? You promised to stay with me until—

"I got a call. Your mom will be home Saturday. She's free."

Ecstatically, he grabbed her, kissed her hard, and started removing her clothes.

"Better make it fast," she encouraged. "Everyone knows. The council elders will be here in half an hour to plan a big party for her at the community centre."

He needed no urging.

Melissa was overjoyed to be home but disappointed Todd did not come to greet her at the airport. A taxi driver met her and explained her fare was gratuitous, and he was to bring her to meet Todd at the community centre.

She entered the centre through the backstage door and was led unto the stage, then startled to see the whole community waiting for her.

The mayor in his ceremonial Inuit regalia bowed and said, "On behalf of the people of Natuashish, we welcome you home."

The whole group stood up and began applauding. Having a criminal record, she was perplexed at the contradictory response. Although happy, this was not how she wanted to be honored. It was so overgenerous it bordered on sarcasm.

She found her voice and responded apolitically, "Thank you, Mr. Mayor, ladies and gentlemen, boys and girls. I sincerely appreciate your enthusiasm and loyalty, but I do not deserve such respect. By law, I am a criminal, and that is what I taught all you young people to avoid when I was your role model, a chore I loved so much. To accept such idolization is contrary to God's laws. While I do not regret what I did . . ."

The statement caused a tremendous applause and standing ovation drowning out her words. After the noise abated, she continued, "I regret that I am no longer permitted to continue as your counselor. Thank you again from the bottom of my heart. I must now find Todd."

"I'm here," came a voice, in Inuktitut, from a walking shadow, dressed in an Inuit caribou skin suit and sealskin boots, from behind an artificial iceberg prop.

She stared, confused; it sounded like Todd, but his voice was much more mature and forceful. He came and hugged her, as the audience cheered. Tears streamed down her face. When the din died down, she responded in Inuktitut, "What are you doing dressed like an Inuit Spirit?"

He faced the audience and made his rehearsed pronouncement. "It is my privilege, on behalf of the Inuit and Innu of Natuashish, to christen you, my mother, *Spirit of the North*, to continue to convey your wisdom to our youth and hereby make you an elementary schoolteacher."

Melissa was flabbergasted. The audience stood up and applauded again.

"Todd, sweetheart, I'm a criminal, and you're still in your youth. You know it's disrespectful of you to dress in that outfit, when you're not an Inuit or Innu elder to give such honors."

The mayor stepped forward and bowed. "Naglingnig has been an esteemed Inuit for the past year and has been granted such discretionary powers for his commitment to our people. The council of elders was unanimous that you, Mrs. Clarke, possess the spirit of both our people and the North. It would honor our people if you'd accept."

She found his name, Snowflake, almost amusing but realized it fit him perfectly. The audience was silent, awaiting her decision. She knew it would be illegal to accept such a position of trust.

"Mr. Mayor, it would be an honor, and I want to accept, but I now have a criminal record."

He bowed again. "By white man's law. Our people see you as a good and just spirit that can fight evil in any culture. And you speak Inuktitut better than most of our own children. Please accept."

She bowed and said, "It is the greatest honor of my life." But she knew it was only temporary since she would be going to England in July.

There was a standing ovation. She looked at Todd and cringed as he handed her the raw walrus meat. As she ate, the audience cheered.

"You are now one with the North," proclaimed the mayor. Then, turning to the audience announced, "Let the festivities begin."

As the drums began to roll and the traditional dancers emerged from behind stage, she held Todd and cried. "Todd, I always knew you'd survive. Joella will too."

"I've seen life through their eyes, Mom. I really am one of them now."

A week later, Todd rushed into the house to get his knapsack to head out on the barrens and saw his mother sitting quietly in the armchair.

"Lois's late. Is she here?" he asked joyfully. Then seriously, added, "What's the crowd doing with the police over at Lois's place?" grabbing and biting into his favorite caribou sandwich that she had prepared for him. He missed Lois in his bed each night, but his mother's cooking mostly compensated for it. When she looked up, he could see she had been crying.

"You still miss Dad, Mom?" he queried, somewhat scornful.

She shook her head. "Did you show your father's sex pictures to anybody?" she asked softly, surprising him that she knew.

"No. Nobody. Except the slimeball!"

"Don't call your father that."

"I was just being kind, Mom," he cynically apologized, going and hugging her. "Is he okay?"

"They're at the Tulugaq place. Tammy's dead," she answered candidly, beginning to cry again. Todd froze, unsure if he had heard correctly.

"Dead?" he repeated skeptically.

She nodded.

He felt as if he had been stunned by a rock-centered snowball. Tears came to his eyes. "Dead?" he whispered again, as if it were too unbelievable to accept. He put his sandwich down and hugged his mother again, tears forming in his eyes. Now remorseful for his actions, he ventured, "She got killed in a Ski-Doo accident?"

"No," she answered, almost sobbing. "She committed suicide."

He felt icy cold, too traumatized to speak

After a long silence, his mother asked pitifully, "Why would she kill herself? She was such a good kid. I liked her; she always obeyed."

Yes, always, mused Todd, still too dazed to respond. His mother handed him the sickening sex photo. He felt weak and nearly fainted, not wanting to view her anguished face again. The portion of the photo containing his father's picture had been cut away. Sitting slowly on the sofa beside his mother again, he asked with incredulity, "How did you ever get the picture?"

"The police found it in her shirt pocket, sealed in this envelope, close to her heart. It was addressed to you. Read the back."

He unwillingly turned it over and read:

April 19, 2001

Todd,

I love you, and I know you liked me too. I know you saw all your dad's videos since you sent him my picture, and I'm sure you don't want me now. I'm too ashamed to face you. Don't hate your dad, because hate means having no love; he had none. Tell your dad I forgive him. Always remember me.

Good-bye,
Tammy

Todd began to cry openly, tears falling on the sofa, as his mother, also crying, tried to console him.

"The police said she had been high on glue ever since she came back from Goose Bay. Last night, she drank a full bottle of moonshine." She paused to catch her own breath. "Then she hanged herself."

Todd remained silent and, between his own sobs, wondered what she was doing in Goose Bay and why his father had blackmailed her. He knew he could not keep his mother's promise; his father had to be stopped.

After another long pause, she managed, "Wilbert was the person cut from the picture, wasn't he?"

"I'm sorry, Mom. I tried to protect you. That scum bucket raped a lot of kids here."

"Now Tammy's going to hell because of him," she sobbed, shivering uncontrollably.

Todd held her in his arms for a long time as she convulsed. "No, Mom, she just escaped from hell."

Every eye curiously stared at Todd as he placed a large bouquet of yellow Arctic poppies on the foot of Tammy's casket and a small bouquet of white Labrador tea flowers at the head, then knelt, folded his hands in a prayer stance, and whispered something to her.

He was not a singer, and everyone was surprised when he stood up and began to sing "Amazing Grace" in Inuktitut.

"Tatamnamiik, saimaninga. Piulilaurmanga, tautungnangaa."

Lois reluctantly joined in, mostly out of embarrassment of Todd's atrocious singing, then her brother, Cecil, with his deep base voice, then Melissa.

"Naningmanga."

As Tammy was lowered into the grave, everybody was singly loudly, the sound echoing off the high cliffs in the Valley of the Spirits.

"Maana, tautukpunga."

It was the saddest occasion of Todd's life. Others seeing his grief and tearful face began crying as well; soon the whole gathering was weeping openly. The atmosphere was inexplicably touching; even tough, heartless Cecil was sniffling.

As they later walked somberly toward home, Lois could see Todd was distressed and asked softly, "Tea flowers? That's odd for a funeral."

"White was her favorite color. And she was the only young person I know who liked Labrador tea."

Lois wondered how he knew, since he had never gone near her poor shack.

"What did you say to her?" Lois asked, trying to understand his peculiar behavior.

"I told her when the *sky livers* returns, I'd get them to look after her for me." Tears were again rolling down his face. Lois was puzzled.

"What's wrong? You didn't hurt Tammy. She adored you."

"I know," he said regretfully, "but I could have saved her."

"What are you talking about?" she asked astounded. "She became a glue head!"

"Don't say that, Lois," he cautioned, instantly angry. "We all have our own personal hell."

That part is certainly true, thought Lois, *but not only in Tammy's situation*. Tammy lived next door to her; she knew her since birth. They were poor, but her parents were good to her. She had never seen Todd so strange and troubled. She felt it best to drop the subject, recalling recently he was acting strange and secretive. It scared her; he had a faraway look in his eyes. She cringed at the thought he might kill his father.

Contented to be back at home in her old routine with her friends again, Melissa was beginning to readjust to domestic life, but her divorce was becoming a contentious issue. For a month, Wilbert refused to sign the papers unless the house was sold, and he got half its value. The family vehicle, snowmobile, boat, and other accessories he wanted. And Todd was to repay the $10,000 he had advanced him.

She was finding it very distressing and wanted a speedy resolution, but Todd wanted to give him nothing in return for remaining quiet. Melissa still loved him and wanted to be reasonable, but she loved Todd even more. And in the end, she agreed with Todd, and now her husband was suing. She could not remotely imagine a more heartbreaking end to twenty years of happy marriage.

She decided to go to Goose Bay to consult her lawyer on her rights.

With Todd's mother away in Goose Bay, Lois came to sleep with him. It was past midnight, and after making love, she soon fell asleep, but Todd was not tired and lay there thinking about Tammy and wondering if the sex picture caused her death. It was an opportune time to fast-forwarding through all his father's sex videos to see how many others were sexually molested. Joella practically lived at his house.

There were almost a hundred tapes, and it was time-consuming. He almost cried several times at seeing the innocent young girls—almost kids—from several other communities that his father serviced being savagely raped. There was not one adult girl among them. He now knew his father had taken advantage of his position and had selected the preteens and early teens to come to him in private to pick up the cheques for their parents. Such evil was chilling. He hated his father with passion but was nonetheless baffled why no one had reported him.

At three, disgusted and exhausted, he was about to go to bed when he noticed a familiar face. He was stunned beyond belief when he realized it was Lois. Being tired, he rubbed his eyes and checked again. It couldn't be. He replayed it again and again and again. He tried to rationalize it must be a look-alike, but to no avail; it was Lois. He was at a loss to explain it. She was the quintessential battle axe, a fighter. A person who would attack the devil if he materialized. He had to recheck it several times more. It never entered his mind that she could be one of them. How could she let it happen? Even more hurtful, she was crying. He had never seen her cry. Tears came to his eyes.

He jumped with fright when he felt Lois's arms around his neck, quickly shutting off the screen.

"Come to bed, Todd. It's late."

They went to bed, but he still could not sleep. Lois's pictures were haunting him. He just held her tight for a long time.

"What's wrong, Todd?" asked Lois drowsily. "You're pretty lovable tonight."

"I'm going to England in July to get away from here. To study at Oxford like Uncle Winston wants," he blurted out.

She was instantly awake. "You're leaving me just like that?"

He saw a terrified look on her face, and he felt sorry for her. "I have to get away. I watched all the videos." Then he saw her eyes fill with tears for the first time.

"And?" she sniffled

"You were in one."

"I asked you before who was in your father's picture. I guessed it was Tammy. I was scared it was me," she cried, tears dripping on his back.

"Good Lord, Lois, why didn't you tell someone?"

"Survival. For me and my family. Our cheque was extra big. I guess he told us all the same thing: 'Tell and I'll cut off your welfare.' My parents suspected something. Cecil did too and wanted to kill him, but I didn't want you to know or get hurt. I've always liked you as much as Joella did, Todd." She was now crying openly.

"Joella knew?" asked Todd disbelievingly, as if not wanting to hear the truth.

"Yes, but we loved you anyhow."

"Someone would have believed you. I do."

"You do now! Who, Todd? Why would the police believe the Ikkuseks? Poor criminals. Did you trust us a year ago?"

He felt overwhelmed, fully aware it was an absolute truth; nobody had believed him either.

She began to ramble, almost incoherently. "We're drunken Eskimos, white man's trash. We're like your mom's little pet poodle, thankful just to get a bite of food. Who'd believe us? Did they believe Joella? Five years, Todd, *five years* for nothing. It's best to keep your mouth shut. I'm not tough. We have to live somehow. Who'd tell something like that? I was eleven, thought it was my fault."

She was now convulsing and deeply ashamed he knew. She continued, "How could your mother be an angel and your father such a devil?"

Todd was shattered and spoke almost in a whisper. "I don't know. I'm so sorry, Lois. It hurts that I have a father like that, but I don't feel that way." He felt deeply humiliated and guilty.

"We have a saying in Inuktitut, Todd. 'What will you do once you know?' You knew about Tammy and did nothing. You're still protecting him. And you're still leaving me for Joella. Love is not something you borrow for convenience. I'm Inuit, but I still love like everyone else," she sobbed uncontrollably.

Todd hugged her tightly, not knowing want to say. She was correct. He finally managed, "I love you too Lois, and I'm so sorry. That's why I have to leave. I'm too embarrassed to live here. It shows I'm a pretty weak person too. But still, one thing puzzles me. Why would your family adopt me and your people make me an Inuit, if they knew what my father did?"

"When you're poor and uneducated, you're forced to be merciful; love and forgiveness is all you have to offer. They don't blame you."

"Who was the cameraman, Lois?"

"I don't know, but once again, 'What will you do once you know?'" she answered, almost choking. "He wore a face mask and didn't talk. *Pijariiqpunga*!"

"Pijariiqpunga?"

"It means *that is all I have to say*, Todd. *Let it lie*."

Todd held her as she sobbed for a long time.

Feeling vulnerable and defeated, she relented, "It's okay. You learn to hide it and live with the pain. As I told you in the cave, you didn't live in the real world. Joella was the pure and tough one; nobody raped her. I only acted tough. You two belong together."

He started to cry. "I'm not tough, but I'll promise the *sky livers* I will change it!" For the first time, he realized how strong Joella really was.

"No, Todd, you're white. It's fearless Inuit, like Joella, who's already changing it. But you can help her. Get a law degree like she wants you to."

For two weeks after the birth of her baby, Joella was held in hospital for monitoring. She was refusing to eat and was becoming increasingly lethargic, talking to nobody except Justin and Susan. Severely depressed, she cried many times a day and kept reminding them that the doctors murdered her daughter, stressing that the baby was kicking inside her stomach on the operating table.

Susan took her to Shady Lawns Cemetery where she saw the grave plaque with the engraved name, *Baby Joella Adams*, and placed flowers on it. But it only deepened her depression. Now she cried nightly to see Todd to apologize for losing his baby.

Justin did his best to help, but after a month and seeing he was losing her, he notified the staff that Joella should be told the truth that her child was alive for her sanity, but he was threatened with dismissal. Susan, knowing the agony of being forced to give up her own child, was not so submissive and secretly told Joella that she had seen her baby, that it had been adopted, but that was all she would say. Justin refused to substantiate it when Joella confronted him but promised he and Susan would help locate her child when she was released. Within a week, Joella was almost back to normal, eager to begin the search for her daughter. She had also formed a bond with Susan and Justin.

In his spare time, Todd scanned and rescanned the videos looking for a clue to the cameraman's identity. On a couple of occasions, he tried to discuss Lois's ordeal with her, but she refused, saying the memories hurt too much, and all he had gleaned from her was that his father would pick her up near the church in his car, and he always played a game by blindfolding her, because it was illegal for anybody to know where he dispensed government cheques after hours. She knew it was at just one location, not very far, and it was always at night. Todd was intrigued why young girls would allow themselves to be subjected to such a ritual. Besides, there were only a few miles of road in the community. The pictures had to be dubbed. If so, by whom? He knew nobody in the community with such skills. Certainly not his father: a computer dummy.

He felt defeated.

Returning from the police station, Lois saw Todd sitting quietly near the fireplace in the dark with that faraway look in his eyes again.

"I'm sorry for taking a fit the other night, Todd. I know why you have to go to England. I'm really proud of you. Most guys your age would run from being a father."

He was puzzled at the accurate guess. *Almost too accurate*, he mused.

"What are you talking about?"

"I know, Todd, but I swore to tell nobody."

He tried to think of a way to ask her how she discovered the secret, without admitting to it.

She stared at him with a troubled look in her eyes.

"What's wrong, Lois? Still mad at me?"

"Joella ran away with a drug dealer to look for her daughter."

He was stunned; Joella would never do such a thing.

"They told her the baby girl was stillborn. How can they be so mean?" she moaned.

Todd could see her face contoured in pain but nonetheless became angry and assailed her for making such brainless allegations.

She felt offended at his lying and, for once, retaliated shouting, "Stop lying, Todd! Otherwise, you'll become your father."

He became silent and felt a surge of fever at her poignant prognosis. Could it be true?

There was a long period of silence.

Sorry for her brief outburst and spiteful response, she calmed down and asked solemnly, "Why didn't you tell me Joella was pregnant?"

He said nothing, knowing he was trapped in his own deceptive network of silence.

"You still don't trust me. That hurts, Todd. I did everything you asked."

He just stared at the fireplace as his eyes began to water.

"You remember Justin in Vancouver, the guy I invited here?" she continued, now back to normal, handing Todd an e-mail. He eagerly read with astonishment. "Susan told her the baby was adopted by white strangers. She was trying to find out who, but Joella ran away to find her. But I'm smart enough figure out your aunt has her."

Todd was positively astounded.

"It's a boy," he finally said solemnly. "Why would he help you?"

"There *are* good people in the world, Todd. Susan got fired for telling her the truth to save her from going mad." She paused and added shyly, "He likes me."

He stared at her with tears dripping off his chin, too distressed at the news to respond.

"But that's not the reason I invited him."

"I'm sorry for not telling you. I'm selfish and didn't want to lose you too."

"I love you, but you only need me. I even risked a criminal record for you, and you shut me out."

Todd hugged her tightly as they cried silently for a time before their grief exhausted them. Feeling repentant, for an hour thereafter, he revealed his very soul to her, down to the tiniest detail. Finally relaxing, he requested she not communicate with Justin anymore, in case someone saw her e-mails. He then jealously asked, “Why did you invite him?”

“You can be so stupid at times. Hate is clouding your brain. Justin is our ticket to keep in contact with Joella while you’re in England.”

“Our?” he asked puzzled.

“When you really love someone, Todd, you always love them, even after they leave you.”

After supper, Todd went with his mother to the church and prayed for Joella. Later, they went into the office where she usually balanced the church books. Looking around, he sensed a familiarity, like he’d been there many times before; but he hadn’t. He checked all the items on the desk, walked around it, and looked into all the drawers, rumbled through its contents, much to his mother’s dismay, who sternly reminded him he was in the house of God.

He scoured the ceiling and the overhead fan and the large Persian rug in the centre of the floor, then checked the titles of some of the books on the shelves that completely covered the end wall. He had an eerie feeling, like he had been there a hundred times before, but he could not put his finger on it. His mother was disappointed at his inquisitive meddling into other people’s private property and assailed him.

Then, like a miracle from heaven, it hit him.

At the edge of the carpet was a hardwood-tiled floor. The walls were birch paneled. More astounding, there was a black leather couch. He recalled Joella telling him she scratched the pastor’s penis on a leather couch in the church. He was absolutely stunned. It was the video sex lab. The cameraman had to be Pastor Cornelius.

Above the couch on the wall was the mysterious clock. On the face of the clock was a picture of Jesus, as a shepherd with a staff, leading lambs. The implication of the sinister blood-chilling parody nearly traumatized him. He stood there speechless, recalling his father always went to church to pray after supper, took his briefcase with him, and issued cheques from the church office.

Equally disturbing, the clock on the wall indicated just after eight.

"What's wrong, Todd?" asked his mother, concerned.

"I won't need your services anymore, Mrs. Clarke," said the pastor, startling both Todd and his mother, as he silently entered the office. "I've been transferred to a new diocese."

He glared at the camera hanging around Todd's neck. But however awkward or repulsive the situation, his glare gave Todd an idea. Todd bowed respectfully and requested a picture of his mother and him for her posterity. Surprised at the pastor's sudden disclosure and Todd's inappropriate request, she stood up confused but ready to comply out of courtesy and respect for the church. The pastor hesitated, knowing it was probably a trap, but eventually smiled and agreed. Todd positioned them strategically on the black leather sofa. He took several wide-angle snapshots, encompassing the clock on the birch-paneled wall and the hardwood-tiled floor. He then gave a wide, intimidating grin, bowed again, thanked the pastor, and they left.

They had only walked a short distance silently homeward before Melissa eventually spoke. "Pastor Cornelius is leaving because of your tapes, isn't he?"

"Because I know. I took the picture tonight to prove to you he was the person who operated the camera for the slimeball's rape videos."

"Hush, Todd! I don't watch sex tapes. Besides, your father destroyed them."

Todd's mouth fell open at the brilliant inspiration. He hugged and kissed his mother. "I love you, Mom! Dad will agree to all your terms within seven days."

"No, Todd, I'm being unfair. Court's in two weeks," she said sadly. "And I'm dreading it."

"You can't close your eyes, Mom, and hope it will just magically disappear."

"Todd, you must learn to forgive!"

"First, stop the abuse, then forgive. I'm turning the two slimeballs in. I now have the proof."

"Hush, Todd!" She stopped and, facing him. "Vengeance is mine, saith the Lord."

"Where was your Lord when ten-year-olds were being brutalized by his chosen representatives? Turning water into wine at wedding feasts for other drunks? Too late for that now, Mom. The bastards have to be stopped."

"Hush, Todd! That's wicked."

Lois was shocked at the wording of the e-mail Todd had given her to be transmitted using the police computer and was reluctant to do it but loved him too much to refuse. She patiently waited until both officers had left for the night and, with trembling hands, obeyed but erased the file seconds after sending it.

May18, 2001

Listen, Slimeball,

You believe you destroyed all the tapes, but I made two duplicates of each and every last one. I've included a few samples as proof, including one of Lois. I know you killed Tammy, but Lois is stronger; she's a secretary at the police station. And Cecil hasn't seen the pictures yet either.

Now, you're blackingmailing Mom? Your plan to destroy her didn't work, scum ball. Mom is now an elementary schoolteacher and a lay preacher in the church. Hurt her again and you'll have to deal with me and Cecil.

I know who the masked cameraman was in your torture videos: Pastor Cornelius. He knows I know, and like you, he's now run away too.

Everybody here is now scared of me and Cecil. Cecil is now the wilderness tourist guide officer and carries sidearms, a scope-equipped, high-powered rifle, and is a crack shot at one hundred yards. In jail, Cecil says Bubba loves pedophiles.

Get the picture?

Here's my minimum demand to make you and your problem go away: all clauses in the divorce papers that Mom wants. $5,000 to Lois for rape.

In seven days! The demand will be $1,000 interest with each day that it is not paid.

PS: Note this letter was sent from the police station where Lois works; only Lois can erase it from the computer servers. Upon payment! Even then, it stays on the server until it is written over. Maybe years. Only I can remove it from the memory banks.

Your Worst Nightmare,
Todd

Chapter Six

The Dream Catcher

It's only when you're young and have nothing that you can do everything.

Scared, sweaty, hungry, and crying again, Joella sat on her filthy cot in a tiny run-down housekeeping hotel room and stared at the dream-catcher package in her backpack and sneered silently, *If there were any Great Spirit up there watching over me, I wouldn't be in this mess.* She now believed the only two good people in the world were Todd and his mother. For three days now, she had been locked into a room to prevent her from escaping until her criminally insane abductor, Skelly, could persuade or coerce her into agreeing to take drugs and become a prostitute. She figured if she would never see her daughter, this was where she was going to die, and she planned on going down fighting.

A week ago when Susan promised that her friends on the Vancouver downtown east side would help her locate her baby, Joella had no idea these friends were pimps, drug dealers, drunks, and mentally retarded people; and once again, she had to defend herself. Susan protected her for two days, but soon the stress of her being fired got the best of her, and she succumbed to her old drug-and-prostitution habit and was now lying unconscious on the adjacent filthy cot being eaten by bedbugs, and Joella was left alone to control Skelly, a sadistic pimp and drug dealer, who carried a knife in his shoe and a gun under his arm.

The filthy, stinky cockroach-infested room was hot and damp, with water dripping into a can on the floor from the bathroom of an equally grungy snake pit above. The walls were encrusted with years of dirt that partly covered the vulgar graffiti and spattering of dried blood. The single dangling lightbulb in the centre of the room was barely bright enough to illuminate the greasy hotplate on which she was boiling a bucket of water. She knew Skelly would be high, or drunk, when he returned, and this would be her final chance to escape. She had her plan down to an exact science. It would land her back in detention with maybe a life sentence, but she had nothing left to lose. She would never find her baby this way.

At midnight, she heard him stomping noisily up the dark cluttered stairway and hid behind the door, clutching the bucket of boiling water with rag-covered hands. As he entered the dark room, she threw it directly into his face, scalding her wrist in the bargain. He fell to the floor without making a sound, as she dropped the bucket, jumped over him, and fled in terror down the stairway, out into the street and ran for dear life to the only place she knew, the Salvation Army *Harbor Light*s' flophouse where she had eaten a week earlier. She knew when Susan sobered up, she would have to inform police what had happened; the scheme was her idea.

Upon arriving, she found a long lineup, with *Harbor Light*'s filled to capacity, and began to panic. She asked several people for a quarter to phone the detention center, but nobody would stop or speak to her, and one john almost dragged her into his car. Not knowing what to do, she paced the streets until daybreak in a daze, staying close to the twenty-four-hour restaurants for protection. But even there, the criminals, johns, and drug dealers were prowling. At first light, she hid in a nook by a hot air exhaust duct near a Tim Hortons restaurant, covered herself with newspapers, and fell asleep.

Todd returned home from school to see his mother holding a letter and hugging Lois, both smiling. His mother excitedly explained to him that Wilbert had willingly agreed to all the conditions of the divorce and had generously given Lois $5,000 to go to Vancouver to help locate Joella, saying she always knew Wilbert was a friend to the Innu and Inuit. She was ecstatic that he had recognized his failings and was now a changed man. His true character was shining through. She forgave him.

Lois winked at Todd, then eagerly related to him how she had spent an hour communicating with Justin, who was going to help her. Todd felt an instant surge of jealousy but soon realized it was Joella who was his true love.

Todd hugged them both, then whispered softly to Lois, "You don't have to spend your money that way."

"You'll understand why one day, Todd, how much I love you. Justin told me what to do, but it has to be kept a secret. We have to make up a lot of posters."

"Were you behind this, Todd? You promised me not to harm him. Did your bribe—" his mother began, with a troubling look on her face, now sensing something was amiss.

Todd could see his mother was instantly let down and hurt.

"Please don't ask. I only promised I would never let you down, Mom. I didn't hurt him. Now you're free," he interrupted, kissing her. "And believe me, the slimy scum ball hasn't changed."

Excitedly, Justin took a week's holiday from work. He felt like a kid with a new toy or an infatuated preteen on his first date. He met Lois at the airport and took her to her hotel. He was impressed at her high degree of preparation that was evidenced by the four large boxes of posters she had brought with her and her detailed Google maps showing all the strategic locations throughout the lower mainland.

To get better acquainted, he spent some time helping her with her chores, which she carried out with almost fanatical dedication. Within a day, thousands of posters were stapled to poles and bulletin boards throughout the downtown area, plus ads were placed in eight different newspapers requesting Joella to contact Justin.

Justin's propensity to help and his unpretentious, rugged nature quickly brought Lois close to him. They connected immediately, as if by some magic hand of fate. She wanted him to stay at her hotel for the night but knew Todd trusted her. That made her feel guilty. She felt she had now found her true soul mate but wondered, if so, how she would ever be able to tell Todd, knowing he'd be hurt. Todd had raised not only her status but also that of her whole family, far above the mentality level of their small community. He certainly deserved her loyalty and respect. She was now trapped in a love labyrinth in which she had no experience. Her days of making love for fun were gone. Todd had changed that too.

I will have to solve that problem later, she mused. *My first priority is to find Joella.*

Lois went dejectedly about her chore for a full week with Justin by her side treating her like a princess. Then, after a week of searching and failing, early Friday morning Justin got a rare emergency call requesting his return to work for a few hours.

"Don't worry, we'll find her," he encouraged her. He then hugged her, told her he'd probably be late, but would pick her up for the movie, and rushed off.

She immediately felt lonely. On Sunday, she was returning home; she now doubted if she'd ever find Joella.

Joella was awakened from her brief restless nap an hour later by a mean-looking two-hundred-pound prostitute named Cantella, who practically dragged her inside and bought her a meal.

Cantella was loud, obnoxious, and known on the street as *The Big Injin*. By her own admission, she was pure evil, not caring if she, or anybody else, lived or died.

After eating, Cantella invited her, and four other prostitutes, to her home that, to Joella's dismay, was a cardboard makeshift shack underneath a viaduct, where she received a crash course on survival in the urban jungle. As they prepared their fixes, they gave Joella some basic ground rules: get a big partner for safety, use a condom since most fucking men were dosed up or HIV positive, learn how to identify good drugs and who to buy them from, where to get free food and welfare. The lecture went on and on.

Finally, Cantella stopped, and Joella got an opportunity to explain her unique situation: that she did not use drugs or do prostitution and had just escaped detention to find her child. Cantella laughed for a long time, joking to her friends that the Virgin Mary had come to live among them. Pointing to the *Union Gospel Mission* just across the street, she advised angrily, "Get the hell out of here while you can. It's only when you're young and have nothing to lose that you can do everything. You wanna end up like us?"

Joella opened her backpack to get a hand napkin.

Cantella saw the dream-catcher package and realized Joella was a native Inuit. Soon they began to mock her for her stupidity in aboriginal beliefs. "The shamans didn't fucking help me," Cantella sneered sarcastically, as she injected her arm with heroin and passed the needle to her friends. "Open it, and you'll get a stupid fucking whale-bone charm."

Joella, now terrified, moved farther away from them, sat on a rock, and pondered Cantella's advice, as her friends slowly drifted off into oblivion. It was true. If there ever were an ideal time to get the hell out, this was it. Also, the time had come to open her catcher package.

She wondered what Todd and his mother would think of her now that she had injured, maybe killed, another person. She reached for her mother's package as tears streamed down her face. She glanced cautiously at her now-lifeless friends as she ripped it open. To her surprise, it contained a piece of hard bread, a small ornament pasted unto a map, and a letter. Frantically, she tore open the letter and saw a $50 bill drop out. Quickly stuffing it into her pocket, she began to eagerly read.

> My only child, Joella,
>
> I know you hate me and don't think much of me, and I know why. Because I'm nothing. I was born into this life and not strong enough to get out, but you are. My life ended when I married Tuk, but yours have now just begun. Since you have now reached the lowest point in your life, you must have now seen the world with your own eyes. Eat this bit of hard bread; it was blessed by the Great Spirit who told me to suffer my

fate to help others. It will give you the strength to go to the nearest church, any church, and show them this letter, tell them your story, and their god will lead you back to life. Trust me they will know what to do; the Great Spirit told me so the day you were born. All mankind is just one family.

Tuk is not your father. I made the mistake of marrying him so you could have parents. No one must ever know this except you. Your father was a young archeologist graduate I worked for when I was fourteen. Joe Ellan is one of the people in the criminal's graveyard below Whaler's Lookout back in Davis Inlet where we place the mysterious flowers each year on the first of August. It was the day we first made love there. He was here searching for the trail of Franklin. Joe loved me and knew I was pregnant, wanted a girl, and wanted you called after him, so I named you Joella. He was going to take me back to England when, they say, he fell off Whaler's Lookout, but I found out later Tuk had Quinn kill him when he found out that I slept with him. They buried him in the criminal's graveyard.

Joe said half breeds are always smarter and prettier than their parents and wants you to be a movie star. Keep fighting and don't let him down.

The fifty dollars is for a new teddy bear. The bear that you carry with you was given to me by Joe to keep for you. It must be worn out by now. It will be a symbol of a new beginning. The Great Spirit forgives you for all the mistakes you made. It will take time, but he will make things right for you.

This map will lead you back to your roots. It's an Inukshuk, the spirit of our people. That's who you are. Be proud of it.

Your stupid mother

Joella was astounded. She had no idea her mother was smart enough to write such a sophisticated and thoughtful letter. She began to sob uncontrollably. Turning to her drugged-crazed friends, she exclaimed, "And I thought she used her welfare cheques for booze!"

"She opened her stupid dream-catcher package?" Cantella noted to her street friends, slurring her words. Opening her eyes, she turned to Joella and mocked, "Did the shaman make you wise?"

"Yes!" she answered, still sobbing. "But the dream catcher didn't filter out the bad ones."

"Here goes the Virgin Mary again with that voodoo crap. We have a tough time understanding your dumb Inuktitut or whatever 'skimo language you speak."

"I'm going to turn myself in, get my baby back, and become a movie star."

Her friends roared with laughter.

"That fuckin' Vietcong on Davies is an asshole," Cantella said angrily. "He sold you shit."

Without saying another word or looking back, Joella picked up her backpack and headed directly for the nearby mall where she bought a large $40 teddy bear and christened it Joe Ellan at a water fountain in the name of the sky livers.

With the remaining money, for two hours, in sheer panic, she phoned the detention centre trying to reach Justin, the only person in which she had any faith, refusing to talk to anyone else. Then finally, just before lunch on Friday, she heard the sweetest voice in her life. It was Justin.

Between her sobs, she again vented her soul to cleanse her conscience about her tragic escapade. He managed to calm her down and assure her that everything would be fine, since he had already conditioned the authorities that as a minor losing a child, she was under severe stress and not responsible for her actions. He made her promise not to tell anybody, especially the police, what she had done until he had the opportunity to assess her mental stability, warning they would put her in a mental asylum.

Justin agreed with Cantella's suggestion to go to the Union Gospel Mission Church like she had planned, and he would make arrangements with Father Bolden for her to rest for a day, noting all relief centres were already on the lookout for her. Tired and confused, she promised to obey everything he said.

Entering the church, she found a serious-looking old priest in his faded sermon robe and two nuns waiting for her. The smiling nuns directed her to a private room, gave her some clothes, ordered her to take a bath in disinfectant, to eat the meal laid out for her, and then take a nap. She needed no urging. She stared for a few seconds at the opulent room; it was as if she had been just been reborn and moved from hell into heaven.

When the nuns left, she knelt at her bed and said a prayer of thanks, especially to her mother. Within an hour, she had bathed, dressed, eaten, and was fast asleep in the comfortable bed.

She awoke ten hours later to the feel and sound of someone snapping an electronic tracking device on her ankle and a smiling giant towering above her.

"Welcome home," greeted Justin.

At lunchtime, a knock came on her hotel room door. Lois opened to find a jubilant, smiling Justin. She hugged him excitedly, believing he returned just to be with her.

"Good news. I had a girl phone me today," he stated enthusiastically.

Lois was devastated; he had a girlfriend. She felt stupid, jealous of a girl she didn't know, by a boyfriend she didn't have.

"We can cancel our movie," she whispered sadly, quickly recovering.

"No. No. I like to go. Don't you want to know her name?"

He was beaming and causing her deep embarrassment.

"No. Please don't," Lois answered, gently moving away from him. "I have to keep putting up posters. I know the city now."

Justin, conditioned long ago at being rejected by females, accepted his fate but still managed to shout with glee, "From Joella!"

"Joella! Oh my god!" she screamed, returning and kissing him hard on the lips before she gained control of her emotions. Then apologizing, added, "I'm sorry, I just got excited. Is she okay?"

Justin, thrilled that Lois cared a little for him, answered, "She's fine. But I have to run back to debrief her before the vultures devour her. We'll talk about it tonight." He kissed her and left.

Lois was ecstatic. She rushed downstairs to the computer and sent a long e-mail to Todd to break the good news.

Safely cowering in her prison suite, Joella nervously anticipated her fate. But it was not to be the agony of her first defensive killing. Recriminations began almost immediately in the media, who had already picked up the objective of Lois's numerous posters and newspaper ads, and was followed the events; but this time, the blame was aimed exclusively at the managerial incompetence of the youth detention centre.

Even the institution considered Joella an innocent victim since her personal caretaker had assisted in her escape. Unknown to Joella, she was considered their star inmate, the intelligent one most likely to succeed. Every effort was made to keep her silent. Any knowledge of her forced adoption, Susan's firing, or her killing of Skelly was vigorously suppressed with a court-ordered news blackout.

But Joella was still positive her baby was not stillborn, and Susan was now taking a rap for her. Her new designated warden was Vanessa Khan, the black single mother who guarded her in the hospital. She was kind but the no-nonsense type who followed strict protocol.

Her only friend was now Justin, a psychologist, who refused to let anyone else question her. She was puzzled how protective he was of her after what she had done. But however humble she now felt, she did not give up hope her child was alive and was convinced that her baby had been adopted, since Justin had promised her he had good news regarding her baby if she finished her sentence without further incidents. She felt defeated and now set her goals on education. And even though she had finished her grade eleven with all As, she decided to continue with summer classes in grade twelve to keep her mind occupied and speed up time.

"You're very popular," said Vanessa, on her daily rounds, handing her a newspaper.

Joella scanned the headline:

> UNIDENTIFIED TEENAGER ACCIDENTALLY KILLS MURDERER IN SELF-DEFENSE
>
> No charges will be laid against the teenager who was a victim of Tom Bradshaw, an escaped murderer from San Quinton. However, a former prison worker of the teenager, Susan Kamanirk, who counseled her to escape, is being held as an accomplice. On May 30, 2001 . . .

Joella was stunned at her streak of good luck. The sky livers were indeed watching over her. She threw the paper down in disgust and glumly returned to her computer to continue her studies, not wanting to relive that horrible experience. Yet Susan's fate was bothering her. She knew Susan's dismissal and returning to drugs was her fault. And now possibly prison time as well. This was the second time another person had taken the fall for her actions.

"Good morning, Vanessa. Joella, I have something to cheer you up," said Justin entering her unit, also on his daily routine, handing her a color flier. She took it out of courtesy and placed it on the desk.

"Read it," he ordered. "It was found on the community bulletin board downtown. There's thousands of them all over the place."

She glanced at it to see on it a photograph of her and Todd taken two days after she killed Quinn. Her face was red and bruised, her lips swollen, and both her eyes were black, yet she was smiling. Below were the words:

> Keep smiling and come home, Joella; you promised to marry me. Whatever you did, I forgive you. *Negligevapse.*
>
> Naglingnig

"He still loves me," she whimpered, almost crying. "How could he know I ran away? There's no—"

"Shhhh! He knows you've been found too. He knows everything," Justin interrupted in a whisper. Then added, "Look at this."

Turning to page 10 of the newspaper, he pointed to a large picture of her and Todd taken atop Caribou Lookout when she was only six, with the caption, "Happy Birthday, Sweet Sixteen, Joella. Naglingnig."

"He remembered!" she cried.

She realized Todd must be in Vancouver and closely following her actions but had no idea how he knew or how he obtained the money to pay thousands of dollars for travel or to buy expensive newspaper ads. She felt rejuvenated, became very excited, and tried to speak. "Todd is here, Justin, looking for me, and—"

Justin put his finger over her mouth and ordered sternly, pointing to the cameras. "Don't talk." She stood up, hugged him, and whispered, "Oh, thank you."

"It's forbidden to discuss that subject with Joella," warned Vanessa.

"I'm her psychologist," he retorted. "And I saw you show her the newspaper clip."

Vanessa gave a defeated smile and walked away.

Lois never felt so contented and relaxed; she was so comfortable with Justin that she stayed for another week after Joella was found. She seemed drawn to him like a magnet.

He was equally intoxicated by her. She was crude but precocious, tough but feminine, carefree but sensible. He loved everything about her. She was modest but spoke her mind honestly, even if political incorrect, and seemed to jell with him in every aspect. She was his dream, but she was Todd's girlfriend, and he did not know how to approach such a delicate, intimate topic with any female outside of work, much less discuss his innermost feelings. He was much older at twenty-four, not good-looking, well over two-hundred-twenty pounds, broad at the shoulders, and his nickname was Bruno.

He was thankful Lois was open and honest. He never felt more relieved than when she told him that even though she loved Todd, and he her, she was just his stand-in until Joella was released and that he was leaving to study at Oxford in England after graduating in a few weeks.

For two weeks, Justin had tried to impress her by taking her to fine restaurants and all the local attractions but still couldn't find the nerve to ask her to stay at his place, but armed with the new knowledge now, her last night, he was going to treat her to a grand finale: a musical and a dinner and hope for a miracle.

Having drunk too much, he got the courage to tell her of his lonesome existence. But after such a magic evening, no miracle was needed; she went back to his apartment where she willingly submitted to his advances, even encouraged.

However, tears came to her eyes as they made love, not because it hurt or that she didn't enjoy it but that she felt she was cheating on Todd. Her conscience bothered her. This was not the way to repay him. She had confused feelings and did not know how to deal with them.

After they finished, she cried as she told Justin her dilemma. Her truthful exposé impressed him even more; city girls would rarely relate such intimate details, even in therapy. This was the kind of honesty and fidelity he was looking in a partner, and he did not want to miss his golden opportunity.

"In seven years of university, I have never met a woman I want more than you," he embarrassingly told her, astounding himself that he was actually telling his own feelings to a stranger.

"It hurts, Justin. I love Todd, but it's you I want. I'm insane."

"Is Todd insane?" he asked gently. "As a psychologist, I assure you it's normal."

She just cuddled him and cried. She wasn't so sure. Cees acted retarded at times; maybe it was hereditary.

"I want you too, Lois. When Todd leaves for England, come and spend the summer with me."

"Seriously?" she asked surprised, changing instantly from crying to smiling, unable to believe her good fortune.

"Together we can make sure Joella survives for Todd; that's the least we can do."

"Oh, Justin!" She kissed him for a long time, then said coyly, "Okay. Now, let's try it again."

Lois returned home, rushed excitedly to Todd's house to find them packing, and to be informed his house was being rented in July to the new senior RCMP officer and his family, and they were leaving for England as soon as Todd finished grade twelve in a few weeks.

"You got into Oxford, just like that?" she asked astounded, disappointed he was leaving so soon.

"Money talks Lois," he stated, somewhat repulsively. "My uncle told them I was coming. Understand?"

"What about me?" she asked, almost crying.

"You're coming with us, of course. Aren't you?" he stated questioningly.

She saw the worried, disappointed look on Todd's face, then thought about Justin. This was going to be much harder than had she anticipated and hurt a great deal more. As he came and kissed her, she merely stared at him, searching for an answer and realizing she loved him equally as much. She now felt torn.

"We got your ticket, dear," said Melissa pleasantly, casually going about her work. "We had to wait for you to come back to get your passport."

Lois just stood staring into space, lost in limbo, with no idea how to break the news. She realized they now considered her an integral part of their family. A tear rolled down her face. She quickly wiped it away.

"Don't worry, dear," Melissa added softly to calm her. "Winston got you into Oxford—"

"I told him you wanted to do business," Todd interrupted, now puzzled, as he returned to his packing. "You can change it. First though, you have two major assignments for class on Monday. I did them for you in appreciation of you doing my work for me."

As she stared at him, she now wanted him again, instead of Justin. But he had Joella. He was good-looking and could date any girl. Justin had nobody. Life was simpler when she was crude and obnoxious and knew nothing about love and the outside world. Todd had taught her manners, to dress properly, stop smoking, helped her with her studies, and even paid her to travel with him.

The local teenagers now considered her a bigger snob than Joella ever was. How could she possibly dump him now?

She whimpered softly. Todd and his mother stopped packing and looked up. He came and kissed her again and comforted her, "We would never leave you behind. You're family."

These words cut even more. She began to cry. She did not want to leave her family and go to England. Cecil would no longer be able to protect her there. But then she realized Vancouver was actually much farther away. She hadn't realized parting would trouble her so much. She needed psychiatric advice desperately, but the only counselor was Todd's mother. She felt trapped.

Melissa went and hugged her, advising her caringly, "We know you have no money, dear. We'll pay for everything. And give you pocket money. You can help me with Joe Ellan."

That made the matter even worse. Lois cried even harder.

"Are you sick?" asked Melissa, concerned. She shook her head.

"Is Joella okay?" asked Todd.

"Perfect," she assured him, between the sobs. "Justin and I will look after her."

Todd immediately grasped her problem.

Justin really was a super guy, exceptionally intelligent, he thought, but he was not happy about him stealing Lois. He felt the bitter pangs of jealousy. "We'll talk about it tonight after I finish packing," he promised her sadly.

Seeing his pain, she immediately left sobbing.

"What's wrong?" asked Cecil, as Lois entered her house, still sobbing.

"Todd . . . Todd's leaving me," she stammered, severely distressed.

"What? He had me buy your ticket for him. You're leaving on July sixth" corrected Prissy, puzzled. "You're going with him. We're all proud of you."

Cecil, very concerned, got up and hugged her. "Did he hurt you?" he asked, puzzled. "He changed his mind?"

"No, Cees, I hurt him. Todd would never hurt this family; he's one of us."

I know, mused Cecil, *he's the greatest guy I know*, while glancing at Prissy contentedly correcting school assignments. "Why would you hurt him?"

"I'm guessing she now loves Justin too," reasoned Prissy.

"Yes!" sobbed Lois, covering her face.

Her mother, who knitted incessantly and seldom talked, offered some rare advice. "It's a good spot to be in. Choose wisely. Follow your head, not your heart."

"He's marrying Joella, Mom," she retorted with jealousy. "They got me enrolled in Oxford. To live with them. For free. They're paying for everyt—"

"Then you also know the answer," said Prissy. "Todd is a gentleman, Lois. You must know that by now. He'll understand."

Lois cried harder.

"Don't blame him. You knew that all along," her father reminded her tersely.

"I want them both," she exclaimed repulsively. "I'm fucking insane!"

Everyone laughed.

"Welcome to the real world," said Prissy.

Lois recalled she had made that same insightful statement to Todd just a year ago. She marveled how much adversity had matured them both in that short time.

"That's your ticket out of this wasteland," advised her mother. "You're a damn fool if you don't take it."

All day Saturday, Lois did not show up at the Clarke household. She could not face Todd to tell him the truth. She loved him too much to hurt him. On Sunday afternoon, Todd went to her home to give her the assignments he had completed for her during her absence. He found her alone sitting on the sofa reading a brochure on British Columbia. As Todd entered, she blushed, bowed her head, and blurted out, "I cheated on you, Todd. I'm sorry."

He went and sat by her and responded sadly, "I've already guessed that." He kissed her and added, "But it still bothers me."

"It's not fair, Todd," she mused openly, whining. "We should have met before you and Joella—"

"Life's not fair, Lois. Think about Tammy. And Joella. I cheat on her too."

"A year ago, I dumped guys for fun. I could chew the head off anybody who talked back to me. What's happened to me?"

"You grew up," he said, smiling. "You forced me to grow up too. And I love you for it."

"No. I'm mad like Cees. I want you both."

He laughed aloud and kissed her again. "So do I."

"You don't understand, Todd. I'm going to Vancouver all summer to stay with Justin," she ventured cautiously.

That jolted him, but he managed enough finesse to gain control and, however distressed, answered thoughtfully, "I'm happy for you. Justin is a gentleman. But let's make the last two weeks count."

She kissed him, and within minutes, they were making love like old times, openly on the sofa.

After they finished, they talked for an hour about her trip to Vancouver and her relationship with Justin. She detailed the story of Joella's escapade on the downtown east side and how close Joella was to Justin. Todd, now somewhat forgiving, pleaded, "Look after Joella for me please."

"I promise on my life." She now loved Todd even more and dreaded the day she would have to say good-bye at the airport.

As did he.

Chapter Seven

Secrets from the Grave

Real loss is when you lose something you love more than yourself.

Joella placed Todd's poster and newspaper ad under the glass on her desk for moral support and, for the next three months, settled comfortably into her new reality of studying eight hours a day. By September, she had once again earned the privilege under the merit system to attend classes at her private high school and to attend movies during daytime, unescorted. All her restrictions had been removed, and she was again fast regaining her position as the star inmate of the institution. She enrolled in an acting class to honor her father's request. She cooked nearly all her meals in her suite, and with her cooking experimentation producing some curious dishes, members of the senior staff did occasionally drop by unannounced at mealtime just to sample her unique creations. Traditional Newfoundland and Labrador food was as foreign to the staff as the multinational meals in the cafeteria were to her. She became the little darling of the staff.

But inexplicably, to her fellow inmates, she was no sweetheart and was treated with disdain. And ironically, they avoided her almost as if she had the plague. It was a cruel paradox that she was considered as part of the establishment. This made her lonely, but it also made her feel safe. Her only real friends were Justin and Vanessa, who was constantly sending mixed messages.

On BC Day, she cooked a feast of old-fashioned Newfoundland jigs dinner with turnip greens, pease pudding, and roast duck, with bakeapple pie for dessert. Amusingly, the whole staff showed up at her place for dinner. It was an unusual grand affair for her, and like the others, she overate.

Later that night, Vanessa heard Joella screaming for her daughter and rushed to her bedroom to find her sweating profusely and shivering. "Joella, wake up! Wake up!" she yelled, shaking her.

After sitting up, it took some time for Joella to recognize her surroundings, stop convulsing, and gain control. "My baby was crying for me. She's lonely," she sobbed.

"Your daughter is dead, Joella," Vanessa answered sympathetically, rubbing her hand over her face. "You saw her grave."

"But I didn't . . ." she began, and then suddenly stopped. This gave her a brilliant idea. If she had the body exhumed, she would be satisfied. "Thank you, Vanessa. I'm okay now," she finally offered, lying back down and closing her eyes.

For the remainder of the night, she lay awake conjuring up a scheme to exhume the body. Finally, near daylight, she was confident she had a workable plan in place.

After three months in England, Todd was still reeling from the shock. His uncle's house was a hundred-year-old three-level twenty-four-room stone mansion situated on a sloping hill on a one-hundred-acre estate, overlooking an artificial lake with swans and a small cultivated forest in the foreground populated with white-tailed deer. Pebbled walkways, adorned by multicolor flowers on each side, snaked their way through the impeccably manicured lawns and trees. He felt as if he were in a Disneyland theme park.

There was a guesthouse as living quarters for two cooks, a butler, a chauffeur, two gardeners, and a horse jockey. There was a stable with two thoroughbred horses, a separate underground cellar for vintage wines, and a twelve-car garage with an equal number of expensive antique cars.

And there were only two of them. *This is English arrogance at its worst*, though Todd.

Even more mind-boggling, he was given a private bedroom that, in itself, was larger than their house back in Labrador. It had twelve-foot ceilings, a floor-to-ceiling fireplace, two leather sofas, and walls adorned with numerous ancient relics, medieval paintings and murals, and electric torches. Several life-size medieval armor-clad statues stood as sentinels over a huge bed with a canopy. Interconnecting was a large alcove for an office and an English sheepdog for company. The unpainted cedar-raftered ceiling contained numerous spears, crossbows, and coats of arms. He felt like a page boy straight out of King Arthur's castle in Camelot. But it was equally enchanting.

To add to this opulent lifestyle, his aunt Emily wanted him to drive her Porsche to class, which was only a few miles, to reflect their prestigious position and to further enhance his status, but he loved to jog to stay in shape. Like his mother, his aunt was always calm, saying she never went anywhere without Winston, and he had his chauffeur drive his antique Rolls-Royce.

Todd felt miles out of his world. Even meals were a drawn-out affair to mimic the long-established etiquette of the royal family.

Yet amid this medieval fantasy world tapestry, he was unhappy and homesick. He missed the crisp nights of Labrador, the migrating rush of the caribou, the lonesome call of the loon at dusk across a calm lake as the sinking sun tinted the water into a crimson glow, the chilling howl of the wolf on a moonlit night with the Northern Lights dancing in the sky above the snowcapped peaks, the beckoning smell of salt ocean water with the meandering pods of whales frolicking among floating icebergs. He longed to be home with the friendly, honest Inuit, with whom he had a natural bond. But, most of all, he felt guilty about living this lifestyle while Joella languished in prison.

He was now a world away ensnared in a life that was the opposite of what he cherished or wanted.

After living a dream summer with Justin, Lois was beginning to feel like a housewife and was strangely contented in that role. She still missed Todd but was now sure it was Justin that she truly loved. She was intrigued; for a large educated man, Justin was uncharacteristically gentle and loving.

At her first crossroads in life, she was forced to make a major decision: whether to remain with him—like he had been insisting—or return to Newfoundland to attend college in which she was enrolled. She was homesick for her family and the rugged Atlantic atmosphere. Being Inuit, 75 percent of her school tuition and lodging was paid for by the federal government, and that was an opportunity too good to waste. But Justin wanted her to attend Trinity College, just four blocks away, and live with him. The problem was that she was not a city person. But, in some ways, Abbotsford was really a small rural city in the country. She felt torn. Todd's heart was in Labrador, as was hers. And sometimes, she felt she wanted Todd again. And this was the day she had promised Justin to give him her decision.

She heard the door open, ran, and threw her arms around his neck and kissed him.

"How's my Bruno?" she joked. "Did Popeye's spinach cause you any trouble today?" She was hesitant to tell him she could not decide.

"Popeye is leaving the end of September," he announced solemnly. "And I'm taking her position as director next week."

Lois glowed with happiness, danced on her toes, and squeezed him with glee.

"I'm so proud of you," she almost squealed. But she could see he was strangely serious. She stopped and became nervous. "Is everything okay?"

"I don't want you to leave, Lois," he whispered, feeling awkward and uncomfortable. Before she could respond, he took out a little box from his pocket, knelt on the floor on one knee in the hallway, and offered her an engagement ring. "Please stay and marry me," he almost begged.

Her mouth fell open. It was the shock of her lifetime. He had never once mentioned marriage in four months. She was barely eighteen. The suddenness left her speechless. There was an embarrassing period of silence

"You can think it over, Lois," he whispered again, now embarrassed at her intransigence.

Finally, the shock wore off. She kissed him and answered cautiously, "I don't have to. I want to marry you."

"You sound unsure, Lois. I can wait for you if—"

She took both his hands and interrupted him solemnly, "Justin, please remember, I'm a poor Inuit. Be sure I am what *you* want. I want a husband for life, like Mom and Dad that stay together whatever goes wrong and never cheat on each other."

"I've never been surer of anything in my life," he answered adamantly, as tears came to his eyes.

"Then I'll always be yours," she promised, starting to cry, knowing it would hurt Todd.

Todd had completed four prerequisite courses at Oxford during the summer, mostly to please his aunt, who insisted he become familiar into the stuffy elite protocol before the fall semester began. Surprisingly, he didn't find his peers as intelligent as he had anticipated. In fact, he was equal to most of them, and he was merely average in Canada. However, most were condescending and arrogant, more concerned about image than grades, and he avoided them whenever possible, concentrating on his studies, determined to finish his law degree in four years, when Joella was released.

The girls flocked around him because he drove a Porsche, and somehow, they knew he was of the Howard lineage. But he had problems understanding their language, which was fast and jumpy. Conversations were mostly on his apparent wealth and status as they shamelessly hounded him for dates. He considered none of them friendly, with the exception of a second-year Filipino student, nicknamed Bookie.

Each night, he missed Lois in his bed but had no interest in any of his classmates. Booky was kind and sociable, but not very pretty. However, she was smart, assertive, and hung around with him, yet she would only discuss law.

But more so, when alone, he felt guilty about not telling Joella he had their child. He wanted her to know he had named him Joe Ellan, that he had bathed him, fed him, and even changed his diaper once, and how Joey had brought him even closer to her.

Tears came to his eyes just to think of her unfair lot in life. He wanted her to finish her education, but he did not want her behind bars. He knew Justin and Lois were correct; a court challenge now would disrupt her studies and possibly cause an international flap, with no guarantee of success. His aunt and uncle provided all the necessary funding to have her live as luxurious as the youth home would allow, and then some. He also knew that they were working with politicians and lawyers behind the scenes, and he was left out of the loop for fear of disrupting his own studies, which he soon found was becoming logarithmically more difficult.

Joella skipped classes and went early to Shady Lawns Funeral Home to place flowers on her daughter's grave. She had remembered correctly; her baby's plot was the only used lot in the Valley View section. After scanning the area for visitors, with bare hands, she carefully cut and removed a sod from the adjacent plot the exact size of the plaque. She moved the plaque to the new lot and placed the sod in the previous plaque's position. She placed the flowers on the plaque and said a brief prayer. She removed the tiny numbered marker "Lot No 7" to the new plot. Then, after half an hour of tedious touch-up gardening, she was positive nobody would notice the plaque and marker had been moved forward one space.

She went to the office and requested to purchase lot number 6 in Valley View. Recognizing her from her weekly visits with a detention security guard, they all laughed, as the sexton mocked humorously that it cost $3,000, and that was a tad high for an Indian jailbird.

She took $400 from her pocket and offered to pay for it on installments. They stopped laughing, and after a brief huddle and heated disagreement with the administrator behind the glass, she heard the sexton whisper, "These lots are *all* empty. If she reneges, we'll only take it back."

They accepted her money, hastily registered her in the temporary log, and gave her a deed for plot number 6. She quickly rushed outside clutching her precious legal document and took a deep breath. She had pulled off the first step in her plan as smooth as clockwork and felt like a novice detective who had just pulled her first caper.

Todd took a brief respite from his monotonous library study and went into the university bar to meet Booky, who a day earlier had suddenly broken her law-only credo and had bashfully told him that she had a big secret to tell him. As he approached her sitting alone in the far corner, he walked past the two crowded self-designated private-club tables of the popular college football team, all boisterous cavorting with women and competitive drinking as always. He noticed the two Manchester hopefuls, whom the students called Tom and Jerry, again ridiculing the patrons at an adjacent table. Having seen them harassing Booky several times, he found himself tense, recalling visions of Joella's abuse.

"This is the private football corridor," Jerry informed Todd, smirking.

"Men play football. You play soccer," joked Todd.

Surprised at his belittling answer, the place went quiet. Todd looked around to see all the patrons staring inquisitively at him.

"They say you knocked up a 'skimo and got a little papoose." Tom laughed, getting up and standing in his path.

Todd was startled by the pubic revelation of his private life but soon recovered and became incensed at the brutal insult.

"I just came to speak to Booky," he managed, controlling his temper. He didn't want a negative image here.

"Don't you know why we call the Flip, Bucky, Labrador boy?" asked Jerry, standing up next to his friend. "Because she has buck teeth!"

The two tables roared with laughter.

"He told the class he's specializing in Canadian law and Eskimo language," joked Dunk, their three-hundred-pound strong arm Scottish friend and team goalie.

Everyone roared again.

"My fiancée is Inuit, not Eskimo, and she speaks Inuktitut, peasants. In Labrador, the Inuit have a saying, 'Crows fight for fun and run, but wolves fight to die.'"

Everyone at the two football tables now stopped talking, surprised by Todd's calm response and fearless mentality.

Todd continued, "I hunt with the wolves, and if you don't want Inuit justice, just sit down and boast about your pig bladder skills to your crows. Repeat those words, and I'll show you how we scalp Qablunaats."

Tom was about to hit him when Jerry grabbed his arm. "Not yet. They say your little 'skimo scalped two people."

To Todd, that was the ultimate insult, far past the limit of his tolerance. Instantly, with his right fist, he hit Jerry with the full force of his body in the mouth, knocking out a tooth and sending him sprawling across the crowded table, smashing several bottles, as the patrons scurried out of their way. Just a fast, Todd kicked Tom mercilessly into the crotch dropping him to the floor like a ton of bricks, crouching in pain. Their friend, Dunk, leaped up from the second table to help, but Todd had anticipated their wolf-pack mentality and punched two fingers viciously into his eyes, temporarily blinding him. The bartender dialed the police and yelled for them to stop, as the other football players encouraged their buddies.

Tom and Jerry, now recovered, grabbed Todd together, only to be both slammed headfirst into the hardwood table, smashing several more bottles and upsetting the table. There was instant commotion and screaming from the girls as they yelled for Todd not to kill them. Todd slammed their heads several more times onto the table edge, before throwing them motionless onto the overturned table.

Dunk, now in a boxing stance, was challenging Todd to fight like a man. Todd needed no urging. With his karate knowledge, he gave him a reverse flying kick to his head but was astounded when Dunk remained standing. However, Dunk was momentarily stunned at Todd's viciousness and unexpected response. With renewed determination, Todd kicked him again in stomach, and Dunk fell to his knees. Todd knew he had met his match. He was about to attempt another flying reverse kick to Dunk's head when he heard Booky scream, "Watch out, Blackbeard's behind you!"

He turned just in time to see Booky crash a wooden chair over the head of a bearded person holding a switchblade knife. The person slumped lifeless backward unto the floor. Dogmatically, Todd immediately returned to Dunk, who held up his hands and, in sheer panic, pleaded, "No more please. You got me, laddie."

Within a minute, the campus security was crawling all over the pub, along with a dozen *bobbies* and three ambulances. As the medics carted Tom, Gerry, and Blackbeard away, the bobbies handcuffed Todd to a column, as Booky screamed at them, "It wasn't his fault, dummies."

They grabbed her and handcuffed her next to him, causing a barrage of curses and obscenities to be hurled at the authorities, as the students tried unsuccessfully to get them to understand it was the football team's fault.

Surprised, Todd heard Dunk shout, "We're the bloody blokes here, bobbies. Let them go. We're the bloomin' troublemakers!"

Some students became even more aggressive and threateningly demanded Todd and Booky be released. As the police struggled to get control, Todd and Booky, now tied back-to-back to a column, introduced themselves.

"I'm Arnaq Eetuk, Todd."

"Todd Clarke, Booky."

"It's B-u-c-k-y, not Booky. Like my buck teeth," she explained, deeply embarrassed.

"That's cruel. Why do you tolerate it?"

She said nothing.

He added, "Thanks for helping me. Your name sounds Inuit."

"That's what I wanted to tell you. I'm not Filipino. I said that because I was ashamed of my heritage. But seeing how proud your family was of Joella, I had to tell you."

"How does everybody know about Joella and my son?" asked Todd, both puzzled and angry.

"Your mom is so proud of Joey she tells everybody about him. She's proud you speak Inuktitut and is specializing in First Nations law to help us."

"*Us?*" asked Todd impatiently.

Switching to Inuktitut, she said shyly, "I'm from Goose Bay. My father was a British RAF pilot. That's how I got here. He's proud of me too." She paused. "And I'm proud of him but was ashamed of my mother because she was Inuit. Until now."

Remembering Joella, tears came to Todd's eyes, as he answered in fluent Inuktitut. "If I wasn't hog-tied, I'd kiss you."

She blushed.

As they were being lectured and released pending further investigation, she encouraged, "Don't worry, Todd. We did everyone here a favor."

She has Joella's spirit too, he mused.

Every night, for the next week, Joella splashed water on her face and pretended to wake up screaming for her baby. Each time, Vanessa would rush in and comfort her. By week's end, her recurring nightmares were reported to the administration, which caused Justin to be concerned.

Justin discussed it with her and did a thorough textbook analysis but found no mental deficiencies; quite the opposite, he found her somewhat eccentric for a teenager and unusually clever.

On Monday, Vanessa found the cemetery title deed and, after lecturing Joella for her stupidity, informed Justin. He reported it to the prison director, who called a special session of the medical panel and management to analyze her mental state.

Joella calmly explained to them that the Great Spirit appeared each night in a dream and told her to prepare she was going to die soon and would see her baby. As a result, she had bought a plot in the cemetery to be buried near her daughter. This shocked the panel, recognizing this was a drastic deterioration in just one week. Justin, however, was skeptical and, sensing something was amiss, asked kindly, "What can we do to help you?"

"Bury Joe Ellan in my plot to keep my baby company until I die; she's lonely," she replied quickly, starting to cry, further shocking them. They looked at one another, believing she had gone insane. Vanessa began to panic thinking she had now killed some inmate, this time on her watch.

"Who's Joe Ellan?" asked the confused prison director cautiously.

"My teddy bear."

They all smiled, gave a big sigh of relief, and asked Joella to wait outside.

They discussed the pros and cons of the absurd request for a while and finally dismissed her request. This angered Vanessa, who had to deal with her distress every night and blurted out, "Why not? That's the least we can do after her gross mistreatment. She's lonely. She wants to work in the front office for experience, but—"

"With the confidential files?" asked the director, appalled.

"Do you have something to hide?"

"That's enough!" she warned. "Remember Susan's fate."

"I'll inform the police if—" bluffed Vanessa.

The director incensed, stood up to speak. Justin held up his hand and stated resolutely, "Thank you, Vanessa. I'm taking control next week. In this institution, psychology is my jurisdiction. I'll approve her request."

Vanessa stood up and applauded. The director was furious. As the others squabbled over the decision, Justin recalled Joella and informed her that the request had been approved and ordered her to promptly return to her suite and organize her funeral service, and she was also authorized to spend a few hours a week in the front office for practical experience, noting some files would be confidential and off limits to an internee.

Joella wondered whether Justin was onto her and supporting her. She knew it was an outrageous request with no assurance the funeral home would comply. She was also excited that she was now allowed to do practical work for credits to hasten her degree. She felt like hugging him.

That night, she knelt at her bed and prayed for a long time to both the Christian God and Todd's sky livers.

Step two had been precariously achieved.

A week later, Todd was called to the dean's office to find Arnaq sitting with her head bowed. She had all her textbooks with her. It appeared she had been crying.

"Three world-class football students hospitalized. This is an outrage. This is Oxford! The most prestigious institute in the world! An icon of higher learning! Alfred the Great debated here in 872. And you two brawling like hooligans, desecrating our impeccable heritage—" he began to lecture.

"This dingy stone barn is no more than an elitist pub, where students are formally brainwashed to be pompous and egotistical. But it *is* a relics from the Dark Ages," sneered Todd, angry for having to justify self-defense and guessing he was being heavily fined by the council.

Encouraged by Todd, Arnaq chimed in, "I've been here for a year, sir, and they're mostly braggarts and egomaniacs. Everyone here needs a taste of reality."

The dean slowly rose from his antique wooden desk and angrily faced them. "Two wilderness kids from the Canadian colonies committing sacrilege against a thousand years of history. Dissidents were burnt at the stake here for less."

"The smell is still here, sir," agreed Arnaq metaphorically.

The dean reddened.

Todd smiled.

"We know its history. Why did you call us here?" attacked Todd, equally sarcastic. "We're here on merit, not gratuitous football scholarships or as favors for the elite. I have to study for my law degree."

"You're both expelled!" the dean retorted vindictively.

Step three was a major problem. The funeral home would permit Joella to bury her teddy bear as a healing process for her troubled mind, but it was mandatory that the procedure to be performed by their sexton, and that cost another $400, money she didn't have. She was defeated.

Vanessa found her crying when she came for her final evening reconnaissance check. After extracting her problem, Vanessa unexpectedly volunteered to discuss it with Justin and to take a collection from all the inmates and staff to help her cause.

Joella was puzzled and cautious. She saw Vanessa as a *company* person but halfheartedly agreed.

Even more astounding, within an hour after going to bed, a knock came on her door. She found Vanessa standing there smiling with $400 in her hand.

"It's only a loan. You have to pay it back." Then, in her deep professional voice warned, "And keep it confidential. Our ass is on the line."

"Our?" asked Joella gratefully.

Vanessa walked away without answering.

"Did they figure out Joella's scheme?" Lois asked her Bruno, kissing him excitedly as he entered the house.

"No. They're so darn rigid the inmates can hardly breathe. They're kids, young and restless! It's understandable why they run away. Popeye thinks Joella's crazy."

"She's not, Justin. She's using them. She's only trying to find her baby," Lois explained disappointedly. "You have to help. You promised."

"I overruled their objections and approved it," he stated matter-of-factly, kissing her back.

"I love you, Justin," she almost squealed, kissing him again.

"But the sexton wants four hundred dollars to dig the grave. Damn bloodsuckers! She didn't have it."

"I'll phone Todd—"

"Vanessa and I loaned her the money."

"Oh, Justin. I'm so glad I met you. Let's get married right away before you change your mind."

"You're the best thing that ever happened to me, Lois. I'd marry you tonight if you wanted."

Lois wondered how she ever got so lucky. He was as solid as a rock. Todd was like that too.

Joella turned the funeral procedure into a grand affair with flowers and several inmates from the prison in attendance. As the sexton dug the grave to nine feet—having convinced him it was an Inuit ritual—she filmed the whole process. Finding no casket, she now knew beyond the shadow of a doubt her daughter had been adopted. She could barely contain her joy.

She then had Vanessa film the sexton lowering the teddy bear into the grave, as she kneeled and prayed to the sky livers. And for a time thereafter, she amused the inmates by doing an Indian dance around the grave, chanting some indecipherable ancient Inuit mantra. The spectacle drew curious onlookers until a big crowd gathered around her grave. After she finished the funeral, she got a loud applause.

Joella had never been so happy. *Maybe I can be an actress after all*, she mused to herself, overjoyed.

Step three had been achieved in grand showmanship style.

"Indian dance? You're Inuit, not Innu. Filming a funeral? You overdid it, Joella, don't you think?" Justin smiled as he tasted Joella's newest cooking creation, a local delicacy, something she called padarah. She got up and hugged him.

He pointed to the cameras and ordered seriously, "Control yourself."

"I was excited," she whispered. "You know, don't you?"

"I follow institutional protocol," he lied, aloud and sternly. "Will you now promise me to finish your time and your degree, before you continue your charade? I will then help you."

"I swear!" she promised emphatically. "I know you know where she is. Oh, I love you, Justin."

He smiled.

"I want you to have a copy of the funeral service," she suddenly announced, fetching him a CD. "Keep it until I get out."

He smiled when he saw the title, *Joe Ellen's Teddy Bear Funeral: October 2, 2001.* Now positive of her conniving plan, he agreed. Then staring amusingly at the stack of CDs, he asked, "How many copies did you make?"

"A lot," she answered shyly, bowing her head. "Fifty."

He smiled again and shook his head in disbelief as he left.

Monday morning after breakfast, for an hour, a miserable and repentant Todd halfheartedly related to the Howards how he and

Arnaq had gotten unceremoniously expelled. He was relieved to have finally gotten the disaster into the open after a weekend of indecision on whether to disclose it, knowing he had grossly overreacted.

"Thank you, Aunt and Uncle, for everything; sorry to have embarrassed you," he concluded dejectedly, hugging them. "I must now to go and pack. I'm returning to Canada."

His mother just listened, stunned.

Winston pensively lit his pipe and blew a stream of smoke, took a few puffs, then snuffed it out again.

"By God, we have Howard in the family, Emily," he said proudly to his wife, in his calm stoic voice. "Miles, have my chauffeur bring the Rolls around."

Miles appeared and bowed.

"A favor, Todd," he added seriously, "before you go, run around my estate three times."

"That's six miles," a confused Todd managed hesitantly.

His uncle nodded, patted him on the back, and left.

When Winston left, his mother, now crying at Todd's leaving, handed Todd a letter postmarked British Columbia and labeled *Private and Confidential.* Quickly ripping it open in a state of despair, he read:

> Sept. 27, 2001
>
> Dearest Todd,
>
> I thought this issue too important for e-mail. It hurts just to write it. Justin has asked me to marry him. I agreed, but I first want your blessing; I love you too. Since you are marrying Joella . . .

"This is not my week, Mom," he moaned, with tears in his eyes, putting the letter down. "Lois is marrying Justin."

His mother came and comforted him for a while, then solemnly handed him an e-mail.

"Where did it come from?" he stated emphatically, putting it aside. "What else can go wrong?"

"It came in on your uncle's secure line. It's from Justin. Read it, Todd. He's not supposed to contact us directly."

"How did he know Uncle's direc—"
"Read it!"

October 2, 2001

Todd,

Joella dug up the grave plot in the cemetery and now knows her child is alive. She promised me to now settle down and study hard. I assured her if she finished her degree in four years, when you're finished, I'd help her find her child—with your permission. Good luck with your studies.

Justin

Seeing Todd smiling, she queried nervously, "What is it, dear?"

Todd hugged her.

"Lois has my blessing, Mom. They deserve each other."

Joella was preparing to attend her Monday acting class at noon when Vanessa requested her presence at a special meeting. Entering the conference room, her heart sank. Sitting at the head of the table was the infamous Social Services Director, Drucella Dingley, looking like an angry hyena ready to pounce, with a glum social worker positioned on either side for backup. Two police officers were in attendance as well as a number of medical and behavioral experts, all sitting on one side of the table. The outgoing prison administrator was sitting next to the director of Shady Lawns Funereal Home, Dan Filtree, who also looked annoyed. Justin Patey was at the other end of the table as interim administrator and chairperson.

Then to Joella's horror, she saw the sexton and realized they had discovered she had moved plaque number 7 marker to plot number 8. She dreaded her fate.

After being positioned alone on the opposite side of the table, the meeting was called to order.

"Ms. Adams, our funeral home has been audited. The sexton's records have revealed that lot seven was sold to both you and Social Services. Why did you dig up your daughter's body and dispose of it?" Mr. Filtree pounced mercilessly.

Joella almost fainted. "There was no body in—" she responded, shivering with fear.

"I'll answer that," Justin interjected. "Joella is under severe stress from the loss of a child. I'm sure my colleagues agree I cannot permit this line of questioning."

They unanimously nodded their approval.

"You must turn over the videos you took," ordered Mrs. Dingley angrily, disregarding Justin. "You may suffer from chronic fetal alcohol syndrome, but committing criminal activity—"

"Just one second!" Justin snapped. "Please go wait outside, Joella," he instructed calmly.

"I'll get my daughter back," Joella promised them defiantly as she left. "Even if it's the last thing I ever do."

Everyone began to talk at once.

Justin continued, "If I may also ask the officers to wait outside."

As they left, you could hear a pin drop; everyone was waiting for something drastic to happen.

Justin could barely control his temper. He stood up and attacked, speaking directly to the Social Services members. "It? Mrs. Dingley, her child is a person, not an object! Fetal alcohol syndrome? She has no such condition. You know that! Criminal activity? That appears to be the forte of your Social Services' department. Stop this damn charade now. Or I'll report your activities to these police officers outside."

"Don't threaten me, Mr. Patey. Grave robbing is a criminal offence; she's sixteen!" she retaliated, standing up and shaking her fist at him.

"You know she videotaped the grave digging. Would you like this committee to see it? I can get a copy for everybody; she made fifty and distributed them."

The two social workers' mouths fell open. Mrs. Dingley angrily slumped back down, as did he.

"Mrs. Dingley, you know her baby is not dead."

She stood up again and glared at him again. "Are you calling me a liar?"

"Yes!" he stated obstinately and equally irritated. "But let me finish please."

There was an instant uproar and a call for order. She grudgingly sat back down again.

He pressed on. "Her baby is a boy. His name is Joe Ellan Clarke. I met Todd Clarke, the baby's father, here."

The room went deathly quiet. Everyone was aware that was a serious breach of protocol.

"Todd arranged for his son to be adopted by his rich aunt in Oxford, England, where he now lives on her estate, raising their child as he studies law at Oxford. You see Mrs. Dingley, he's more clever than Social Services. He knew Canadian courts have no jurisdiction in England. Social Services, however deceptive, have been outwitted by a mere teenager. Joella, equally intelligent, knew her child was not in that plot. If you do not wish this made public knowledge, I warn you: do not harass my patient, Joella, again. I will consider this issue solved until she finishes her sentence. Then, I'm sure, you will hear more from her."

The place remained eerily silent as everyone stared repulsively at Mrs. Dingley and pondered the implications of such a damming allegation.

"I will mail each a video copy of the grave digging," he added, now firmly in control.

"It's a breach of court protocol to release that information and illegal to conspire with the father of Joella's child—" warned the outgoing administrator, standing up and now speaking condescendingly on a point of information. At times, Justin believed Lois was right. She even acted like Popeye.

"It is also illegal to dismiss Susan Kamanirk for telling Joella the truth," he retaliated.

She sat quietly back down.

"These are very serious allegation you're making, Justin. If true, criminal activity is occurring here. These occurrences are far above the law," noted one of the behavioral experts.

"Yes, indeed," agreed Justin. "Now, Mrs. Dingley, again, would you like for me to advise the police outside or just contact the newspapers?" He stared questioningly at her. "Or do you want to apologize to Joella and let her finish her sentence in peace?"

"No! Illegal activity must be reported," objected the second behavioral therapist. "That's cruel and unusual punishment for a teenager—"

"It's mental torture for her. I know!" interjected Vanessa.

Stunned, the two social workers stared demandingly at their director's face, which was bloodred, also demanding a credible response. Others at the table voiced their disgust, followed by a period of deafening silence.

"This is a case for our lawyers," she finally noted sheepishly.

"I know you were following a court directive. An apology to Joella will suffice for now. But no further interference for the duration of her sentence. Understood?"

She nodded.

Joella was then brought back in as the other therapists objected strenuously with Justin's instant solution.

"There's been an honest error in judgment, Joella; you did nothing wrong. On behalf of Social Services, we're sorry for accusing you of an illegal act," apologized Mrs. Dingley insincerely.

Everybody stood up and gave Joella big hand.

Puzzled, she stared inquisitively at Justin, who calmly smiled. Once more she wanted to give him a big bear hug, knowing he had somehow saved her again.

After she left, the other behavioral psychologists on the panel assailed Justin for his incompetent decision and for forcing it upon the committee without a vote.

"Yes, she's innocent," Justin mused aloud, somewhat despondent. "And exceptionally smart. But here, at least, she can get a degree for free in a safe environment; let's not deny her that too. It's the real reason she was sent here. Some Social Services decisions are brilliant in their incompetence. I'm confident their day of reckoning will come."

The social services officers flushed.

He stood up and, with the three behavioral therapists still objecting and accusing him of being a dictator, stated decisively, "I will personally see she's taken care of properly. This meeting is now adjourned."

Winston was in an unusual ugly mood at having to wait to meet the dean and wasted no time broaching the subject, refusing to shake his hand.

"Spencer, the Howards fought Napoleon's frogs, the African Boers, the German Krauts, the Japanese Nips, and the Vietcong goons. Now, I have to fight you and my old alma mater? What in bloody hell's happening here?"

The dean cringed, utterly confused and disgusted at the tirade of derogatory racist remarks.

"*Dean* Spencer, sir. What is your point?"

"My nephew was expelled without justification."

"Ah! Todd Clarke. He badly injured three of our top football players . . ."

Winston let the dean vent for a time, then interrupted, "The police report was specific; the ruffians initiated it and should be charged. Are they?"

"That's irreverent and immaterial, sir,—

"Drop your legalese, Spencer; I too am a lawyer. Stick to the facts.

"The fact is our prestigious institution—"

"Don't patronize me," he said, taking out his pipe, lighting it in defiance, and blowing a huge whiff of smoke in his direction. "And an economist. Is this the same football team I sponsor? What were they doing drinking? They're underage. Did your prestigious institution serve them?"

The dean flinched again. He hadn't thought of that scenario. He then recalled that Mr. Howard was its major benefactor in both the football and rowing teams and felt awkward but remained silent.

Winston continued, "Were they given a hearing?"

There was still no response.

"Your tenure has been too long; you've lost control. Power corrupts."

"What is your solution, Mr. Howard?" the dean backtracked, sounding conciliatory.

"Reinstatement: both."

The dean nodded hesitantly.

"And a letter of apology to them. Now."

"That's capitulation," lectured the dean, offended, standing up. "You are free to go."

Howard stood up, faced him, and blew another stream of smoke in his face.

"I'm not a passive student, old boy. Lord Thurston was appalled too. I'll ask him to cancel his gratuitous football ads for your morally and financially bankrupt institution and embrace Cambridge, where he actually attended, and to write a column in his newspaper on this injustice. Good day, Spencer."

"You . . . you know Lord Thurston?" stammered the dean doubtfully.

"He's my sister's husband, old boy." He started to leave.

"One second, sir. These are extenuating circumstances; it sheds a new perspective on the issue. I'll have my secretary invite them back.

"Not invite, beg. Expunge their eviction. It's fair English justice. And I expect the person with the knife to be expelled and the college to lay charges of attempted manslaughter; he's a criminal."

"He's the league's number one full-back—"

"Was, Spencer, was!"

"We'll likely come second to Cambridge—"

"Or there's no team!"

The dean nodded passively.

It was late when Winston returned for supper. Todd was pleasantly surprised to see Arnaq with him.

"We've been reinstated," Arnaq, blurted out, smiling.

Todd was too amazed to speak.

"Is supper ready? I'm a tad famished," Winston asked his wife casually.

"Your favorite beefsteak-and-kidney potpie," answered his wife, smiling happily.

"Mine got a broken collarbone; yours only got mild concussions and lost a few teeth," informed Arnaq, laughing at Todd's astonishment.

"Thank you, Uncle," Todd offered meekly. "How did you manage that?'

"Elementary, me boy. And I'm bloody proud of you two. You're both Howards. Sit down and let's eat."

His wife smiled in agreement, but Melissa was not so sure; Todd was already needlessly aggressive.

Arnaq laughed again at the astonished look on Todd's face, as she began to read a note, mimicking the English accent:

November 12, 2001

Mr. Clarke,

It appears that our prestigious institution has committed a rare faux pas by acting prematurely in expelling you, one of our most outstanding students. Your presence can only contribute to our excellent lineage and reputation. Please return to lectures at your discretion.

Sincerely,
Lillian Crossle
Per, Dean Spencer, PhD

"Bloody right," began Winston as he ate. "Listen and learn, me boy. I said, 'The Howards fought the . . .'"

For once, Todd was content to listen to an hour-long tirade from his uncle in his slow monotonous voice. He even ate the beefsteak-and-kidney pie he so much hated.

Joella, grateful for Justin's help, baked him his favorite oatmeal-raisin-spice cookies for a full week and, when not in college, made him batches of chocolate brownies, which she knew he loved to nibble on as he worked. She noticed he also loved her Newfoundland jigs dinner but always took it home to eat.

Justin, though grateful, asked her not to pamper him, joking that he was already 230 pounds and the staff was becoming suspicious.

Relieved she had not lost her mobility privileges, she decided to settle down for a while until the furor blew over and study harder to finish her courses even sooner.

After a disastrous two weeks, Todd decided to invite Arnaq to a dance at the university club. They arrived late and found the club overcrowded, and the only empty space was the two football-club tables near the bandstand. They nonchalantly sat down, as everyone stared in disbelief.

To their surprise, the bartender appeared and offered them free drinks, explaining they were complimentary for a week. Even though underage, they gladly accepted the hospitality, figuring the student council was rewarding them for civilizing the football hoodlums.

They danced, drank, and chatted happily alone at the two tables until midnight when both were nearly drunk. Suddenly, there was a huge commotion as everyone simultaneously moved away from adjacent tables. Todd looked up to see that Dunk had mysteriously reappeared and was towering menacingly above him. The band stopped; the club became eerily silent. The bartender dialed security. Everyone, now standing, stared at Dunk and Todd, waiting for hell to break loose.

Instead, Dunk smiled, held his hand out, and said in his deep Scottish accent, “I see you’ve accepted my peace offering. I’m Duncan Campbell.”

Todd stood up, shook it, and said, “With gratitude, Mr. Campbell. I’m Todd, and this is Arnaq. You’re welcome to join us. Can we buy you a drink?”

The crowd erupted in an enormous applause and sat back down with a sigh of relief.

“Call me Dunk. A pint of Guinness. ’Tis the least I could do after a bloody stupid start.”

“I remember you now,” said Arnaq, bright eyed. “You’re the boxing champ.”

Todd swallowed hard, realizing he had been fortunate.

Arnaq laughed devilishly.

“And defeated only once,” he boasted, pointing at Todd. Then, looking at Arnaq, added, “You’re a wee one but bloody tough too, missie. Sure you’re not a Highland Lassie?”

Todd laughed aloud and nodded his agreement.

Dunk added, "Are all you Canucks that bloody tough?"

"We're the timid ones." Arnaq laughed. "The tough ones play hockey."

Within a few minutes, drinks began to pile up on the football tables, as other students joined and congratulated them.

"Scots," explained Dunk, nodding toward to the others now crowding their tables. "In Bonnie Scotland, we too have a saying, Todd. 'A bauld fae is better than a cowardly friend.' I've made you two honorary Scots."

The two tables applauded.

"I take it you're Scottish," joked Arnaq, staring at his tartan kilt.

He roared with laughter.

"Scottish by birth, British by law, and a Highlander by grace, lassie."

She laughed hardily and pulled her chair closer to him to better enjoy his company. Standing up, Dunk cheerfully called for the band to play a traditional Scottish reel on the bagpipe and invited her to dance, as most of the patrons then crowded around the dance floor and applauded as he taught her the Hebrides rendition of the sword dance. Todd just sat back the table and enjoyed the spectacle.

"You got us expelled this semester," said an angry voice from behind. "Let's take it outside, 'skimo lover."

Todd turned to see Tom and Jerry standing behind him, smirking sadistically, and three other strong arms farther back waiting for him. He realized they had chosen their opportunity wisely; he was now too drunk to fight them all and held up his hands in defeat. The band again stopped. But this time, his Scottish friends, realizing Todd's predicament, surrounded the troublemakers. One spoke, "Leave him be. He's now an honorary Scot. That means you'll have to fight all of Scotland."

"Ah! Fags in skirts!" sneered Jerry. Tom laughed insultingly. Every eye turned toward Dunk in his highland tartan standing above on the dance floor, with his hands on his waist, watching. Realizing their gaffe, Tom and Jerry looked paralyzed. Arnaq laughed impishly at their dilemma. Todd stood up. Dunk held up his hand.

"This one's mine, laddie," volunteered an infuriated Dunk.

The whole bar erupted in loud applause. Tom and Jerry began to back away, but the Scots had encircled them.

"No. One-on-one is fairer," Todd offered, slurring his words. "Who wants Inuit justice first?"

"No. You're drunk. They're mine, laddie. One Scot, two limeys: a fair fight," boasted Dunk. "Nobody insults Bonnie Scotland," he lectured, offended, suddenly jumping down from the dance floor, unexpectedly grabbing Tom in one hand and Jerry in the other, lifting them over his head, and then, just as quickly, slamming them heavily back down onto the floor. They crumbled to their knees.

"Break it up!" yelled the police, bursting through the door. Dunk backed away and held his hands up in submission. The police simply bypassed him and went directly to Todd, grabbed his arms, and handcuffed them behind his back, and sneered, "You again?"

Instantly, there was a chorus of angry curses from the drunken crowd as everyone began to voice their opposition.

"I'm responsible for this institution. I saw what happened, officers," said the dean, standing up from a table in the dark corner and waving his hand to get attention, surprising the drunken students. The place went quiet. The crowd felt defeated, knowing he favored the football team members.

"Thomas Preston and Jerry Cooper were here illegally; they're on suspension. Now, they will be expelled. Mr. Clarke refused to fight. And Mr. Campbell was reacting to a bigoted, racist insult. If I may suggest, officers, you charge these two with hate mongering against the Inuit."

Ouch. Like the crowd, both Todd and Dunk were taken aback. Hoodlums, yes, but hate mongering?

The police nodded, removed Todd's handcuffs, and quickly left, escorting a humiliated Tom and Jerry to their paddy wagon.

"Mr. Clarke, you're still only seventeen, I believe," noted the dean sternly. "And drunk. Who sold you the alcohol?" staring at the three bartenders. Todd did not answer; now sure he was being expelled again.

"Nobody," interrupted Arnaq. "But I can make a legal case, sir, that the club bar be closed and fined for giving free alcohol to minors," in her class argumentative mode.

The dean smiled, impressed at her instant blackmailing defense.

"I'll take them both home," Todd's uncle, Winston, advised the dean, standing up from the same table in the corner and again surprising everyone.

"I'm sorry, Uncle—" began a repentant Todd, staggering toward him.

"Let's go, Ms. Eetuk," interrupted Winston in his stoic manner. "You both need indoctrination."

"Thanks for the drinks, Mr. Howard," offered a defeated dean, shaking his hand. "You have proven your point."

"No damage done, old boy. Now, you look after yours; I'll look after mine." Then, turning to Todd and Arnaq ordered sternly, "Let's go."

Winston turned to Dunk and shook his hand firmly. "Yes, Scotland the brave. You're a bloody credit to the Highlanders!"

Chapter Eight

A Taste of Reality

In honest hands, poison is medicine; in dishonest hands,
medicine is poison.

Joella sat on her bed and cried all night, staring blankly at the photos of Justin's wedding with his bride blanked out. He looked so happy. Joella was disappointed he had actually gotten married, although she had known for months that he was engaged. He had told her several times that the ceremony was soon, but she had closed her mind, hoping he would have a change of heart. Had she lost a close friend, her only friend? She was terrified of losing his affection and wondered how he would treat her now.

To her, he was the most attentive and loving giant who seemed to anticipate her every need and did his utmost to help her. He alone seemed to know all the details of her native ways. This was not how she viewed big white people. They were supposed to be arrogant and overpowering. He made no advances toward her, but she wondered how she would respond if he did. She was embarrassed by her own feelings and felt guilty for even thinking of cheating on Todd.

Justin had brought her a piece of their wedding cake and, confusingly, some native Inuit bread. But, most of all, it hurt she was not invited to the wedding, and he knew that she would have been permitted. He even refused to show her pictures of his bride, saying only she would like his wife, and in time, after she finished her degree, things would turn out for her, and she'd thank him. But she was now beginning to have doubts. She pushed her face into the pillow and sobbed pitifully.

As she drifted off to sleep, once more, she felt totally alone.

"Where were you all weekend?" Todd called curiously to Arnaq through the Rolls-Royce window when he saw her strolling in front of the university assembly hall Monday evening as his ride pulled in front of the university for his evening lecture. "Uncle wanted to take us to Paris."

"Shall I wait, Master Clarke?" asked Miles, who chauffeured him.

"Just for a few minutes please," requested Todd.

He was surprised to see her wearing a red-blue tartan skirt instead of her usual blue jeans; she looked like a cute Japanese schoolgirl.

She giggled, lowered her head, and mumbled, "Scotland."

"Scotland? he asked inquisitively. "Why? Where?"

"With Dunk. Stornoway in the Hebrides."

Before he could query her further, Dunk appeared wearing the same tartan-patterned kilt accompanied by a beautiful young blonde girl. Todd was amused and laughed. Matched pairs? He mused, *That's not a dichotomy. Arnaq is barely up to your armpit.*

"I see you met my Tara, Snowflake," Dunk said proudly. "She wanted you to come."

It was clear they had spent the weekend together. Todd was impressed but a little envious; he was losing his only female friend in England.

Dunk continued, "And this is Penelope."

After a brief introduction, she handed him a letter and, in the sweetest voice Todd had ever heard, began to plead, "I'm sorry for what Tom did, Mr. Clarke. I'm his sister. Please forgive him and help us."

Todd was astounded beyond words.

She recognized his astonishment at the impossible request.

"You see, Mr. Clarke, we're paupers. Tom was our only hope to help our sick mum. He doesn't hate you. He fell in with the wrong blokes, was their gofer—"

"I can vouch for that," said Dunk emphatically. "Even a Highlander fell for it."

"Please read his letter," she continued.

Todd stared at her long blonde hair and blue eyes, still enthralled, but managed to note, "Penelope is Greek?"

She blushed.

"The name is Greek. I'm English. Mum said I was going to be a royal princess and wanted me called Elizabeth, but my dad loved Homer. Like Tom, he's pigheaded, so he called me Penelope."

The princess part Todd could believe. She was tiny but breathtakingly beautiful. He now knew what the term *peaches and cream completion* meant.

"Are you doing acting?" asked Todd, overwhelmed by the conflicting emotions within him.

She blushed again and looked away. "No, sir, I have to look after my mum. My dad is a useless black hard."

Todd had to swallow hard as Joella's past flashed before him.

"Let's go inside and sit at the *Canuck Tables* with the *Wild Colonial Boys*," suggested Dunk to Penelope, smirking.

"The pub Scots have rechristened the soccer tables and us." laughed Arnaq. "We're now celebrities."

Inside, they drank and chatted for a while as Todd read the long letter. He was puzzled at its contents. It reflected a character completely foreign to that exhibited by Tom. It was well-written; every word and sentence was grammatically correct. He doubted if it were actually Tom's work. He saw Tom as no genius. It reflected a passive loving character of a defeated man. It had to be a fake or a setup. He stopped and stared at Penelope as he digested Tom's humble unorthodox request for forgiveness and his assistance in lobbying the university dean to reinstate him.

Penelope sat quietly with her head lowered, too ashamed to look at him. She felt deeply embarrassed and out of place amid the rambunctious preppie students and the old leathery smell of the prestigious university.

"This can't be accurate!" exclaimed Todd, somewhat irritated at being manipulated. "This letter was written by a professor. And everyone knows Tom's a baron landowner's son."

"Tom wrote it, Mr. Clarke. He's very smart. He is *a* baron, sir. But we're still peasants. You can visit him if you like, but you'll be pretty disgusted."

"You haven't been to Natuashish," offered Todd reflectively.

"I haven't been anywhere, sir."

"Call me Todd. But you're dressed like a movie star, you really do look like a princess," he congratulated her, smiling with amazement.

She blushed again. "I borrowed these clothes from my friend."

Standing up, he reached out, touched her hand, and said kindly, "Miles will take you to our place for an hour. I have to attend one lecture. Then we'll see."

"Me in the Rolls?" she asked unbelievably.

"Would you prefer the Jag then?" taunted Dunk. He stared for a time at her indecisiveness as Todd waited for an answer, then added, "Don't worry, Pen. He's a Canuck."

She smiled embarrassingly and nodded.

Todd returned home to find Penelope with Joey in her arms listening to his uncle grimly relating how he and her father, as invincible teenagers, in the war had captured a bunker in France and how her father had saved his life. Todd then saw his uncle shake the stem of his smoking pipe seriously at Penelope and saw him become emotional for the first time, as he stated emphatically, "Yes, Tom has both brain and brawn but needs guidance. Your father was bloody foolhardy like that too. His pigheadedness got him a lifelong injury. But he saved my life, and for that, I am eternally grateful. You remind Tom of this: 'In honest hands, poison is medicine; in dishonest hands, medicine is poison.' Tom needs a few doses of his own poison to cure him. Todd gave him but a sample."

"He won't heed me, sir."

Seeing Todd suddenly appear, he slowly snuffed out his pipe and returned to his usual calm quiet voice, "I'm popping over with you and Penelope to chat with Gershom."

Penelope put Joey back in his crib, then hung her head, and stated, "It's best not, sir; he's now a filthy drunk. Our farm is an overgrown moor, and our home's a pigsty; my mum's very sick."

"His head wound acting up again?" asked Winston.

"Yes, sir," she whispered softly.

"Why wasn't I asked for help?"

"They're all too bloody stuck up. I wanted them to."

"Who looks after your family?" he asked curiously.

"I do, sir."

He turned to Todd and gave a grin. "She's a good catch, old boy; you know class."

This time, Todd blushed as well, not knowing if he were being facetious or complimentary. His uncle's manner was always convoluted.

In spite of killing two people, having a child, and having done a series of renegade escapades, Joella, by studying continuously, had completed high school by November at the top of her class in just sixteen months, and she was barely seventeen.

She was now enrolled in Trinity College studying for a degree in sociology. To help her people, Justin had convinced her she must first understand all the determining factors, processes, and consequences of internal Inuit and Innu relationships and what caused their society to become dysfunctional. He was keen on having her understand intercultural relations to determine if and how white man's institutions, like law, education, and religion, were contributing to or were directly causing their high-crime and poverty levels or if it were simply cultural shock.

Because of him, she no longer believed the Inuit was an inferior race, but one aspect both frustrated and puzzled her. She felt Inuit, and the females she identified with were Inuit, but all the males she admired were white. To get these answers, she knew she must grasp racial and ethnic differences. And she was part of both worlds.

After breezing through her exams, she stared at Todd's picture on her desk. She so much wanted him to know all she had accomplished and that she was keeping her promise to him. She wondered if he would really wait for her. Or had he already fallen in love with Lois, who worshiped him? She wondered where he was and if he were okay. Justin seemed to think so. Was he forced to live with his father whom he hated? She felt sorry for getting him involved in her troubles. However, she was not sorry he hit his father. She wondered why his father did not try to rape her. He certainly had the opportunity. Todd was right and should defend himself even more. She kept his picture in each of her books for moral support. He eyes watered, and she cringed at the thought she might have lost him.

Their daughter was always first on her mind, and she pondered if she would ever see her. She knew she would never give up trying to find her after being released. A degree was a must to show the courts she was capable of supporting her. Justin told her so, and she trusted him. He even promised to help her when she finished. If it were not for Justin's encouragement, she would have lost hope long ago. He was a real-life angel. She wondered if Justin wanted her; she certainly wanted a person like him.

She marveled how her suite had become a beehive of activity at times, how she was the sweetheart of the group-home staff. Yet all the people who admired her were old, except Justin. She much wanted a young friend whom to tell her problems, but they were all unapproachable inmates. She was still lonely and lived in her own private world.

But now, here in college, her life was anything but private. She had heard whispers that she was an Eskimo who once lived on the downtown east side and was a cheap prostitute. The university students seemed to know all her past indiscretions and avoided her as if she were a rabid pit bull.

All avoided her except a homely ultrareligious guy named Aaron Pringle who was also studying sociology and hung around her in gym class and the cafeteria. They discussed religion a few times, but he was interested only in her hometown and her culture, which she was reluctant to boast about. He sometimes offered to buy her meals and to take her to movies, but her answer was always the same: that she was promised to someone. He was not as assertive as she liked but was a whiz at everything passive, especially chess.

His mother, Barbara, whom he often praised, was a lawyer who gave free legal advice to the poor and minorities, and Joella figured she was as poor and minor as anyone could possibly be. She wanted to ask him to get her to review her case, but she had promised Justin to finish her degree first, and she did not want to openly disobey him. She somehow had to figure a way to do it and keep her promise. And although Aaron was kind and respected her, she continued to chat with him only for an opportunity to broach the subject.

Todd found Tom Preston's place a large farmhouse and more livable than most homes in Natuashish. He was not appalled; in fact, he was amazed at the expansive ten-thousand-acre farm stretching as far as the eye could see in all directions. As his uncle chided a drunken and bedraggled Gershom for not requesting his assistance, he and Penelope located Tom who was chopping wood in the shed with his shirt removed.

Tom even looks like a muscled soccer player, thought Todd. *I may have escaped a bullet.*

Tom looked up in surprise and stopped.

"Hello, Todd, 'tis nice of you to come," he greeted shamefacedly, offering his hand. "You're more of a bloody gentleman than I."

"Your pretty sister influenced me," Todd replied honestly.

His attitude changed instantly, and he stared at Todd angrily.

"He's protective of me," explained Penelope. "He thinks I'm still a child."

"My sister's only seventeen. Half the girls in university stalk you," he remarked, almost disgustedly.

"Not me: money and prestige. They think I'm rich." Seeing Tom almost fuming, he added apologetically. "I was joking!"

"And outside as well, why—" continued Tom, staring at his sister.

Penelope blushed bright red and interrupted. "He was bloke enough to come now, Tom. You're acting like Pop again. Swallow your ego and tell him your—"

"You own this beautiful farm?" asked Todd, still impressed at the spectacular location and wanting to curtail the escalating tensions.

"For the present," responded Tom more calmly, realizing he *was* being arrogant again. "That's why I need to return to university." Then bowing his head and becoming mellow, he added pathetically, "By now, you've guessed I'm only tough at bullshitting—"

"He already knows that. Tell him what you want, Tom," ordered an irritated, impatient Penelope. "Mum needs help."

He flushed and then began to display a more defeated mentality. "Only a bloody asshole would insult a man who had the guts to raise his son while his girlfriend is in jail. Todd, there's no words in my limited vocabulary to describe that immature indiscretion. I'm pretty damn ashamed of my actions, especially for insulting the Inuit. Look around, as you can see, I'm in no position to judge others—"

"Uncle Winston can get you back in college," interjected Todd, somewhat embarrassed at his repentant conduct, not wanting him to rave on.

Seeing Penelope jubilant and her eyes sparkling with delight at his instant solution, he decided it the ideal time to ask her for a date. Turning to her, he continued, "My friend Arnaq dumped me for an oversized Highlander. Now I need an escort for the University Christmas Fest. Would you like to come with me?"

Tom was instantly angry again and yelled, "She's my sister, you bloody bloke!"

"If I can borrow the clothes, I'd be honored," she answered excitedly. Then dejectedly, added, "But I'm afraid I have to look after Mum."

"I understand, thank you," Todd answered, disappointed. "Besides, your big brother would kill me." Turning to Tom and patting him on the back, he added, "Let's go inside and convince Uncle to arrange your return." After a brief silence, he noted, "You see, Tom, the pretty ones don't want me."

After walking for a distance, Tom looked away and offered meekly, "I'll tend Mum, Pen; you need a spell."

"That's the real Tom," said an instant bubbly Penelope. "He's smart too. If you need help in law, he's your ticket. He's not really a braggart, you know. He knows it!"

Really, thought Todd, *our war may have been a blessing in disguise.* Glancing at a glowing Penelope smiling gratefully, he mused, *I may have killed two birds with one stone.*

Negotiations didn't go as smoothly with Uncle Winston as Todd had anticipated. After a week, Tom was still not back in class. Todd was beginning to experience the tough practical side of his uncle. His uncle was adamant that people were to be held responsible for their deeds: a lesson had to be learned. And the price was not cheap. Tom was required to provide a written apology to Todd and Arnaq confessing it was his fault, and agree to testify against the person who attacked Todd with the switchblade at the court's upcoming hearing in just weeks; and, in that, everyone was scared to do, except Todd and Arnaq.

Tom knew that opening up a bitter feud with Blackbeard would create an even more serious problem. Blackbeard was a dangerous hoodlum, but also an excellent soccer player loved by his fans, who would overlook any indiscretion. It became a stalemate until Winston came up with the idea of having Todd's lawyer request a subpoena from the court to force Tom to attend, upon which Tom agreed to tell the truth about Blackbeard's other equally serious incidents as well. The university was then approached to readmit Tom, but still only on a trial basis.

Justin kissed Lois on the neck as she combed her long black hair and prepared for their second annual Christmas party together. "Is my Inuit goddess ready?" he asked. "Not too pretty now. I don't want anyone to steal you."

"Sedna," she responded solemnly.

"What?" he asked surprised.

"The Inuit goddess, the goddess of the sea: Sedna," she repeated sadly.

"What's wrong, sweetheart? You've been down lately," he asked lovingly, kissing her again.

"Life's so unfair. Todd has Penny. I have you. And Joella, an angel, is in jail with nobody. She deserves a nice guy like you, not me."

"I love you, Lois, not Joella. I'm helping her all I can."

"I know, but she needs a break from jail and study."

Recognizing her depressed and anguished mood, he hugged her tightly for a time and said, "The party can wait. Let's plan to spring her."

She forced a smile, happy he had finally made a joke.

For the next ten minutes, Justin held her as she cried and vented some of her past transgressions. She told him how she drank, smoked, even fought, and committed many illegal acts with local boys for fun back in Natuashish, whereas Joella stayed home in a shack, studied, and waited for Todd. Finally, she stopped crying and almost whispered, "You deserve better, someone like Joella."

He kissed her and replied, "I don't care what you did; you're now mine."

"I love you, Justin, but I feel you got a bad deal in marrying me."

He was concerned she might be sick; he had never seen her so moody.

Then for an hour of often conflicting discussion, he unhurriedly helped conjured up a vacation plan for Joella that pleased her. As he hugged her again and prepared to leave, he could tell she was still tense and hesitant. He stared at her, dazzled by her small slim body. She was nineteen but looked more like fifteen. He wondered how he, a lumbering monster with broad shoulders, who actually did look like Bruno, had gotten so lucky.

"In future, I'm calling you Sedna; you're beautiful."

He kissed her hard, then carried her to the bed, and began to remove his tuxedo, and said seriously, "Lois, we need a little Sedna."

Lois never knew a big man could be so understanding and lovable. "This is your big night, Justin."

"I have priorities, Lois. You're number one."

"Justin," she whispered shyly, "I'm already pregnant."

"Why didn't you tell me?" he asked, overjoyed, hugging her hard. "This is truly a Christmas gift."

"I was scared you'd be upset."

"Why?" he asked, astounded, beaming with pride.

"I didn't know you wanted kids yet. Besides, the baby might look like me."

"That's what I want, Lois," he stated emphatically. "This is truly *our* big night. Let's go and tell the world. I'll never again have anything bigger to boast about."

Oh, yes, you will, she mused.

"But let's go."

Two weeks later, Tom sat in the auditorium, barely listening to his lecture. He was troubled and frustrated over the fact his baby sister was falling for Todd, and Todd was to marry Joella Adams. He felt he indeed had learned two valuable real-life lessons for his arrogant, thoughtless actions: that stupidity had a price and that he was no hero like his father, however much he despised him. He now stayed close to Todd and Dunk for protection and treated his sister with more respect, realizing she had indeed grown up. On the positive side, Winston's fierce reprimanding of his father had smartened him up as well. His father was now drinking much less and helping him with chores around the property.

Todd too had a new appreciation of his uncle. He now saw him as a silent tiger that if provoked could take down an elephant. Todd now knew how he had accumulated such a fortune.

But his uncle was also giving and gentle. He insisted Penny—he didn't particularly like Greeks or the name Penelope—whom he now saw as Todd's best friend, go to go university and study fine arts like she wanted. He would advance her the money and provide a servant to take care of the Cooper household to help his friend Gershom. In exchange, Tom would help Todd with his studies, and Penny would stay on his estate to help Melissa with Joe Allan, since she loved kids, thus keeping her away from housework at home. He even approached her college and had her enrolled in acting. This was his part in repaying Gershom for saving his life. His uncle proved to be both a shrewd negotiator and organizer. The ease and speed of which he got things accomplished astonished both him and Tom.

The auditorium went silent, curious why Todd Clarke, now considered the university's tough guy, would be seen on stage at the podium holding a baby in his arms at an open forum for lectures.

"I'm Todd Clarke, and this is my son, Joey," he began halfheartedly, unhappy to publicly expose Joella's incarceration. He merely wanted to dispel the rumor that he was a blue-blood fighter looking for competition that had circulated throughout the university. In truth, he was finding his courses difficult and intended the legal lecture, now at the end of his first semester, to be strictly aimed at course credits.

It began as a simple suggestion by Penelope, but all his relatives jumped on the bandwagon, deeming it to be an outstanding opportunity to publicize Joella's plight and get the best legal minds involved in a credible solution. He knew Justin's scheme for Joella was the best course and trusted both him and Lois completely, but he was having trouble coming to grips with Joey's mother behind bars for self-defense while he wallowed in luxury.

"His full name is Joe Ellan Clarke. My son's grandfather was a British archeologist named Joe Ellan, who died accidentally in Natuashish, Labrador, while searching for the remains of the Franklin expedition. His grandmother is Inuit."

He then handed Joey to Penny, who was proudly standing by his side smiling, and began to speak directly from the heart.

As he continued to give an in-depth exposé of Joella's imprisonment and tell the story of both his and Joella's life, he found himself became increasingly emotional and began to orate with a passion he didn't know he possessed. For twenty minutes past his fifteen-minute time allotment, he continued uninterrupted by the examiners, as the audience listened spellbound to the teary-eyed university tough guy defend a double murderer and appalled that such an injustice could occur in a progressive country like Canada.

Realizing he was being overdramatic, he toned it down and calmly ended by urging everyone to petition the Canadian government to review her case and help secure her release.

Surprisingly, he got a standing ovation that was initiated by his examiners.

Next day, he got a bigger surprise when he received the highest marks for the most convincing argument.

The dean personally congratulated him and remarked, "That was a brave lecture, Mr. Clarke."

Joella was tense when she was summoned into the conference room. She wondered if she had done something wrong or omitted some detail. Maybe it was about her daughter? She sat fidgeting before the panel with her hands folded obediently on the table and staring questioningly at Justin.

He spoke seriously, "Joella, the institution has received your report from the college. You aced every subject?"

"I didn't cheat; the courses were easy," she attacked, disappointed he would think she was plagiarizing.

Recognizing her anxiety, he smiled and explained, "Oh no. This is the annual official review by Social Services," pointing to the two officers.

Joella was angry instantly at their sight and stood up. "Where's my daughter?"

"We are accessing your progress in order to give you—"

"All I want from the Qablunaat Gestapo is my daughter back."

Ouch. Justin recognized she was maturing faster than he had anticipated and needed some direction in real-life experience. He insisted on a few minutes alone with her, knowing from his psychologist perspective that such derogatory racist attacks would only inflame matters and strengthen their resolve.

After an emotional five-minute rant on her part, he managed to cool her down enough to explain the purpose of the review and how to answer their concerns to achieve the best results.

Hesitantly going back inside, she sullenly apologized to them and proceeded to answer their questions more rationally but was nonetheless having great difficulty controlling her temper, which she did solely to please Justin.

After a full hour of exhausting grilling, the senior worker gave her the synopsis. Since being incarcerated, her behavior was beyond reproach, her college marks excellent, her obedience record impeccable, and as a result, she was being granted a reward: a pass with adequate funds for a two-week Christmas holiday away from the institution.

She stared at them puzzled. She had killed two people, escaped from jail, dug up an empty grave, and was forever searching for information to find her daughter. She smelled a rat.

"But on condition that you give up searching for your daughter," noted the younger social worker cautiously.

"Blackmail?" she almost squealed.

This infuriated her, but before she could further assail them, Justin snarled, "She has already promised me that. It's in my report. Don't Social Services ever do anything except talk? What else do you want from her?"

"In that case, Ms. Adams, you may vacation anywhere in BC with a court-appointed escort," the senior officer replied quickly, wanting the unenviable task behind her.

Justin realized they were trying to use his vacation request as a bribe to silence her for some unknown reason. He guessed someone, most likely Todd's relatives, were working behind the scenes on her case, and Social Services were feeling the pressure. That bothered him even more. "I have already chosen an escort for her," advised Justin.

"We have to approve—"

"I'm her psychologist; that's my jurisdiction. I had it court approved."

They were annoyed at his domineering attitude but nodded and silently left.

"You had it preapproved?" Joella asked inquisitively, standing up. "You didn't ask me."

He nodded.

"Who is it?" she ventured cautiously, wondering if he too had now deserted her.

"A lawyer named Barbara Pringle from Minority Rights. Two weeks at Whistler in Christmas. Skiing. Is that okay?"

She was flabbergasted. She recalled how she loved to ski with Todd for days. Her mouth fell open, but no words came out. Obviously, his marriage had not changed his feelings toward her; in fact, that illegal act proved he now paid her more attention.

"Use it wisely. And remember your promise," he ordered.

"You set this up, didn't you? How do you know all these things, Justin? You're a god!" she whispered emphatically.

"No. But it was a goddess's idea: Sedna's." He laughed amusingly as he walked out.

Christmas Day 2001 didn't start well at the Howard household. It was snowing heavily, and his guests were two hours late arriving due to the storm. It was a somber mood as everyone tried to make up lost time in order to follow their age-old festive traditions.

Todd knew this would be a lonely day for him. As he sat quietly next to Lord Thurston and his family, all dressed in their finest festive clothes, in his uncle's huge ballroom staring forlornly over the huge festive Christmas table, a table capable of seating a hundred guests, fully laden with sumptuous food of every kind, waiting for the queen's own table etiquette to be followed, a tear escaped his eye. He felt embarrassed by the opulence. He would trade it all for a quiet paddle in a kayak among the icebergs or just a stroll on the rugged Labrador barrens with Joella munching on bakeapples or pemmican.

"Your new friend doesn't look happy, Penny," whispered Emily, breaking the silence, as everyone rigidly waited for the butler to carve the oversized Christmas dinner turkey, aided by two servants standing on either side of him, courteously offering him the silver cutlery as per their standard protocol. "Is he in trouble again?"

"No, ma'am," she answered, picking up Joey from his high chair and wiping his hands, then glancing at Todd, somewhat defeated herself. "I can't make him happy. I tried. He misses Joella. This is his second Christmas without her and—"

"It's not you, Penny, sweetheart. Joella used to spend all her Christmases with Todd. I miss Wilbert too at this time of year," offered Melissa, also with a tinge of melancholy.

"That bastard was as evil as the Hobbes of hell," Winston stated in his consistent stoic manner, bringing everyone back to reality. "The past is dead, Melissa. Get on with your life. Lord Calvert wants you to escort him to the opera. Go!"

"Hush, Winston," chided Emily. "Melissa makes her own decisions."

Everyone stirred and took a breath, relieved the stuffy atmosphere had been broached.

Recognizing Penelope's displeasure, Todd got up, took Joey, and kissed her on the lips, making her blush. "Let's enjoy our meal, Penny. It's *not* you. It's that Joella always came to our home on Christmas Day after dinner just to get the leftovers from our table to survive. She once told me it was always her best meal of the year: our scraps. Now she's languishing in jail for self-defense while I wallow in this luxury."

"We're poor too, Todd," she reminded him jealously.

"With a ten-thousand-acre farm on prime real estate?" asked an astounded Lord Thurston.

"Let's say grace," interrupted Winston. Then, turning to Penny, promised, "That'll change for both you and Joella."

Everyone bowed as Penny stood and recited the ritual blessing. "God, bless this food, which now we take, and feed our souls for Jesus's sake."

Everyone said *Amen*, and the feast began.

Todd, too distressed to eat, fed Joey, who waved both arms and legs begging for more food as he shoveled it into him.

Just then, Miles burst into the room in a flurry, trailing snow behind him, and bowed. All looked up in surprise at the rare interruption.

"Yes, Miles?" asked Emily kindly.

"There's an entourage of dignitaries here to see Master Joey, madam."

"Entourage?" queried Mrs. Thurston doubtfully.

"I'm guessing fifty, sir."

Everyone looked at one another stunned, then stared at Miles waiting for him to continue.

"And a lorry full of presents for him."

Now everyone was amused.

"Good god, man, 'tis Christmas Day. Have you been nipping egg nod on the job, Miles?" asked Winston piercingly.

"Not yet, sir. But we are two hours behind."

Winston gave a slight grin at his clever answer.

Before Winston could give consent, an old man about ninety hobbled into the dining room waving an old wooden walking cane, panting, chased closely by an equally old woman.

"Where's my great-great-grandson? What in blazes have you done with him?" he attacked.

The old lady scolded him, then turned to the household, and bowed. "Sorry for me husband, sir. He's grumpy these days. Rheumatic fever in his joints. I'm Dianna, and this is me husband, Chester Ellan. Our great-granddaughter, Chelsea—pointing to a young woman among the full entourage now standing behind them—heard Mr. Clarke's lecture about Joey and Joella. And Ches wanted to see him before he passed away. He's ninety-five."

Todd instantly recognized Chelsea from class. He stood up with Joey still wiggled in his arms and his mouth open reaching for food. Todd was so amazed his mouth fell open as well.

"Set fifty more paces," Emily ordered the chefs jubilantly. "Get all the domestics to help you. Hurry! Hurry!"

"About time you asked us!" complained Chester. "Bloody weather! We were supposed to be here yesterday. Damn planes! Horse and buggies were faster."

Everyone now laughed and began to relax.

"I'm Mildred Ellan. Joe was my son," offered a very cultured older woman patiently waiting in the back, bowing.

"How can you be so sure our Joey is your grandson?" a skeptical Winston asked her, disappointing everyone.

"Reasonably so. We've spent two weeks checking it out," replied an impeccably dressed gentleman standing next to her. "I'm a barrister at Old Bailey. Joe was my brother."

It was still an incredible coincidence. Winston was not so sure. There was a period of silence.

"Joe had a tic," offered another lady, smiling shyly. "He always wiggled his nose when hungry. Does Joey?"

"Yes!" replied Penny, Melissa, and Emily simultaneously, totally amazed, as everyone stared at Joey in Todd's arms wiggling his nose and struggling for more food.

"And I got two bloody good lawyers working on *Joe Ella's* case too," threatened Chester, shaking his cane at them. "And not those Old Bailey sheep-wig potbelly Oxford phonies."

Everyone laughed again.

For the next hour, Joey became the undisputed star as he was overfed, hugged, kissed, squeezed, prodded, and mollycoddled like a new stuffed toy by everyone in the entourage. Dozens of stories were exchanged at a record pace as the festive meal lay untouched on the table and as Chester Ellan complained incessantly about everything that was wrong with Britain.

Penny could see that Todd was the main focus of all the young girls, and she was just his servant, as they queried her about him and *his* posh estate. It made her insanely jealous and very angry.

Finally, everyone was formally introduced, and they all sat down to feast, when Chester suddenly stopped grumbling and asked civilly, "What's me great-granddaughter, *Joe Ella*, like, Todd?

The place went silent.

Todd's eyes filled with tears, and he almost choked as he answered honestly, "She never complained, sir, but she certainly has your fighting spirit."

Everyone gave a thunderous applause.

Chester finally smiled and promised, "Don't worry, me boy. I'll get her out."

"I'd give anything to find Joe's remains," noted his mother solemnly. "He needs to know he's loved."

"I know where he is!" exclaimed Melissa. "Joe already knows. Aglari and Joella placed flowers on his gravesite every year. But you'll need a DNA test; ancient Inuit and Innu peoples also used the area as a burial ground for criminals."

Todd, like the others, was stunned by the revelation, recalling Joella telling him that she and her mother placed flowers on an unknown gravesite below Whaler's Lookout every year in August, as he stared at Penny, who looked positively wrenched.

Returning to reality, for the first time, he grasped that Penny was in love with him. He reached across the table and kissed her on the lips to the dismay of all the other young females. She rebounded with a proud smile.

"Because of you, I give a lecture to expose Joella's plight and found not only help for her but found her father and my future in-laws as well. Penny, you're not only hardworking and beautiful, you're intelligent. You'll be a famous movie star. Joella will be proud of you. You have made this undoubtedly my best Christmas gift ever."

Penelope blushed. It wasn't the end result she wanted but knew it was the best she could hope for.

While Whistler was a reprieve from the monotony of the group home and study, skiing with Aaron at night along the groomed well-lit trail among the oversized trees did not have the charm as skiing with Todd on the treeless open barrens of Labrador. She missed the Northern Lights, the frosty air, the howl of the wolf, and the crackling of the snow.

Though kind and considerate, Aaron was talkative with a city mentality, who boasted about his knowledge of the local wildlife and the world-class cultured nature trails, whereas she and Todd would always be quiet and reflective as they watched the wildlife, and let nature talked to him.

She still felt lonely.

Mrs. Pringle was surprised to see them return after only a few hours.

Joella was frank as she explained it was not skiing like she thought, why she did not enjoy it, and wanted to get down to business on finding her daughter.

She also requested to return to the group home so she could enroll in another course to finish earlier, explaining if she could finish in three years, they would possibly release her on good behavior.

While disagreeing with her sense of urgency and not wanting to lose a rare two weeks of paid work at a world-class resort, Mrs. Pringle reluctantly agreed to return after one week. She also knew the sooner Joella began searching for her daughter, the more comfortable she would feel.

Joella sat on the floor in front of the fireplace and immediately began to tell her side of the story.

Mrs. Pringle could see by the painful expressions on Joella's face that it took a lot of courage and dedication for her to relive her tragic past and relate the most intimate details of her poverty-stricken life to a stranger. But she was also finding it difficult to accept that Joella was actually telling the truth; it seemed like an open-and-shut case for both the authorities and the judge.

She let Joella laboriously relate the events chronologically for almost an hour without interrupting. She was impressed by her intelligence and attention to detail. She concluded that Todd was her life, and his mother was her idol. After finishing her third martinis, she spoke, "Take a break, Joella. I have the picture. You're an excellent witness. Did you tell them this story already?"

"Many times." Seeing Mrs. Pringle's questioning face, she elaborated, "You don't understand. I'm Inuit."

Mrs. Pringle blushed. She knew she was guilty of that same bias many times but never more than in this case. She went and mixed herself another strong drink. Returning, she promised, "Joella, take the two weeks and stay here and enjoy yourself. I want to make you a special case."

"You have to first trust me before you can help me. I need someone to believe me," pleaded Joella.

"In the real world, lawyers don't care a damn if a client is wrong or right. The key is to get them off." She paused and took a big swig of her drink. "But, in this case, I know you're innocent. I trust you."

Joella went and hugged her.

"I'm your lawyer, Joella," she warned, smiling. "Not your mommy."

Chapter Nine

The Secret Search

Two wrongs don't make a right.

Susan Kamanirk was released from prison on New Year's Day, 2002, one year early, on good behavior for her part in Joella's killing ofTom Bradshaw. Her prison wardens were impressed at her resolute spirit and dedication. She was a model prisoner, attended all the prescribed lectures, had aced all the courses; she had spent her time well. She physically trained faithfully for two hours each day and studied detective work unrelentingly, promising the authorities she would to start her own private-eye business upon release, and they were all routing for her.

Inside however, emotions were different. She was a bundle of churning hate that did exercises only to release her tensions. She was now on a one-way mission. She had made herself a solemn oath that she too, like Joella, was going to find her own daughter, who was now twelve, even if it were the last thing she ever did. And she knew if her precarious plan failed, it might well be.

She was convinced that she was twice imprisoned for simply living as an open and honest Inuit, and wanted to settle the score.

Her last prison term was merely revenge for telling Joella her child was alive. She now knew the details of the inner workings of the prisons and police stations, as well as how to gain access to Social Services files.

She spat on the floor as she walked out, promising herself that she would never again return to prison alive.

Joella quickly rebounded from the shock of Justin's marriage, and with his insistence, they sat down to lay out a new curriculum to better achieve her desired results. He counseled her to enroll in more political science classes as electives to gain practical debating knowledge to beat the white man in the courts and especially the media; people tended to believe what they read. He also advised her to chose a few easier psychology courses in good parenting such that could best influence the authorities in getting get her child back.

That amounted to her full compliment, but both her real father and Todd wanted her to do acting, and she somehow had to try again. While past courses showed she was very good at traditional Inuit skits and dances, it clearly demonstrated the she was nothing short of terrible at mainstream acting; all the roles reflected a white man's fame-and-fortune mentality, with overinflated egos; and these she found repulsive.

But something else was now bothering her. Even though Justin seemed to treat her even more affectionately, for a week, his co-workers had been excitedly patting him on the back and shaking his hand, and he would smile, something he rarely did. She guessed he was being promoted to a more prestigious institution. He certainly had the right credentials: education, respect, even size. That had to be the reason for his treating her so well and why he was so adamant about planning her life.

Finally, Joella got up the courage to admit openly, "I don't want you to leave, Justin. I'll have nobody."

"Leave?" he asked, puzzled.

"I know. I saw everyone congratulating you on your new post," she explained sadly, staring at the wall.

To her astonishment, he laughed out loud.

"Oh no, Joella. We're having a baby girl."

That hurt her more than his leaving, and she began to cry instantly, startling him. Seeing his surprise, she stammered, "I'm . . . I'm . . . happy for you, Justin, but it hurts to know I may never get my own daughter back."

"I'm positive you'll see him, *her*, but I do not know if you'll get her back.

She stopped crying and asked curiously, "How can you be sure?"

"I told you. Sedna is looking after you."

"Sedna is a myth, Justin."

"Oh no! She's my goddess."

Todd's single lecture had produced amazing results in just three months. It had struck a social nerve among the senior students who took up the challenge to compete to see who could produce the most positive results. In addition, legal experts from the university, eager to earn favor with Winston Howard and Lord Thurston for sponsorship money, were competing to provide their superior assistance.

But it was Chester Ellan with his sleazy political connections and rabble-rousing mentality that produced the most results. The Canadian politicians, as a result of his bombardment of legal letters threatening to make the issue public, were concerned it might become an international embarrassment and ordered Social Services to expedite the matter.

Social Services were not only appalled at Chester's conniving and underhanded methods of extracting the facts but stunned at his in-depth knowledge of the actual events, including confidential in-camera court transcripts. They began to panic that the truth would be leaked to the press and tried to contact Joella's original lawyer to organize a plea bargain for a lighter sentence, only to find *that* lawyer no longer represented her and her new lawyer was Barbara Pringle, whom they considered a minority rights fanatic.

It had all the ingredients of mushrooming into a nightmare for Social Services.

Much to the dismay and embarrassment of Social Services, on the first of April, Joella sent out birthday invitations to all the staff for her daughter's first birthday party. It was immediately squashed, and she was reprimanded with a warning that if she insisted on perusing that line of blatant disobedience, she would lose her privileges. With Justin's directive, she quickly offered a written apology.

But, to her surprise, on April 4, 2002, Justin, Vanessa, and most of the staff showed up with gifts of money, recommending she use it to get a head start when she was released. She knew it was for her daughter's search and their subtle way of helping her. And once again, she also knew Justin was somehow behind it.

Justin, the last to leave, patted her on the back, smiled, and encouraged, "You're growing up, Joella. You're learning to play the white man's game."

"I'm not white, Justin," she answered almost repulsively, then felt regret for possibly offending him.

"Think that statement over, Joella. Good night. It was a great party."

When he left, she sat on her bed and mulled over his statement. Did he know she was a half breed?

After making love, Penny turned to Todd and cautiously asked him if he could also talk to his uncle to help get Jerry back to Oxford in return for him pleading guilty and testifying against Blackbeard.

"You know Jerry?" he asked, surprised and a bit jealous.

"They own the farm next to us."

"The big one with the ten silos?"

She nodded.

"His sister Portia is my best friend. Jerry makes her loan me her new clothes. They're rich."

"Why didn't I meet her?"

She blushed.

Todd guessed the answer. “Why?” asked Todd, a little annoyed since the hearing was in just two weeks.

She bowed her head and answered softly, “I love you, Todd. You’re my first love. But you already have a family and are going to marry Joella. Jerry has always liked me, but Tom kept him away. I’ll need someone after you leave me. I lived all my life at home and don’t know anybody. Blackbeard is the bad one, not Jerry. Tom told me everything. He talks to me now.”

Todd felt a surge of guilt. “Did he tell you to ask me?”

“No. Portia did.” She blushed again.

“Did Jerry agree?” Todd ventured curiously.

“Yes. But he’s too high-strung to admit it.”

Todd kissed her and promised, “For you, I’ll do my best, but you know my uncle.”

“You deserve better than me anyhow, Todd,” Penny moaned, in a whimper. She didn’t know, but the converse was true. Penny added, concerned, “But not Portia. She’s pretty loose.”

Todd felt a tinge of guilt but speculated that Portia really was more down to his level.

Justin was both anxious and concerned when he entered the crowded boardroom and sat down. How Social Services could be so incompetent and naive as to request a panel of experts to assess—more accurately justify—their birdbrain proposal to have Joella released early to a halfway house boggled his logical way of thinking. To him, halfway houses were undersupervised, understaffed drug pits with roaming sex predators and the mentally insane, which actually prevented reintegration into normal society. Joella was presently a well-adjusted teenager who had almost unlimited freedom and had settled in contentedly and was working diligently on her studies to complete her degree to correspond with her release. And she was not yet halfway through. He knew the meeting was going to be a challenge for him, and he was going to be cast as the dark knight by everyone.

And he was right. He first gave each of the experts, many of whom were merely hired puppets by the Social Services, an opportunity to give their professional opinion.

He heard a complete exposé on him from the beginning of his tenure, how the board was frustrated with his history of lenient dealing with teenagers, how they were continuously aggravated by the fact that he would not even entertain the idea of releasing any juvenile to a halfway house, how he considered it a breeding ground for crime, how he argued the government was patently wrong in its implementation, and how the government bureaucracy labeled him arrogant, headstrong, and incompetent.

Even though he was taking a beating and it was a stone wall against him, he was the administrator with the veto, and when his turn came, he used it without hesitation. Even when he was accused of blatantly contravening governmental policy, a dictator, who disregarded the democratic panel of advisors, he was steadfast. He made it clear that his theme policy was to be enforced: the interest of the internee came first, not money or government expediency.

They threatened to petition to have him replaced, openly accusing him of being too young and inexperienced for a senior position. He retaliated by subtly warning them he had the power to dismiss the board. Social Services responded by cautioning him that his approach may be criminal. That brought out Justin's ire. Standing up and pointing his finger, he responded with a scathing remark that silenced the panel. "Let it be known, I have sound evidence that the government is pressuring Social Services to release Joella, not on compassionate grounds but out of fear that international press will uncover her illegal incarnation and the equally illegal apprehension of her child, based solely on racial stereotyping, that she's Inuit." He paused and took a drink of water, reflecting on his last statement, aware it was not totally accurate, but had used it only for shock effect. "I offer anyone here the right to challenge me on that issue, now."

The Social Services representative angrily jumped up to challenge him.

"Include Susan's dismissal in your rebuttal," he warned, before she had a chance to speak.

She sat back down.

"Be cautious, my friends. Joella now has a full-time spitfire lawyer," he added, more subdued. As an oddball child himself, Justin knew the temptation to turn to gangs or criminals for friends and support. Experience had taught him to stand alone. Realizing he was on shaky ground, he adjourned the meeting and angrily walked away.

Like Tom Cooper, Jerry Preston soon got a taste of the harsh reality required to have his misdeeds forgiven and regain his university position under Winston Howard's direction: restitution or compensation to his victims, plus a written apology, even if they did not know or request it.

Jerry found that harsh and oppressive and flatly refused, he had once thrown a can of paint over five expensive sports cars belonging to football players from Cambridge University, their main rival. Winston quickly solved that by suggesting he obtain the value of the damages and give the money to charity. Again, Jerry refused but soon acquiesced after Winston suspended the talks, accusing him of being a spoiled brat, a sniveling coward, which required a stint in the military to learn some discipline.

This incensed an already-embarrassed Jerry in front of his family. His father had tried for years to have him join the forces, but the military represented the mentality he detested.

After a full day of mostly losing battles, Jerry Preston's lawyers finally wrote a cheque on behalf of the defeated Prestons for $12,000 to the Salvation Army.

Winston then offered Jerry his hand and lectured him sternly, "Listen, Jerry, you have a big ego. You follow the strong, not the righteous. Learn to be fair, not mean. You have to solve that first if you want to be a leader. Tom had the guts." Then figuring Jerry had been disciplined enough, he mellowed and gave him his reward. "Lord Thurston reserves one position each year at the university. It's yours. Don't let him down."

A red-faced Jerry reluctantly shook his hand and managed, "I won't, sir." As Winston walked away, Jerry mused, *I can see why Todd is so bloody tough*.

But it still took another full day of intense negotiating with the crown prosecutor by three defense lawyers: one for Todd—supplied by his uncle—and two for Jerry, to plea bargain and to obtain immunity from prosecution for their past infractions. In addition, like Tom, Jerry agreed to be placed on probation for one year. In return, Blackbeard's lawyer would not be permitted to deviate from the knife-attack case. Neither was happy with probation, but both knew the alternative could be much harsher.

"What's wrong, my Bruno?" asked Lois when Justin entered the house, leaving her cooking and kissing him on the nose. She added, "I made you that stuffed squid that you like."

He kissed her back and sat slowly down and placed his hands on his head and related mournfully, "They wanted to release Joella early."

"That's great news," responded Lois, beaming, confused at his depressed state. "What's wrong?

"I'm not sure I did the right thing. I prevented it."

"What! You prevented her from being released." Tears came to her eyes. "How could you, Justin?"

It was the first time he had ever seen Lois angry and disappointed at him. He noted she was being more irritated and testy as of late. He wondered if she was growing tired of him; the few girls he had dated before her grew bored with his passive mentality in short order and moved on.

"It was a tough decision, Lois. I kept her in the group home for her benefit."

Lois was stymied. How could keeping a person in jail be a benefit?

"Her benefit? Group home? Call it a correction facility, behavior modification, youth detention, or even a palace; it's still jail, Justin." She wondered if he wanted Joella and started to cry. "I thought you loved me."

"Oh, Lois," he said tenderly, getting up and hugging her. "I love you more than life itself."

"Then why do you love Joella?"

"Are you okay, Lois?"

"Then why are you keeping her there?"

"There she's safe. Has a suite better than ours. All amenities provided, including free university. If she leaves, that becomes expensive. She has no money. How can she? And halfway houses are dangerous. She's smart and needs a helping hand in life. Our system is damn unfair to young people."

"Halfway house? They want to send her to halfway houses? She's a teenager."

"For the next three years. That's insane. Not because they care; they're being pressured. For image. To say she's released. Technically. I want—"

Lois became calm and interrupted, "Why halfway? At the rate she's going, she will finish her degree in two years there and—"

"Because to the system, she's a number."

Lois felt foolish at her outburst and attempted to apologize. "You are so smart, Justin. Why did you marry a nobody like me? I'm just a stupid Inuit."

He smiled and kissed her again.

"You know how much I love you, Sedna. Joella is fortunate in having a loyal friend like you. Let's go see your gynecologist again tomorrow. You've been down lately."

"You think I'm crazy, Justin?" she asked inquisitively.

"Of course not. I meant physically."

"I'm just jealous." Then bowing her head, she ventured cautiously. "And I'm having twins."

Justin couldn't believe his ears. Before he could find the words to express his euphoria, she continued, "I'm sorry; I've been so tired and moody lately."

"Why didn't you tell me?" he asked, jubilant.

"I was scared you didn't want two babies."

"A boy and a girl?" he asked unbelievably, beaming.

She nodded.

"Twins?" he almost squealed. "You can get twins in that little tummy?"

She smiled. "I'm sorry I'm touchy."

"I like to be touched," he said jokingly, lifting her up in his strong arms and holding her straight out. "There must be a god, Lois; otherwise, I wouldn't be blessed so much."

It was the first time she had ever seen tears in his eyes. She smiled with pride, marveling how such a big strong man could take so much abuse and still remain calm and forgiving.

Joella was relieved her first year of college was behind her and she had completed a record thirty-six credits and had won the institutions Come-Back Achievement award and a $1,000 scholarship. She had defeated all the Qablunaats, and the college students were now viewing her as talented as well as tough. She figured in three more years—by May 2005—at the present rate of progress, she would have her degree complete. However, acting was a losing proposition; she wanted to drop it. It took two nights each week away from studying.

She walked proudly into the conference room with a big smile on her face expecting a big round of applause to be started by Justin. As she scanned the twenty or so administrators at the table, her smile changed to one of concern.

Justin pointed for her to sit by next to him, then hit the table heavily with his gavel, and said sternly, "This panel is now in cession." He nodded to Mrs. Albright to commence.

Joella saw the senior office administrator as stern and direct but always fair to everyone. She had no idea what to expect but knew it involved her, being the only inmate present.

"Congratulations, Joella."

Everyone gave a silent applause as Joella managed a forced smile and said softly, "Thank you."

"Get to the point, Stella," ordered Justin impatiently.

Stella stood up and began. "Joella, you are studying sociology and have been given permission to attend psychiatric profiling sessions with other patients for practical experience and college credits. Thus, you have access to all the confidential file cabinet."

"Yes, but not all."

"Did you see the H file?"

"No!" she replied adamantly.

"Did you ever open the drawer?"

Joella became concerned. "Only once, when I first started: by mistake. Why?"

Nobody spoke.

"Karen Collins asked me to get the H file for her."

"Did you?"

"No! I opened the drawer and realized it was confidential and told her I wasn't allowed. Why?"

Stella Albright nodded to Karen Collins.

Karen stood up and spoke. “She didn’t give me the file. I didn’t see what she did with it.”

“I didn’t touch it, Karen. You know I didn’t. You said you’d get it. Someone please tell me why.”

“It’s missing,” said Justin calmly.

“That was months ago. I didn’t take it,” she reiterated, nearly crying. “My stolen daughter would be filed under A. I’m an Adams.”

“The K file is also missing,” informed Mrs. Pringle.

Tears filled Joella’s eyes as she began softly, “I swear to the sky livers, Justin, I’m innocent. Why am I always blamed? Because I’m Inuit?”

“Because stealing is a criminal offence–”

“You may sit down, Mrs. Albright. Ms. Collins,” ordered Justin tersely, I’ll take the floor from here. You may go, Joella. Nobody is accusing you. We’re checking all the internees.”

Joella left in a daze, guessing she was being framed by someone in the office because she was considered the snob of the institution. She too often wondered why she was given such an elaborate private suite.

Todd came to his mom’s private prayer room, wondering if her request was a special occasion, and sat beside her.

“God wants you to mend your ways, Todd, before it is too late,” requested his mother kindly, however reluctantly, not wanting to offend him.

It was the first time his mother ever asked him to have a motherly talk. He knew his uncle was encouraging him to be more assertive, and he was responding, mostly out of necessity. Lois had taught him that same basic principle. Penny had already subtlety warned him several times that overconfidence becomes aggression; that was Jerry’s and her brother’s mistake.

“I don’t make trouble, Mom,” he answered honestly and just as kindly, smiling at her overreligious zeal and kissing Joey. “You, Joella, and Joey are my life.”

“That’s not what I want to talk to you about. As a teenager, your dad was a womanizer too. To be fair, it wasn’t all his fault.

Young girls threw themselves at him. I did too. I was young and didn't see the danger."

That hit Todd like a bullet, shocked his passive religious mother was insinuating he could become a pedophile. Or even that pedophiles were made, not born. He quickly realized she was more intelligent and observant than he had given her credit. Her abrupt and calm approach to such a delicate subject left him silent.

"Had you thought of the consequences of getting Lois, Arnaq, and now Penny pregnant?" she continued seriously. "How would Joella feel?"

He was stunned that his conservative mother was discussing sex with him at his age, even though he knew she had been a successful youth counselor with females since he could remember. "Girls are smart enough to know today, Mom," he finally managed.

"Penny doesn't. She's only seventeen and has been sheltered, sweetheart. We talked. Neither did Joella."

He couldn't believe his ears. She had gained the confidence of Penny as easily as she did all the other young people she had helped. He had no credible defense, because he knew she was absolutely right. Penny would willingly do anything he asked without complaining. He realized he had been taking advantage of her youth. He was again quiet.

"I'm not scolding you. You're young too, but wiser. Adversity does that. Just remember, children are the responsibility of both parents."

He reached and took a laughing, wiggling Joey from her arms and kissed them both. "Don't worry, Mom, I'll solve it. I'll never let you down."

"What's the panic?" asked Barbara Pringle as she entered Joella's onsite suite. "You know I don't get paid to make house calls. Aaron pressured me."

Smelling Joella's cooking, she removed her coat and casually tasted Joella's creation of baked seafood.

"Lobster? Who supplies the lobster? I don't live this good."

"My daughter was adopted by rich white people. She lives in a mansion," Joella blurted out.

"How do you know that?" coughed Mrs. Pringle, caught by surprise with a mouthful of food.

"Someone told me."

"Someone? Do you have the files?"

"I told you. No!"

"If that's true, aren't you happy for her?"

"Yes, but she belongs to Todd and me. She was stolen. That's unfair. She's not a toy poodle."

"I agree, and I know it hurts, but children are not property, Joella; parents are just temporary caretakers. Life's not fair."

"Money's not everything."

"I'm afraid in juvenile law it is. And in court, you get the law, not justice." Now concerned she had the stolen files, she added, "Welfare of your child is most important, not yours."

Joella, not wanting to disagree further and lose her free legal services, halfheartedly handed her a handwritten note:

> Joella,
>
> Your baby was adopted by a rich white couple whose daughter was killed in a car accident. I haven't found out where the mansion is located yet but meet me at the corner of Yale Road and Rose Street at 9:30 on Friday, May 13, 2002. I have a big surprise for you.
>
> Your best friend

"Where did you get this? Who's your best friend?" asked an anxious Mrs. Pringle.

"Justin is my best—my only—friend. It was left on my desk in class. Maybe they have my baby."

Mrs. Pringle mulled it over and found that ludicrous but nonetheless troubled at the remote possibility.

After discussing and disagreeing over a dozen or more possible scenarios, Joella decided it best to turn the note over to Justin; he always had the right answer. But she was silently irritated that Mrs. Pringle was proposing to have the police attend their secret meeting. With that, she would never agree.

Todd sat at the football tables with Tom, Jerry, Penny, Dunk, and all the other Scottish students in the special reserved position for him and Bucky at either end, on centuries-old wooden chairs, with their names engraved on the back, along with other famed figures throughout its history. His mind wandered as he drank his free beer. Just two years ago, he was a wimp in the unknown backwoods community of Natuashish, Labrador. Now he was the hero of one of the world's most prestigious universities and dating a princess.

But he soon despaired. He doubted he'd ever be famous. His academic performance did not match his popularity, and he would soon have to free his princess. He was struggling with law, and it was now his former enemies, Tom and Jerry, that was keeping him afloat. At times, he wanted to quit, but each time, Penny would delicately remind him of his promise to Joella, who in spite of all her hardships and adversities, was struggling on heroically, tops in her university.

He knew Penny was right; the least he could do was to get his degree and help Joella's people as promised. He wanted so much to be alone with her in those backwoods wilds of Labrador; here he was out of his natural environment. He hated the college's stuffy, elite, pretentious protocol.

"I have a big announcement to make," Dunk bellowed to be heard above the din of the revelers, suddenly jumping up, attracting everyone's attention. He reached down and lifted Arnaq from her honored-guest chair next to him and placed her in the centre of the two tables as everyone stood up, waiting for something exciting to happen. She looked both puzzled and scared. She was again wearing her Hebrides tartan skirt to match Dunk's kilt.

To everyone's surprise, he suddenly dropped heavily to his knees on the floor in front of her, sending a chair flying. He too looked nervous, as those at the table moved away and waited in captivated anticipation for his response. Some wondered if he had a heart attack. Students from nearby tables quickly gathered around to view the unexpected exhibition. The place then went eerily silent. Todd watched spellbound and concerned. Dunk had once told him that sudden death ran in his family.

Dunk slowly reached into his pocket, took out a tiny box, opened it with shaky hands, and presented it to Arnaq. Then in an unnerving, wavering voice, the giant of a man struggled to calmly articulate his true feelings. "This was . . . was . . . the . . . the ring my great-great-grandfather gave his bride after the Battle on the Plains of Abraham in Canada after the defeat of the French."

He stopped and took a deep breath to conjure up the courage. "Tara, I would be honored—as would those ancestors—if you would wear this Campbell heirloom and be my wife. Bonnie Scotland loves you too."

It was so sudden and unexpected everyone just looked silently at one another, breathless at the unexpected turn of events and didn't immediately react.

She quickly took the ring and placed it on her finger.

He smiled and quickly stood up, relieved.

"Yes! Unconditionally, yes! Absolutely, yes!" she almost squealed with delight, kissing and hugging him. Then joking in her legalese, added, "And without malice or prejudice: yes."

The surprise soon wore off, and the pub gave a thunderous applause. Soon a parade of congratulations began, and the drinks began to pile up on their table. Both Dunk and Arnaq glowed.

Todd was stunned that Arnaq didn't even hesitate. They had dated only a few months. He could not imagine two more culturally diverse people being so like-minded and happy. Yet he saw them as the quintessential odd couple.

Seeing Todd's silent disbelief, Dunk explained, "In later life, laddie, when you look back, you won't regret your mistakes; you'll regret your missed opportunities."

Todd did not answer. He was staring at Penny who was hugging Jerry as they celebrated. He knew they were equally compatible, that the time had come to release her. He had an unfamiliar sinking feeling as if the world had just deserted him. He wondered if he would lose Joella as well.

He never needed her more than just now.

Joella was apprehensive as she was fitted with two miniature video cameras while being introduced to three female and two male plainclothes police officers that would be staking out the route and monitoring her safety. She felt guilty about spying on someone who might be trying to help her. But Justin pointed out it was for her protection, and she knew that it was a real possibility it might be an ambush by some of the more envious inmates, who had often made threats about her preferential rich-bitch treatment. And several of these were dangerous criminals who had walked away.

Arriving at the designated location, the male officers had Joella watch from the safety of the ghost car until her contact should appear. For a time, she scoured the area but saw no one except two figures casually strolling back and forth along the sidewalk. As the appointed time passed and nobody came to meet her, she figured it was a hoax. But after waiting for another few minutes, it became obvious that the two figures strolling were also expecting someone as they continuously scanned the streets. Joella tried to identify them but was unable in the semidarkness. She was now very concerned; there was no mention of a second person.

Impatient after an hour of wasted time, the officers had a brief five-way phone police consultation and decided to have Joella get out and stroll the sidewalk to check everyone in sight. The three female officers on the street carefully approached the two figures and reported back to the two male officers, who were with Joella in the ghost car, that it was just a woman with a preteen girl.

The police requested Joella to get out of the car to identify them. She refused, suspecting a trap. She did not know anyone with a young daughter. But after a few minutes of persistent, aggressive prodding and with the police strategically positioned, she reluctantly got out and began to walk toward the two females but was shivering with fear. Vanessa as her personal prison guard followed closely behind out of concern.

When about fifty metres away, Vanessa recognized the larger shadow. "That's Susan Kamanirk!" she yelled to the three policewomen. "Get her! She's wanted!"

Joella was stunned.

"Run, Susan, run! They're plainclothes police," screamed Joella, quickly recovering, as the three female policewomen bolted toward Susan with guns drawn yelling *police* and ordering her to remain silent.

"Joella, I found my daughter, Theresa, after twelve years!" she yelled back, overexcited, as the three officers viciously slammed her to the ground and handcuffed her as if she were a dangerous terrorist. "She still loves me! Your child is alive too, Joella; she's with To—"

One officer viciously clasped her hand roughly over Susan's mouth and angrily ordered, "Shut up!" The male officers grabbed Theresa with the fierceness of an attacking pit bull and dragged her next to Joella for her safety.

Within seconds, the commotion was over, and as the ghost car containing Susan screeched tires away from the curb, Joella could still see her struggling and screaming for her daughter.

Theresa, traumatized at the outcome of the meeting, stood staring unbelievably into Joella's teary eyes. Finally, Theresa burst out crying and began to ramble incoherently.

"My mom told me you were her best friend. Some friend. She saved your life and spent over a year in jail for it, and you turned her in. You're not Inuit; you're a Qablunaat. You don't deserve your daughter. You're just a traitor."

As the officers intervened and led Theresa to another car, it broke Joella's heart to hear her plead pitifully, "Please, pretty please, don't make me go back there; I want to stay with my real mom," and then the officer's heartless reply, "Your real mother is nothing more than an east-end druggie and a lying criminal."

"That was a classic takedown," explained the younger male officer proudly to Joella after Theresa left. "We suspected it might be Kamanirk. She kidnapped her daughter a week ago."

But Joella wasn't listening. She was lying nearly lifeless and utterly distraught in a tight ball on the ground with her knees into her chest, her hands on her head, too weak to stand, almost choking on her own sobs.

How could she have been so naive? She should have known the missing K file was for Kamanirk. Never had she felt like such a loser. It had been engrained in her psyche since childhood that there was nothing more despicable in the Inuit code of ethics than to betray one's culture, and she believed it absolutely. To double-cross the *one* person who had risked everything to help her, the *one* person who had the files on her own daughter was not only appalling, it was an unforgivable act. Now all hope was gone. She knew nobody would believe her this time.

With Vanessa's help, Joella slowly recovered from her depressive state with Theresa's words still ringing in her ears, "and spent over a year in jail for it." She recalled her mother also spent time in jail for her. As she was led, defeated and lost, to the police car, she pleaded, barely audible, "Please kill me, Vanessa. Please."

She knew her life was about to spiral out of control. Even Justin had double-crossed her.

Back in her suite, Joella begged to meet Susan and her daughter to apologize, but both the police and the institution adamantly refused. She wanted Vanessa removed as her personal guardian; that too was refused. She went to her bedroom, slammed the door, and locked it.

With no one to turn to, for the next week, Joella did not eat or attend classes. She stayed in her room most of the time and cried, refusing to speak to anybody, even Justin. She felt deeply hurt and betrayed that Justin had allowed her to be used by the police.

But Justin did believe her. He imagined how he would react if Lois or his unborn twins were to be taken away. He had never been so infuriated, and for a week, the whole institution gave him a wide berth. Everyone knew that he blamed Stella Albright.

Others with authority in the institution believed Joella as well; all were equally disgusted at the underhanded and draconian methods used by the police but, more so, deeply embarrassed at having being so cleverly manipulated. Even Social Services, already desperately trying to keep the lid on a seething international public relations nightmare over Joella's incarceration, didn't want the situation exacerbated or another equally unjust incident.

To entice Joella back to reality, the institution took up a collection out of pity and shame and disguised it as a reward for her help in capturing Susan, offering her a three-day escorted trip to Disneyland.

But to Joella, that was the ultimate insult: blood money. She refused to even dignify them with an answer, just shook her head, and quickly left their presence. She no longer trusted anybody.

Each day for the full week, Justin visited her, but she would not even look at him. He calmly explained that it was not the institution's fault. But whatever approach the institution used, the result was the same: deafening silence.

After suffering a childhood of mean jokes about his oversized grotesque body, Justin had a natural understanding of other's problems, but in this case, he was at a total loss to understand her tenacious persistence in apologizing to Susan. He did not want to consult Lois on this issue now that the twins were due any minute, and she was often depressed herself, but realized she might be his only hope.

Todd sat thinking about Joella and musing in his own world in his elaborate study, staring at Penny sitting close to Jerry. Both Tom and Jerry were turning out to be loyal friends, and they were busy laying out a simplified framework for Todd's legal argument for tomorrow's exams. They knew he was close to failing and were trying hard to assist him.

Todd felt he had hit rock bottom again. But, for Joella's sake, he had to find a way to go forward. Her words kept ringing in his ears: "You're not simple, Todd; people say that because they are jealous." He knew he wasn't simple, but here, he was out of his league. Being defeated in his practical exams by his fellow law students with the words *irreverent and immaterial* did not bother him, but to add the words *and incompetent* infuriated him. He found it derogatory and abusive, with no place in law.

He felt Lois and Arnaq had not deserted him but had moved on. Now he had to conjure up the courage to ask Penny to do the same. He was now as much in love with her as she was with him. Fortunately, like him, she was realistic and practical.

Penny and Jerry were always smiling when together and understood each other's idiosyncrasies, whereas Todd felt more like a foreigner from a different culture; at times, he had trouble even understanding Penny's language. He felt it also possible she might be staying with him out of gratitude to his uncle for rescuing her family. She was a natural leader. Even in her own household, they all obediently followed her directions. He realized Tom was really a good brother in protecting his sister with such extreme devotion; she was certainly naive to the ways of the cruel world.

To add to his problems, Joella was on a hunger strike, and all his thoughts were with her. It consumed a great deal of his time consulting experts on how to help her and communicating directly with Justin, who was very busy himself. He was spending precious little quality time with Penny, except sleeping with her each night and felt he was taking advantage of her innocence as his mother had pointed out, and he loved her too much to destroy her life. The time had come to release her for her own good. This was going to hurt both of them.

But he still could not find the courage to tell her.

With his refusal to release Joella early to a halfway house fresh in her mind, Lois went nearly ballistic as Justin grudgingly and mournfully related the recent events and his failure in helping Joella.

"The Inuit don't have Bible commandments, but we're not savages. We live by unwritten values, our ancestors. Susan is not a criminal. Theresa is her own daughter! Stolen! She just took her back. Sharing, not stealing, is our way. We believe all life is sacred; every living thing must be treated equally with respect, even animals. We must only take from the earth as much as needed, nothing more, Justin. We're all, even this earth, gifts from some Great Spirit, somewhere. Joella feels a traitor to her own people. Inuit forgive and help each other. To betray a trusted friend in need is an unforgivable disgrace. Justin, I told you, only you and Todd understands us!"

She was shouting out the words and crying as she desperately attempted to rationally explain Inuit mentality and how the white man's mindset reflected their racist bias toward them. She kept sobbing and adding at the end of each sentence, "Justin, I told you, only you and Todd understands us."

But it was only after she finished her tirade that he really did understand their position. For the first time in his life, he began to truly appreciate another culture's perspective and felt the praise that everyone heaped on his psychiatric abilities was unwarranted. He had failed to grasp one basic principle: forgiveness. Joella was studying desperately to help her people after all her mistreatment.

Lois's instant solution was for her and Justin, with an Inuit counselor who could speak Inuktitut fluently, to visit both Susan and her daughter and apologize on Joella's behalf and explain the facts. They too needed to know that they were loved and not deserted.

Although he found it unorthodox and nearly impossible, he was impressed by both her intelligence and the simplicity of the solution.

After she calmed down, to her surprise, he kissed her and readily agreed. "If they don't, I'll go the news media on behalf of both of them." Kissing her again, he offered, "You should be the counselor, not me."

She couldn't believe he wasn't even angry at her. Becoming apprehensive, she pleaded, "I'm sorry, Justin. Please don't leave me. The Intuit is very emotional about some things."

"And rightfully so. White people *are* arrogant. Leave? I'm fortunate to have a goddess like you, Sedna."

She stopped crying and stared at him with a confused look on her face, knowing she had grossly overexaggerated the facts. The truth was: she knew no Inuit or Innu who was as understanding and lovable as him.

Joella was getting weak and disoriented after more than a week of only water. She was no longer sure she wanted to live without her daughter and friends. She now understood the hopelessness many of her people suffered and why so many committed suicide.

As she prayed for a miracle, unexpectedly, a young woman entered her suite, tripping the alarm, and placed a small bowl of her favorite pea soup and some fruit on her coffee table. Joella staggered over and reset the alarm, wondering if she were hallucinating.

"I'm Jamie Decker," said the stranger kindly but firmly. "Vanessa insisted on being reassigned. I'm new here; and younger, so I guess they figured we'd have more in common."

She took two letters from her pocket and placed them near the food and continued, "Eat if you want, but you'll be happy with the letters. Justin is in his office if you want to talk with him later."

Joella glanced at the two letters. One was labeled "To Joella from Susan Kamanirk" and marked "Private & Confidential." She quickly ripped it open and began to eagerly read.

> Hi, Joella,
>
> Today I had a visit from Social Services, Justin Patey and a close friend of yours. I'm not allowed to tell you her name. They explained what had happened. I know that it was not your fault. Please start eating again; a dead mother is no good to her child.
>
> I cannot tell you very much since this letter has to be okayed by Social Services. But I swear to all the Inuit gods your child is alive, and I know where. You know Social Services disagree with me on this, but they still agreed to let me tell you anyhow. That tells you something. Believe me, the end will be happier for you than it will likely be for me.

Tears streamed down Joella as she stopped and took a mouthful of the tasty soup.

> Stealing my daughter was wrong even though she was stolen from me. She is back with her adopted parents, who are well-to-do Inuit, but she is still unhappy there. Justin and your friend got me a good lawyer, and I am now released into their care until my trial hearing. He is also working on me getting visiting rights to Theresa. Justin arranged a police-escorted visit to Theresa's foster parents' home, and I talked with them and Theresa for two hours. I also now know how hard it is for them to lose their only child. They said they will testify on my behalf to keep me out of jail and will give me unlimited visiting rights to Theresa if I get a job and stay away from drugs. They said we can raise Theresa together. I believe that is the best I can hope for.
>
> So I am now a big chef in a truck stop. I sling hash. A far cry from my counseling and caretaking

> position at your group home. You see revenge doesn't help, Joella; don't make my mistake. You're on the right path. Beat the bastards at their own game.

Joella smiled. That's the Inuit spirit. She then took another mouthful of soup

> Justin Patey is a better friend than you're allowed to know. Trust him, Joella; I do. He forgave me.
>
> Remember, your life is better in jail than it was at home. I'm not allowed to visit or talk to you, but Social Services said I can write you at any time as long as the letters go to them first. I would like that.
>
> You can give the letters you write me to Justin Patey.
>
> Still your true friend,
> Susan

Joella cried as she gulped down the bowl of soup and hungrily devoured a banana. She hoped Justin would forgive her too.

After eating all the fruit in the bowl, she tore open the unmarked envelope.

> Hello, Joella,
>
> Since you don't talk to me anymore, I assigned the new sociologist trainee to you. You two may have more in common than we did. One word of advice: take the trip to Disneyland, then get back to your studies. I promise things will turn out for you.
>
> Justin

Joella burst into Justin's office with tears flowing down her face as he was angrily reprimanding two inmates for dereliction of their duty and began to stammer, "How . . . how . . . could you dump me? You're the only friend I have. Jamie is not Inuit like us."

He laughed, went, and hugged her as the other two inmates watched surprised at his sudden change of personality and the preferential treatment.

"His rich bitch has returned," sneered one inmate.

"And likely his pincushion," the other responded, just as sarcastic.

"Welcome back, Joella. You won again. I'm proud of you," he interrupted. "But you gave everyone a scare," as he waved the two inmates away and pointed for her to sit down. After they left, he added more sternly, "You're my only patient. You know I'm not Inuit."

Joella stared at him with a lost look on her face.

"Why only me? Then how do you know so much about us?"

"I'm an administrator in charge of this facility, not a practicing psychologist. And my job is much more than reprimanding employees and inmates. I see the big picture. You'll understand when you finish your degree. Susan already knows."

"I'll do what you want if you still be my psychologist, my friend."

He sat down and became very serious. He decided that in college, she was now mature enough to understand reality.

"Question is, Joella, are *you* an Inuit or a Qablunaat? You need to do my *Truth Table*." He paused, waiting for her answer.

She was too stunned at his abrupt change of attitude to answer and his uncanny knowledge of Inuit and Innu customs. She had never seen him so callous and demanding. She wondered if he knew Tuk wasn't her father. She remained silent, not knowing how to answer.

"Joella, in real life, you fight for what is yours with the help of friends, not try to kill yourself. That's a coward's way out. A lot of Inuit do that. Are you just another coward?"

She wanted to apologize, but he continued to lecture her, unabated. "You live in a modern suite. You attend college: *free.* You're allowed to travel: *free.* You have a personal guardian, a private lawyer. You live better than I do. Remember, you're in jail; and for jail, that's not reality. People love you more than you know, and you don't appreciate it. I suggest you start acting your age."

She was taken aback by his unorthodox direct behavior but knew he was correct and tried to justify it by stating meekly, "I'm Inuit and not very smart, Justin," beginning to cry again. "I have only you. Please don't dessert me."

"You're insulting my intelligence. That's not true, and you know it. You're tops in your university. I suggest you start applying your knowledge." He became pensive and noted unhappily, "I've done everything I'm allowed, and more. And you still don't trust me. I can do no more. Your actions are impacting my relationship at home, and with the board. They're going to dismiss me."

The thought of him being fired on her behalf horrified her, as memories of her mother, Todd, and his mother, and Susan all flashed back; all had tried to help her, and all had paid the price. She had the knack for destroying lives. "I'm so sorry, Justin. Tell them I won't bother you anymore. I'll stay away." She started to leave with tears streaming down her face.

He relented. "I'll try just one more time, but if, and only if, you don't ask any more questions. Just believe me. If you do, they'll dismiss me."

"Oh, Justin, I swear to all the Inuit and Christian gods," she promised passionately. "I'll do exactly what you say."

"Then go and get ready for your trip to Disneyland."

"God answered my prayers, Justin," said Lois sadly, holding her newborn twins close to her chest.

"Mine too," he answered happily. "Joella accepted your peace offering."

He kissed her and offered to take the twins. She refused. He noticed she had been crying. His meal wasn't ready as usual but realized she had just gotten out of the hospital.

"Are you ill?" he asked, concerned. "Do you need a helper for a while?"

She shook her head and gave him the twins, then took two first-class airline tickets from the babies' nursing bags, and showed him.

"The Howards gave us a two-week European tour in appreciation. Todd wants to see the twins."

"Wow! That's very generous. Great! We both need to get away," answered a surprised Justin. "Then why are you sad?"

"We travel the world with twins, while Joella's baby was stolen, and she's in jail."

"You know Todd has their child, and she's free enough to travel to Disneyland." He paused. "Please tell me your problem, Lois. I thought you would like to see Todd again."

She began to cry. "That's the problem," she sobbed. "What if I still love him?"

That was a scenario he had not considered, and it jolted him. Once more, his lonely past flashed back. He could not even imagine a life without Lois and the twins, but he controlled his anxiety and answered, "I want you to go. Freud would say that's just human. I love my mother, but I would not choose her over you. I love you enough to let you make your own decisions, even if he's what you want."

"You know he's not, but I'm still scared."

"Tom said you nearly failed, Todd. I gave him a good tongue-lashing for letting it happen. He and Jerry promised—" began Penny testily, as she entered his room and saw his gloomy face. She went and hugged him.

"No, it's me," Todd interrupted dejectedly, kissing her. "Please sit. We should talk."

She sat quietly on the bed staring into his eyes wondering if he were quitting law and returning to Labrador. She watched as he twisted his hair and stare blankly at Joella's pictures on the wall. He was finding it distressful to verbalize.

"Mom says I'm unfair to you. I know it's true, but I love you. Joella's waiting—"

"What? You treat me like a queen," she whispered, confused. "I live here in a mansion, free—"

"Please let me continue, Penny. What I have to say hurts."

For the next ten minutes, Penny listened in silence with tears in her eyes. She knew he would probably leave her sometime but felt she was being dumped prematurely, believing Joella might also meet someone else in the next three years. Todd had been her only lover. How could he leave her so soon? They hadn't even as much as quarreled. Besides, she had become attached to Joey. But she felt Todd must truly love her too if he followed her and Jerry's actions so closely that he could read their emotions. She knew his statements were mostly true. It was apparent to everyone Jerry wanted her. She started to cry. "I love you too, Todd. Why don't you stay with me until Joella is released? I can make Tom help you more."

"Because I love you, I must let you go. I can see you and Jerry are as well-matched as me and Joella. Tom and Jerry will still help me. I still want you to stay with us, but if we stay lovers any longer, I will forget Joella. My loyalties are becoming blurred."

"You should live for today, Todd; you may be dead tomorrow," she lectured as she stood up to leave. She saw tears came to his eyes as he twisted his hair again.

"I didn't tell you all, Penny." He paused to formulate a credible answer. "I'm scared I'm like my father."

She had no idea what that meant, but it had an ominous ring, and it was clear he had genuine concern for her. She began to wonder if she could become a victim of his fighting mentality. She kissed him on the cheek, as tears dripped from her chin, and replied mournfully, "I'll always remember you as my first love, Todd."

As she closed the door, Todd stared at Joella's pictures on the wall and analyzed his life. He wasn't in the land that had his heart. He was failing in his studies. The person he wanted was in jail. He was surrounded by beautiful females in a sea of riches yet totally miserable and alone. He knelt down and prayed to the sky livers to help Joella, then, standing up, promised her pictures on the wall that come hell or high water, he was going to become a lawyer for her sake and go back home to help her people in the land he loved.

He went back to his studies with renewed vigor.

"That's an odd request," said a puzzled Joella. "I already give you a picture of me each month. What do you do with them?"

"They're for your family later. A DNA profile may help you identify your child or a relative," Justin offered awkwardly, believing it to be the only logical response she would accept. "It's expensive; you should have it done now."

Joella thought it over for a while and wondered why she had not thought of it before. But it was still unusual. "I don't like blood tests," she responded shyly, seeking an excuse.

"Just give me a lock of hair or a toenail. I'll do the book work from your files and give you a copy of the report."

"It isn't for the crime lab record, is it? I don't want—" she began nervously.

"It's not for the courts. They have your record now."

She was still undecided.

"I swear nobody will know except us," he lied again, knowing Lois would have to know since she did all the direct communications with Todd.

After a few minutes of discussion, she followed his instructions, got a pair of scissors, cut off a large chunk of hair, placed it in an envelope, and handed it to him.

"You're the only person I do trust, Justin." Then smiling, she asked, "Did you ever eat Newfie fish and brewis? I have some on the—"

"Yes," he answered flippantly. Lois had cooked it many times. "But I'm not fussy about it."

"You've been to Newfoundland?" she asked, surprised.

"I thought you meant fish and chips," he responded, blushing.

Part II

Justice

Chapter Ten

The Truth Table

This above all, to thine own self be true.
—W. Shakespeare

Fall 2004

After her client, a Vietnamese refugee, left, Joella relaxed and stared at Justin's picture on his desk and reflected her four-and-a-half years in jail. The end was near.

By staying busy, the last two and a half years just flew by. She had stuck to her promise to Justin, concentrated mainly on her studies, spent a great deal of her spare time working with nonprofit child-find agencies, and toiling with Mrs. Pringle to meticulously prepare herself for the court challenge on April 4, 2005, her daughter's fourth birthday and the day she was to receive her degree. She had kept a calendar and crossed off each day before praying each night. April 4 was labeled, *Zero Hour.*

Justin had successfully kept the Social Services at bay and had somehow secured for her a generous start-up grant from the federal government that was given to exceptional inmates as a Come-Back Award, plus a position as a sociologist working with new immigrants to help them absorb the cultural shook of integrating into their new Canadian society.

The award she accepted, but refused the career position, indicating she had a daughter to look after and was going to work only with Inuit and Innu.

Adversity had matured her far beyond her last teenage year. She was no longer the star inmate, but now almost a star employee, who was consulted by the staff whenever adjudication was required to deal with, not only Inuit cases but all First Nations people's cases and most other minorities.

Three months earlier, she had received the formal notice of impending release from the courts, and had she signed a secrecy covenant not to launch a challenge custody of or even search for her apprehended child, she would be released immediately to work at her new position.

The blackmailing tactic nearly caused her to go berserk, but Justin counseled her to remain calm and refuse, as did her lawyer. She quickly grasped their logic. Now, more world wise, she knew how to manipulate the system and, thanks to Justin, knew how to play the white man's deceptive games. She controlled her temper and gracefully refused, indicating she wanted to finish her degree in the safety of the institution.

With some of her clients able to pay a token amount, she had saved $5,000 and was able to pay Mrs. Pringle a minimum fee for her services, and it was paying dividends. Her three cases were fully prepared and registered with the courts for the target date.

She knew them from memory.

Case one: Joella Adams versus Social Services—her nemesis—to reveal the identity of her daughter's foster parents and associated details and to prove Social Services committed deliberate fraud and deception by apprehending her daughter without parental consent.

But first, Justin's wanted her to just sue for visitation rights to determine if her daughter were happy with her adopted family before going for full custody, but she was scared her daughter might not love her if she waited too long. It galled her that her child went to a white family who, likely by now, had instilled in her a condescending view of the Inuit. She agreed with Justin out of courtesy. But deep down, Justin knew it was only a ploy to get information and that any procrastinating would only be a ploy to gain her child's confidence before going all the way.

Case two: Joella Adams versus Shady Lawn's Funeral Home to regain monies paid, plus an undisclosed amount for pain and suffering in its criminal affiliation with Social Services.

Case three was contingent upon the outcome of the first two, a long-term fight to have her alleged crimes expunged to regain her honor, compensation for mental distress, and pain and suffering for her years in jail, against Social Services, the correctional institute, and the country's justice system, in short, the government.

A month earlier, Social Services, unable to bribe its way out of a legal challenge, in conjunction with the courts, backtracked and tried to release Joella, believing Barbara Pringle's service was free only to inmates and the unemployed, and Joella, having a professional career position waiting, would not qualify, thus, could not be represented by her.

But, in an ironic twist, Joella had Mrs. Pringle successfully obtain an injunction preventing her release and threatened to sue Social Services if she were not allowed to complete her education.

Social Services, realizing Joella was now even more unmanageable due to her education, her acquired sophistication through character acting, and her own legal counsel, was at a total loss on how to deal with her. With the whole messy affair was about to explode, they quickly conceded and, to save face, praised her career aspirations.

Justin too was praising her abilities on a daily basis and begging her jokingly not to abscond with his position. They were now almost equals, but she still saw him as her savior.

Curiously though, he kept telling her that all her frantic legal work was for practical experience only and that it was not necessary to sue for her child. He was now positive things would work out for her beyond her wildest imagination, and on that special date—April 4, 2005—a miracle would occur. While it encouraged her, her life had been a lesson in tragedies, and she expected no miracles.

Todd, Tom, and Jerry were inseparable, and with Dunk and Arnaq, they had become affectionately known as the QCs, the Queen's Councilors, because some two years earlier, Lord Thurston had arranged for them to be invited to the palace to dine and debate a preselected subject—colonial rule—with the Queen on her birthday, a ritual that had existed for the university since its inception when Alfred the Great debated at Oxford in 872.

However, the true basis of their companionship was more sinister; it was an alliance born mostly out of fear and necessity. At the trial, Ranjit Singh Palmar, alias Blackbeard, on being sentenced to five years in jail for attempted manslaughter, had warned the court that when released, he would seek restitution, if his criminal friends didn't take them out first.

In fact, the contentious six-month trial had taken a heavy toll on all those involved, including the Howards. Todd was indeed cast by the news media a blue-blood prizefighter, who had an illegitimate son by an incarcerated teenage murderer. The prestigious university was publicly embarrassed that an undesirable like Blackbeard, a well-known member of a criminal gang with a lengthy record, was able to slip through their airtight screening process because he played football. The Cooper family's fall from grace to poverty was mercilessly exposed in great detail, and as a result, the Preston household was divided and quarrelling over Tom's upcoming marriage to Penelope because of the Cooper's embarrassing financial status.

All this drew the trio closer, and Todd emerged as the undisputed winner since he was barely scraping by in his law studies and was being tutored by both Tom and Jerry. Todd knew the university gave him undue credits for his courses because of his association with the Howards, Lord Thurston, and his one visit with the Queen. Image was everything to the university, and it was aggressively advertised.

None of this notoriety mattered to Todd. He enrolled in the easiest courses, took the minimum required, registered in night classes, and even did practical charity work with the homeless for credits. His priority was not prestige; he was following the path of least resistance to complete his law degree at any cost to return to Joella and Natuashish.

One of the few bright spots in Todd's life of endless study and parenthood in the last two years since Penny left was Portia. After hearing Penny was dating her brother, she hounded him for dates, and being lonely and suffering a breakup hangover, he finally accepted, and soon they became friends and lovers. Even though Portia was exceptionally intelligent, could act sophisticated and charmingly pretentious at public appearances, in private, she was cruder and a more aggressive than Lois in her rebellious years. There was no love or affection involved in their relationship, just simple animal lust, but it filled Todd's desire for female companionship.

Portia rationalized her actions by explaining she was a modern girl and that her name meant *pig*, and Todd rationalized his by actually considering her a pig. He figured by dating that type of loose person, he was keeping his promise to both his mother and Joella.

Another bright spot had been Justin and Lois's first visit. For two weeks, Todd had felt at home as he and Lois reminisced old times as they travelled across Europe. He often smiled as he thought of how astonished they were when they saw his uncle's estate and how happy Justin was when he took Portia with him. It had been the respite he needed from study. And, seeing the improvement, his uncle had paid for two more trips for Justin, Lois, and the twins over the next two years.

Staying in England was only bearable because of the love Todd received from Joey. Returning to Canada would mean leaving Joey behind, and that he would never do. Joey was now his shadow, and all his relatives were proud of him. It took up a great deal of Todd's precious study time teaching him to read, play games or telling bedtime stories about his life back in Labrador, but it gave his life meaning and direction. Often, he would fall asleep before Joey did and find his assignments unfinished in the morning.

Now, there were only six months left to complete forty credits before Joella would be released. He and his relatives had a grand finale organized for her on her first court date. Forty credits was an insurmountable challenge for him and knew he would likely fail, but Jerry, who was still jealous over Penny's relationship with him—knowing she still preferred Todd—was spending huge amounts of time improving his substandard assignments. Jerry knew he had to get Todd out of the way before Penny would set a wedding date.

Joella had just finished the last of her clients and sat staring pensively around Justin's empty office, feeling guilty. It was with conflicting emotions that she had just counseled a First Nation's woman to leave her four-year-old daughter in a foster home with a white family until she could properly care for her. She could still hear her drunken curses and shouts of *traitor* ringing in her ears as she had her security dragged her away, screaming. Joella pondered if she had chosen the right career. She could never have imagined having to have to make such heart-wrenching choices. She knew precisely how the woman felt. However, she also recalled the horrors of her own childhood in an abusive home and was confident it was the right decision for the child, but it did not make the decision any easier.

She wondered what her own daughter would look like at four, being only one-quarter Inuit. Did she have a nice name? Was she smart? Did she look like Todd or her? Her eyes became moist at the thought of her daughter calling strangers, Mom and Dad.

Zero Hour was fast approaching, and she was both eager and apprehensive. As she thought about it, her heart began to race and her hands became sweaty. She wasn't scared of taking on the world; she was scared her daughter might not love her. What could she possibly say when they first met? "Hi, sweetheart, I'm your mom. I just got out of jail for murdering two people." Times like this, she felt like crawling into her secret cave back in Davis Inlet and hiding. She now truly understood hopelessness and why so many of her people committed suicide.

After she reclaimed her daughter, her next task would be to locate Todd. He would be easy to find; he would still be studying at Memorial University for his master's degree, most likely already having completed his undergraduate degree. He probably majored in electronics or computer science; he really was a whiz in that field. After five years, she felt he was by now too sophisticated to associate with a jailbird; he was always out of her league.

What would he think of her now? He knew she had run away on the downtown east side. Did he think she was a junkie and a prostitute like so many other Inuit and Innu? Tears flooded her eyes.

"Superb! Everyone on the panel concurred with your decisions," congratulated a delighted Justin, startling her as he stomped heavily into his office from the observation post next door with two-way mirrors.

"That last assignment was downright mean, Justin," she responded solemnly, wiping her eyes.

"It was reality, Joella; get used to it."

"I now feel like a traitor to *my* own people," she lamented.

"And who are they?" he asked, becoming serious.

She was silenced by the surprise response; he knew she was Inuit.

"I know you've now nearly have your degree and just as good an analyst as I am, but I want you to do an experiment for me."

"What kind of experiment?"

"The real-life kind. A truth table?"

"On what?"

"You. I want you to discover who and what you are."

"I'm Inuit. You know that," she almost scoffed.

"*Do* I? Maybe. Do *you*?"

She was taken aback at his almost-insulting, racist remark. Such statements were uncharacteristic of him. She didn't answer.

"It's not only *who* you are; it's also *what* you are." He could see that she was offended and hesitant, so he made it an order. "This will be your final practical assignment in this institution related to your studies. You will get six college credits, not three. You have the next three months to complete.

She recovered and readily agreed, realizing that would be an easy six credits, and he was helping to speed up her degree.

He took out a file from his desk and handed it to her.

"What am I proving? What are my principle variables?"

"I told you. *Who* and *What* you are. Read the file. You only have to verbally identify for me the *truth* you derive from the exercise."

She perused the large folding chart and was astounded at the numerous headings in an intricate maze: Race. Class. Male/

Female. Rich/Poor. Environment. Good/Bad. Religion. Friend/Foe. Hate/Love. Cause/Effect. There were at least fifty interrelated variables.

"This is a life profile," she blurted out, disappointed at its complexity. "And it's very convoluted."

"So is real life. It's been downloaded to your computer; you only have to answer truthfully."

"It can have millions of possible conclusions. A college will never agree to that," she noted, concerned about doing useless work.

"They will! And for you, there is only one answer, unless you lie to yourself."

Joella recognized what Justin was trying to accomplish and was nervous about discovering her true inner self. She was acutely aware she had killed two people and wanted to put her past behind her.

"They encourage me to give this exercise to all my prize inmates, and you're my first major success story," Justin added proudly. "There is no final exam; you get your credits by merely completing it."

"It's simple to do but hard to answer honestly," she mused aloud. "Why?"

"If you don't know who you are or where you came from, you won't know where you're going. 'This above all, to thine own self be true.'"

She smiled at his awkward attempt at poetry—he was no bard—and answered definitively, "I *am* true to myself. I'm Inuit, from Natuashish, Labrador, and I'm going to help them when I get out."

"Just Inuit? Not Innu or white? You're in for a shock of reality."

She appreciated his concern and agreed, knowing, as did he, that a truth table was like all computer models: garbage in, garbage out. She smiled as she gave him his desk back.

Todd walked into the dean's office and saw his diploma still sitting on his desk. He prepared for a degrading lecture on his incompetence. He felt he had not only disgraced the university but all his relatives and colleges friends by not finishing and receiving his diploma at the annual convocation held a week earlier. He still had six more credits to go, all practical. Organizing Joella's grand finale had taken up all his time.

Especially disappointing was having to forgo his graduation photo on his uncle's wall of honor with other famous Howards.

"Mr. Clarke, you borderlined in finishing your degree."

Borderlined? thought Todd. *I would have failed, but my friends kept me afloat.* Not knowing what to expect, he remained quiet, aware he had not yet completed his credits, speculating that his uncle ordered the dean to help him solve his problem. His uncle continuously reminded him that he did not have to be the best, just do his best, and opportunities would present themselves. He certainly had done his best, and then some.

"Mr. Clarke, I have been informed why you had been busy in the last few months. I understand it had charitable legal connotations that should be recognized. Nonetheless, to receive this prestigious parchment before you return to Canada, you must a sign a pledge to finish five hundred hours of pro bono work representing the Inuit and First Nations of Natuashish, Labrador."

Todd's heart soared; he felt reborn. He knew his uncle's trademark. That would be a labor of love. But five hundred? That was certainly excessive; then everything his uncle demanded was excessive.

"You have now grasped our prestigious institution has a very high standard . . ."

No kidding, thought Todd, *I'm only here because Joella brainwashed me into believing I was a genius*.

"Considering nearly half has dropped out, you did splendid."

Splendid? Now, that's bullshit, mused Todd as he forced a smile.

Looking pleased for a change, the dean added, "But that is all irrelevant and immaterial—"

"Please don't use the words, *and incompetent*," interrupted Todd dejectedly. If he heard the phrase *irrelevant, immaterial, and incompetent* one more time, he felt he'd probably smash his desk.

The dean stood up and offered Todd a rolled parchment in one hand and shook Todd's hand with the other.

"Mr. Clarke, any recipient of this sheepskin is not incompetent. The photographer is waiting for you in the theatre. But first, permit me a word of advice from experience. The undertaking you're about to embrace would be insurmountable to any top graduate of this esteemed institution that I've known during my tenure, including myself. You have the right mentality to succeed and a noble purpose to achieve it. However, your knowledge has yet to be translated into wisdom. Stay close to your uncle. We don't live in a perfect world."

"I appreciate your advice," managed Todd, knowing all too well about an imperfect world.

"*Bonus fortuna, meus amicus*," the dean encouraged in Latin.

"*Nakurmiik*," Todd replied in Inuktitut.

As Todd walked pompously down the outside path where Alfred the Great was said to have strolled, toward the theatre holding his sheepskin, he said proudly to himself, *We've made it, Joella; now let's take on the fucking world.*

Joella's degree was complete with the exception of the credits from Justin's *Truth Table*. She eagerly went to his office to get a transcript for her final six credits and was shocked to see the large Kraft envelope still sitting unopened on his desk. The unorthodox project had proven to be her most frustrating course; it had taken three months of her labor.

"Congratulations," Justin announced excitedly, quickly standing up and shaking her hand. "You did it; you have your degree."

"But you didn't read it," she said, sorely disappointed.

He passed her back the large stuffed envelope and calmly responded, "Not my business. I just wanted *you* to know who you are. What *truth* did you derive from it?"

After the surprise wore off, she answered cautiously, "Be proud of my Inuit heritage?" guessing he might know it was only marginally true.

"Now you know; burn it."

Those words cut like a knife. She was elated her degree was complete but troubled about her true identity. Until the truth table came along, she had never questioned her heritage. Frustrated the table hadn't readily produced the conclusions that matched her convictions; she had rejected the table results and fudged the inputs until it generated her desired outcome, the person she wanted to be: Inuit. *I'm Inuit, not white*, she reminded herself silently for assurance.

Chapter Eleven

The Miracle

Happiness is only real if shared.

April 4, 2005. Zero Hour. This was it. The day she had looked forward to for four years. Her daughter's fourth birthday. The stage was set. She had just this morning picked up her bachelor's degree diploma. The battle was about to begin.

I'm ready to fight the devil. Bring him on, Joella encouraged herself as she took the witness stand, prepared for any eventuality. She had no notes; she had gone to court after hours and practiced for this moment with her lawyer numerous times over the years. She knew the legal section of the Bill of Rights and Freedoms almost from memory. The answers were meticulously scripted and burned into her memory. Her legal research into child adoption was flawless. She took a deep breath.

"All rise. This court is now in session, Judge Wilson presiding," announced the sheriff as the judge entered and took his chair."

To her dismay, she heard her lawyer announce, somewhat reluctantly, "Before we present the opening arguments, Your Honor, I have just this moment received a note from the court clerk that a recent lawyer to the bench is here, with a large entourage requesting pro hac vice to enter the hearing and address the court on behalf of Ms. Adams before any evidence is introduced—"

"Objection!" yelled the lawyer for the Social Services.

"Objection, Your Honor," parroted the lawyer for the Shady Lawn Funeral Home.

"On what grounds, gentlemen? No opening statements have been presented."

There was an embarrassing silence.

"Did you know about this person, Ms. Adams?"

"No, Your Honor," she answered apprehensively, standing up.

"Is this a friendly witness, Mrs. Pringle?"

"I'm not sure, Your Honor. From this secretive memo, he appears somewhat aggressive and arrogant. He claims he has just graduated from Oxford in England with a law degree. His name is Nag-ling-nig. I'm not sure if that's the correct pronunciation, Your Honor. He demands the court—" answered Mrs. Pringle cautiously, concerned it might be a clever highjacking.

"Demands, Mrs. Pringle—?"

Joella sat down and began to cry instantly, surprising everyone and interrupting them both.

"Are you well, Ms. Adams?" asked the judge gently.

"Fine, Your Honor. Naglingnig is my daughter's father. I haven't seen or heard from him in five years. Please let him speak."

A brief hush of confusion fell over the courtroom. Then, once again, there was a chorus of objections from the defense counsels. The lawyer for Shady Lawn Funeral Home called for a recess. The Social Services lawyer wanted to first investigate to see if it were a hoax.

The judge shook his head and hit his gavel on the bench angrily. "No more procrastinating, Mr. Jones, Mr. Hanson. If he is the child's father, he too has a right to know if his child is alive." He nodded to the sheriff to admit them.

As Todd entered the court with Lois on his arm, a handsome four-year-old son, and three-year-old twins by their side, Joella's heart sank. Dozens of older people filed in and filled the visitor's gallery.

Joella's worst fears had been realized. He had forgotten her and married Lois, her only friend, and she had patiently waited for him. She sat down and put her head on her knees and began to sob uncontrollably.

"I am Todd Clarke, Your Honor, but my Inuit name is Naglingnig," he said proudly. "My service is offered pro bono, if required. I would like to request a private session with the bench. This issue is best settled out of the limelight—"

"State your case, Mr. Clarke. The hearing hasn't started. Ms. Adams has waited over four years for a decision. Procrastinating and sidestepping will not happen in my court."

"I have been made an honorary aboriginal elder and represent the Innu and Inuit of Natuashish, Labrador. My service is also pro bono to them for six months. I can state categorically, and prove, that Joella's child is alive, well, and in the care of excellent parents."

The judge smiled at his juvenile exuberance; he couldn't be more than twenty-two years old.

"Such generosity is very impressive, Mr. Clarke."

Joella stopped crying and stared at him, suddenly rejuvenated, overjoyed he had taken her advice but wondered why he had a slight British accent. She already knew her child was alive but wondered how he knew. It hurt deeply to see him with Lois; he had grown into a handsome gentleman, and Lois, though now a lady, had been a conniving, licentious teenager. Now they had three children.

"Objection! Pure speculation. The child's body was stolen—" the lawyer for the funeral home began, waving his arms. The other lawyer added his protest simultaneously.

Infuriated, the judge slammed his gavel on the bar.

"One more interruption without grounds and I'll accept Ms. Adam's submitted version of the events."

The two defense lawyers meekly sat back down. The judge nodded for Todd to continue.

"I would like Lois to approach the bench."

The court went deathly quiet.

Showing off his wife and kids, thought Joella. *He promised to marry me.* Although disappointed, she knew five years was a long time to wait. She also knew Lois worshiped him. She speculated he must have gotten her pregnant when she went to prison; the twins were part Inuit, but strangely, his oldest son was white, but he looked like Todd. *It was my fault too*, she chastised herself. *I told him to go with Lois.* Nonetheless, she was still grateful he had gotten his bar license and was helping her people.

Instead of questioning Lois as a witness, Todd turned to the young boy and said, "Approach the bench and tell the court where you live."

Both defense stood up, but the judge pointed his finger at their seats and gave them an icy stare. They sat back down.

Lois stood by the witness stand as the boy climbed in the box without direction and adjusted his mike, then asked Todd seriously, "Should I address the bench or you?"

Everyone laughed.

"Always the bench."

"Sorry, I forgot. Oxford, England, Your Honor," he said boldly, in a clear confident British accent.

"Why did you come to Canada?"

You could hear a pin drop. Like the whole court, Joella was intrigued. How could Todd and Lois live in England and represent her people? She was amazed; his son was a cultured little gentleman and obviously familiar with court procedure.

"My dad moved here to live with my mom."

"Who's your dad?"

The kid smiled.

"That's a silly question." Everyone laughed. "You know you are."

Joella was still confused. She was correct in that it was his son. But why would he display Lois's children like trophies in front of her? That was cruel.

"Who is your mom?"

He pointed to Joella.

"She is, but she doesn't know it."

Joella stood up, speechless, almost amused. It couldn't be. She only had one child: a girl. Besides, the boy was white. What was Todd trying to prove? Was he now an unfriendly witness working for Social Services as well? She was both puzzled and disappointed that he was not supporting her. Her lawyer opened her arms and looked at Joella as if to ask, 'Do you want me to stop him?' Joella was too confused and hurt to respond.

"Tell the judge your name," Todd continued.

"Joe Ellan Clarke, but my friends call me Joey."

Joe Ellan? Joella couldn't believe her ears. Her mother had told nobody except her in her dream—catcher letter.

"And these other people?"

"All *them*?" questioned Joey, wide-eyed and a little confused.

Todd nodded.

"That's my great-great-grandma. Her name is Diana Ellan. She's nice," he answered, pointing to an impeccably dressed very old lady in front.

Everyone laughed quietly.

"And that's my great-great-grandpa." Turning and leaning toward the judge, he whispered, "He's really, really grumpy, Your Honor. He complains a lot about the weather, the government, the—"

The judge smiled.

Everyone laughed louder.

"Thank you, Joey," interrupted Todd quickly. "They're all his relatives on his great-great-grandfather's side, Your Honor. You see, Joella's biological father was not Tuk Evans but Joe Ellan, a British archeologist. Mr. Ellan's relatives have since removed his remains from Labrador back to England. Proven by a DNA samples provided by Joella herself. Fifty of Joella's relatives are so proud of her fighting spirit they came from England to see her in person. They're—"

Joey's great-great-grandfather stood up and started to applaud and, shaking his old wooden cane, interrupted angrily, "Bloody right!"

Soon all were applauding.

Joella was positively flabbergasted. Her child was a boy. Not the girl like she had so fervently believed. But how could Todd possibly have known her father's name? He seemed to know everything about her life. And why was Joey white?

"*My* son?" whispered Joella after the din died down. The place went deathly silent again.

"My aunt and uncle adopted our son, Your Honor. They were under a strict court injunction—however illegal and inhumane—to prevent them from notifying his mother—"

The Social Services lawyer quickly jumped up and challenged cautiously, "Objection. Irrelevant, immaterial, and incompetent, Your Honor."

"Sustained. Stay with the subject at hand, Mr. Clarke," warned the judge.

Todd flinched at the word *incompetent* but managed to continue, "And they lived up to the letter of the law. They have the custody records here," pointing to them sitting in the front. They stood up, bowed, and held up the documents. "But I have him now."

"May I hug him, Your Honor?" asked Joella shakily, with tears streaming down her cheeks.

"Take one-hour recess. Into my chambers," he ordered the lawyers impatiently.

Todd headed to meet Joella.

"Especially you, Mr. Clarke. Bring those documents."

Joella approached her son and muttered nervously, "Happy Birthday, Joey. I'm your mom."

"Ah, Mom! I know that," he answered confidently. "You remembered my birthday. Dad said you would."

After ten minutes of emotional hugging and chatting with him, she turned to Lois, hugged her, and said appreciatively, "I'm happy you married Todd, Lois. What's his twin's names?"

Lois laughed joyfully.

"Say *hi* to Joella, Joella, Adam."

Joella hugged the little girl and boy, severely stressed that they were not hers and Todd's. *He used my name*, she mused. *At least, he cared for me.*

With tears in her eyes, she begged forlornly as she held Joey, "Take good care of *my* Joey, Lois. Be sure he says his prayers before you and Todd go to bed—"

"Sleep with Todd? I would never cheat on my Bruno; he's my hero."

"Who's Bruno?"

"You *know* my husband."

She felt a surge of happiness and guilt, but still utterly confused. She wondered who would be tough and crude enough to marry Lois.

The Howards intervened and hugged Joella and, in record time, happily explained that it was really Todd and his mom that raised Joey, that their custody was in name only—to beat the system—because Joey's grandmother had a criminal record, stressing that she had appealed her conviction and had been released from jail in less than a year, at which time she and Todd had moved to England to live with them. Now that Todd had his degree from Oxford, they had just moved back to live in Natuashish.

Joella couldn't believe her luck; everything positive was happening for a change, and at lightning speed. Todd appeared from the judge's chamber and hugged her.

"Mom says congratulations. She's behind, trying to reign in our uncivilized home front," he began, as casual as if they had just parted yesterday. "I got an acting role for you in a movie."

She was puzzled by his confident, aggressive mentality. She had just spent five years worrying over his mild manners.

"Oh, Todd, I'm afraid I've failed you. I didn't fare very well in acting. But I tried. Honestly."

"You can play this person's role well enough. Believe me."

"Who is she?" she asked confused.

"Joella Adams. You're going to act out your life story, in your own movie. It's from your diaries. I entitled it *Never Confuse Justice with Truth*."

"You have enough money to make a movie?" she asked, puzzled.

"Hell no! I'm a bloody peasant. But I spent enough time waiting for you to write a book. Our Joey owns ten percent of MGM though."

"*Our* Joey?" she asked even more confused.

He held her tight to his chest. He could feel her tears on his shirt.

"I'm the one who now has full custody."

"All these years, I was fighting *you*?" she asked emphatically, appalled.

"And blimey, you're still a handful," he joked.

"You won't believe it, Todd, but I finished my degree like you wanted." After a pause for strength, she lowered her head and added, "And I stayed faithful all these years," suddenly shy for the first time. Then jealously, asked, "Why is Lois here?"

"I know you did," he answered casually. After kissing her on the lips for the first time in five years, he explained confidently, "Because Lois is still your soul mate. She dumped me and married your prison shrink when she was eighteen. How do you think we took care of you all these years?"

There was no end of surprises this day for Joella. "We? Took care of me?" she inquired doubtfully.

Life in prison was no picnic for me, she mused. *It was one of loneliness and continuous study.* She tried to think of who the shrink could possibly be. It could be that chain-smoker from her first jail in St. John's. He was a rugged outdoorsman. Her only true supporter was her psychologist. But today, she was too happy to challenge such a minor slip and dismissed it.

"Did you not have a private suite there?"

"Yes. They treated me better than the others. Why? I'll never know." She wondered how he could have known.

"Were you molested there?" he asked seriously.

"No. They were all terrified of me because I was a double murderer."

"You didn't murder anybody. My uncle paid for your suite, and they weren't scared of you. Lois had Justin secretly warn all the inmates you had full-blown aids, and 'skimos had a habit at spitting on people if they came too close."

She looked at Lois with a most astounding yet appreciative expression on her face.

"Gentle Justin Patey is your husband? You're his Sedna?" she said emphatically. "Oh, Lois, God truly blessed you! If it weren't for—"

"God had nothing to do with it. You make your own world."

"Justin told them I had aids?" she reflected incredulously.

"He's my Bruno," interrupted Lois, beaming. "I had to do something. You'd never have gotten out if you kept killing rapists; the fuckin' world is full of them."

Joella stared at Lois with her mouth open and, for the first time, realized Lois was much more intelligent and practical than her.

Lois continued, "That was all I could think of." Seeing Joella still speechless, she added, "It worked, didn't it? Who do you think organized all this?"

"Justin?"

"Hey! And me!"

"Oh, Lois, you *are* a goddess." Then, becoming concerned, she asked, "Why isn't Justin with you then?"

"Theresa stole a car and crashed it. He's defending her in court today by acting as her shrink. She got into Susan's illegal drugs and . . ." Seeing tears appear in Joella's eyes, she quickly cut it short. "I'll tell you later. Justin will solve it. He solved you, didn't he?"

Joella rebounded and, looking inquisitively at Todd, asked, "How did you ever find my father's name?"

Putting his hands on her shoulders and staring into her eyes, he recounted forlornly, "The last words you mother ever said to me were words of desperation to help you: 'Love her, Todd. And love means forgiving. Joella's father is Joe Ellan, not Tuk. She's only happy with you, and happiness is only real if shared. Share it with her.' That was two days after you liquidated Quinn."

Her eyes again flooded with tears as she hugged him tightly, thought about her mother, and felt a deep surge of guilt for the demeaning way she had treated her.

The judge returned to the bench, slammed his gavel, and brought the reunion celebrations back to reality.

"Mrs. Pringle, does your client have two children?"

She looked at Joella and nodded.

Joella stood up. "No, Your Honor. Social Services deliberately lied to me. They told me I had a girl."

The Social Services lawyer jumped up and yelled, "Objection! Unproven."

The judge pointed to his seat and ordered angrily, "Overruled. Sit down."

"Mrs. Pringle, does your client wish to hear her case for shared custody of her child?"

"No, Your Honor," Joella answered quickly. "Joey already has a good parent."

The lawyer for Shady Lawn Funeral Home stood up to speak, but the judge quickly hit the gavel on the bar and warned him impatiently, "I had the custody papers authenticated, Mr. Hanson. This case is now stayed." Then, pointing his finger at him, he commanded sternly, "Into my chambers. There are issues of contempt of court and perjury that must be addressed."

As the judge stood to leave, he turned to Joella, "Off the record. Consider restitution for your mistreatment. You're a credit to the Inuit, Ms. Adams. Do keep fighting. And you're correct, justice and civility has not yet reached your people. And, as you found out, we too have a long way to go." Turning to Todd Clarke, he nodded slightly and gave a sly grin. "But it looks as though their future is brighter. Good luck, Ms. Adams."

As the loud and boisterous Ellan clan filed joyfully out of the courthouse, Joey took Joella's middle finger, pulled it, and said with eager delight, "Dad said you're even prettier than your pictures, Mom."

The word *Mom* again brought tears to her eyes. A word she thought she'd never hear. "Daddy has a picture of me?" she asked, surprised.

"Ah, Mom. You gave one to Justin to send to me every month. Wow, they're all over his bedroom, his office, everywhere. Justin's strong too; he carried me on his shoulders at Piccadilly Circus."

"Justin and Lois were in England?" asked Joella, again caught by surprise.

"And Jo and Adam. Justin says we're all one big family. But *I'm* right next to you in the family tree on the wall near King Arthur."

Never had she felt so at home and part of a family but, more so, amazed at the incredible gamble Lois and Justin had taken for her, realizing they must have committed hundreds of illegal acts just to keep Todd and his relatives informed every step in her life for the last five years. She was so breathless she did not have an appropriate response. Her attitude toward humanity, and especially white people, had just been radically altered. She finally grasped there was also good and evil in everybody.

Joey shook her finger again, bringing her out of her dream world. "He says you can teach me to scalp Qablunaats."

She laughed devilishly. *No, that's my job,* she mused. "Your dad was joking, sweetheart. He *is* a Qablunaat. I'll teach you to be Inuit instead."

As he hopped, skipped, and jumped contentedly by her side, she mulled over her flippant answer and stared inquisitively down at him: her own son was 100 percent white.

Then the *truth* of Justin's table hit her like a bolt from the blue, and she heard him say, "You're in for a shock of reality. This above all, to thine own self be true." She stopped and tried to honestly analyze her turbulent twenty years of life.

The *truth* was that she was no longer sure which race to which she and Joey belonged. Were they in limbo, trapped between cultures too? She recalled the frustrating results from Justin's table before she so mercilessly fudged the inputs. It was Todd and all his white relatives who had stood faithfully behind her for five years, whereas she had heard nothing from her own family. Justin, a gentle giant and her real-life guardian angel, was also white, whereas Lois, a one-time unsophisticated teenage licentious man-eater, was Inuit but was now a modest, faithful wife a in a fairy-tale marriage with the most understanding person she knew, plus having two adorable children. Melissa was a passive religious servant to the both the Innu and Inuit youth, whereas her husband was an aggressive predator, a pedophile, abusing these same youth. Her own mother was a good Inuit trapped in an unforgiving culture surviving as best she knew how, whereas Tuk, like Quinn, was living lower than the animals. Even her archenemy, the despicable Social Services, had her best interest in mind when they sent her all the way across the country to a *good* jail where she could get a degree.

Justin's words then rang in her ears: "It's not only who you are. It's also what you are." For the first time, she fully grasped it wasn't just one's race, religion, culture, or any single variable in life's truth table that made a person; they were just mitigating factors. It was love and understanding toward all people.

"The truth was: mankind is just one family," she mused out loud, astounded. "Even Mom knew that! She said so in her dream-catcher letter. Justin is really smart." She thought for a time, then continued sadly, "But so was Mom."

"What?" asked Joey.

"We'll teach you to be a good human being instead," she corrected reflectively.

Epilogue

Joella Adams married her *Snowflake* in a severe spring blizzard at Natuashish, three months after the trial. The men of honor were Justin and Cecil, who was on a weekend pass from jail where he was spending time for poaching bear penises. Prissy and Lois were maids of honor. Joella Patey was the flower girl. Chester Ellan, now incessantly complaining about the cold, gave her away. Penny and Tom Cooper, Jerry Preston, and all fifty Ellans attended. The ceremony was jointly performed by a senior community Inuit elder and Mrs. Clarke, as Dunk Campbell played a Scottish wedding march on his bagpipe and Aglari danced a Hebrides sword dance in the background. Joey gave a brief recital to show off his Inuktitut.

It was a multicultural gala for future Inuit folklore as the whole community attended, dressed in traditional Inuit attire, compliments of the Howard Estate, who had his friends from MGM film the whole extravagant affair.

Todd and Joella had a daughter six months later.

Joella is a practicing sociologist in Labrador, after failing dismally at acting as herself in her own movie. She still has her fighting spirit and is a benevolent dictator who manipulates the local laws and customs at will to enforce human rights for all races, not just the Inuit.

After presenting her diaries to the court, she received a formal apology and large out-of-court monetary settlement from the federal government for her wrongful convection and incarceration and to keep the court's *errors in law* a secret.

Penelope Cooper eventually married Jerry Preston; she is now a successful movie actress.

Aariak and Tuk Adams exist in abject poverty in Sheshatshiu, Labrador. Joella tried in vain numerous times to persuade her mother to leave Tuk and live with them in Natuashish, but she adamantly refused, believing the Great Spirit joined them *for better or for worse* until death.

Susan Kamanirk is still struggling daily with her drug addiction but, with weekly counseling, is managing to hold down her truck-stop job and stay out of jail. Her daughter, Theresa, is doing well in juvenile detention under Justin's care.

Todd Clarke is a circuit judge with liberties to impose traditional First Nations justice.

Pastor Cornelius left Labrador and went on to become a bishop in a large diocese in a major northern Canadian city.

Melissa Clarke, who lives with Todd and Joella, is a full member on the Inuit tribal council, teaches elementary school classes, a lay reader in the church, and a respected senior guidance counselor for wayward Inuit females, all in Inuktitut and all without government approval, yet all paid for by the same government.

But in one of life's cruelest ironies, whereas Melissa Clarke petitioned unsuccessfully many times to have her criminal record expunged, Wilbert Clarke, whose pedophilia was never exposed, became an honorary First Nation's chief and was promoted to a senior federal government position with full responsibilities in administering aboriginal affairs in the area.

Never Confuse Justice with Truth.

CPSIA information can be obtained at www.ICGtesting.com
Printed in the USA
242557LV00001B/23/P

9 781456 876845